Edge of the Knife

A. Miller

For W.

Chapter 1

The police found her on a street in Vista Hills, thirty miles from Los Angeles, lying in the landscaped median. A passing driver had noticed an arm among the ornamental roses. When the coroner's investigators arrived, they found Nyman's card in the torn pocket of her jeans.

"Can't park here, sir," a woman said as Nyman got out of his car.

The woman was wearing nitrile gloves and a blue jacket with the coroner's seal on the arm. A group of Vista Hills officers stood in a ring behind her, guarding a taped-off area that included the median and part of the northbound lane.

Farther away, behind a security fence, rose a Spanish Colonial house, silent except for the whir of early morning sprinklers.

Nyman shut the door of the car and stood beside it. He was a thin man in his late thirties, sharp featured and dark eyed, with the ashen look of someone recovering from an illness.

"I was told to park here," he said. "I got a call asking me to come out."

"You're Nyman?"

"That's right."

The woman nodded. "I'm Ruiz. Stay there and don't get in anybody's way. We're about to move the body."

She turned and ducked under the tape, joining a pair of men in blue jackets who were kneeling on the ground beside a gurney. On top of the gurney, already partly zipped up in a white vinyl bag, was the dead woman.

Her eyes were open and staring. Fragments of a pair of horn-rimmed glasses were tangled in her hair. One of her hands, as the men arranged her arms inside the bag, stood out briefly against the vinyl, the fingers long and brown and delicate.

Nyman turned away and looked in the opposite direction, over the top of his car. A line of palms ran along either side of the road, leading back toward the shops and office parks at the center of town. Swimming pools glinted among the houses in the hills.

A voice said: "Stand back, everybody."

The blue-jacketed men were wheeling the gurney— covered now by a nylon sheet—to the removal van. Ruiz followed behind them, shorter than the men but solidly built, with strong square features and black hair starting to gray.

She peeled the gloves from her hands and said to Nyman: "We'll talk in my car."

It was six-thirty in the morning but the inside of the car was already hot. Through the passenger window, Nyman watched the men lift the gurney into the van and shut the doors. Beside him, Ruiz took a pen and notebook from her pocket and said:

"So how long have you known her?"

Nyman kept his gaze on the van. "Less than twenty-four hours. Only since yesterday afternoon."

"She was a client?"

"Not really. More of a potential client. It was a hit and run, you think?"

"Tell me about yesterday afternoon," Ruiz said. "She came to see you? Or you went to her?"

"She came to me."

He had an office, he said, in a strip mall on Sepulveda. Late in the day, if there were no clients to talk to, he'd go to the restaurant next door and sit alone at the bar, watching the cars come and go in the parking lot.

Yesterday he'd watched Alana Bell climb out of an old Toyota and walk to the door of his office. She was twenty-four or twenty-five, as tall or taller than Nyman, with wide brown eyes and lines of tension around the mouth and jaw. Her horn-rimmed glasses and Pacifica shirt gave her the look of a student.

She tried the door, found it locked, and was turning back toward her car when Nyman left the restaurant and met her on the sidewalk.

"Sorry," he said. "Just taking a little break."

He told her his name and held out his hand. She hesitated before taking it, looking from his hand to his eyes.

"I thought you were supposed to be older," she said.

"My partner was the older one. He retired a few years ago."

"But you do the same kind of work?"

"I take the same kind of clients, if that's what you mean," Nyman said. "But my methods are a little different."

Anxiety was deepening the lines in her face. "This thing I need help with—it's something that has to be handled very carefully. There are people who'd be very angry if they knew I was even talking to you."

Nyman glanced at the other cars in the parking lot. "In that case," he said, taking the keys from his pocket and leading her to the door of his office, "we'd better go inside."

The words *Moritz Security and Investigations* were stenciled on the door. The office was a single narrow room with a set of wine-colored chairs, a map of the city, and an old steel tanker desk. There were no photos on the walls, no personal effects. He showed her into a chair and offered her coffee.

She didn't seem to hear him. She'd taken a business card from the desk and was looking at it skeptically, running a finger over the faded lettering. The name Joseph Moritz was printed in the center of the card. Below it, in smaller type, was Nyman's name.

He poured two cups, handed one to Alana, and walked to the window. "All right," he said, leaning against the sill, "what is it you wanted to talk to me about?"

She looked down at her lap and fidgeted with the card, her fingers trembling as they folded and refolded the little square of paper. Nyman said nothing and waited patiently, listening to the traffic on Sepulveda and the wail of a distant siren.

When she finally spoke, her voice was low. "Have you lived in L.A. very long, Mr. Nyman?"

He took a drink and nodded. "Most of my life."

"And you understand how things work? The way things get done here—politically speaking?"

"I wasn't aware anything ever got done."

She gave a grim smile and tucked the card into her pocket. "I used to think I understood it. Coming where I come from, I thought I had it all figured out. The truth is a lot more complicated."

"Complicated how?"

She sat up straighter in the chair and turned to face him. The skin of her left cheekbone, he noticed, was mottled by a bruise.

"I can't pay you anything," she said abruptly. "I'll tell you that up front. I get my stipend in a month, and I can pay you then, but right now I'm broke."

"Stipend for what?"

"Teaching. Or assistant teaching. I'll be a T.A. in a class at Pacifica next semester."

He asked her what she was studying.

"Public policy, but I didn't come here to talk about that. I need help, Mr. Nyman. And I promise I can pay you in August."

The siren outside was getting louder, triggering car alarms on the street and rattling the glass of the window at Nyman's back.

"Sometimes there's a misunderstanding about how the payment works," he said. "I don't expect you to give me everything up front. You could give me a small retainer now and the rest in August."

Alana shook her head. "I'm sorry. I just spent my last dollar on rent."

"Then what about giving me a credit card number to keep on file? As a kind of guarantee?"

Surprise widened her eyes. "I would think my promise," she said in a cold voice, "would be enough of a guarantee."

Nyman finished his coffee. In a voice that was equally cold, he said that he'd like to help, but he wasn't in a financial position to take clients on faith.

"I can tell you're upset about something, but investigations take time. I can't spend time on yours and run the risk of never getting paid. It's happened too many times before."

She nodded. "So you're not even interested in what I have to say. That's what you're telling me."

"No. I'm saying I can't do anything without some kind of guarantee. That's standard practice."

"Mmm. I see."

Nyman kept his gaze on the empty cup in his hand. With another nod, Alana got to her feet and walked to the door.

Without looking at her directly, he said: "I'm sorry."

"Yeah. I'm sure you are."

She let the door bang shut behind her. Nyman went on leaning against the windowsill for a time, then went out the door himself. He paused on the sidewalk and shaded his eyes against the sun.

Alana shut the door of her car with another bang and started the engine. Her face, caught in a shaft of sunlight as she backed out, was bright and wet with tears. He watched her turn out of the lot and drive toward the freeway.

Eight hours later she was dead.

Chapter 2

"And you didn't see her again after that, Mr. Nyman?"

"Not alive, no."

Ruiz nodded and wrote something in her notebook. The heat inside the car had increased, dampening the back of Nyman's shirt and putting a sheen of sweat on his face and neck.

"What about yourself?" Ruiz said. "Mind telling me where you were last night?"

He gave her the address of the Green Door. "I went home around two."

"Other people saw you there?"

"Half a dozen, at least. Some of them might've been sober. I can give you their names."

"Maybe later. Right now, if you don't mind, I'll ask you to follow me down to the office. The D.M.E. might want you to make a formal identification, depending on the family situation. Would you be willing to do that?"

"I guess so."

"Good. I'll see you there, then. You know the way?"

"I'll look it up."

He got out of Ruiz's car, got into his own, took the phone from his pocket, and pretended to look up directions. After Ruiz had driven away, he put the phone back in his pocket and walked across the street to the Spanish Colonial house.

Its sprinklers were still whirring, filling the air with mist. He pressed an intercom button and looked up at the jacaranda that rose behind the gate, its branches thick with pale blue flowers. After several rings, a woman's voice said:

"Yes?"

He leaned forward. "Morning. I'm looking for Alana Bell. She around today?"

"Bell? No, this is the Collinson residence."

"Is it really? My mistake. What about the neighbors, then? Know of any Bells around here?"

After a pause, the woman said: "Who is this?"

He ended the call. Making a note of the name Collinson, he got into his car and drove down to L.A. under a brightening summer sky.

* * *

The coroner's office was in the old county hospital on Mission Road, a red-brick building surrounded by freeways. The noise of traffic followed Nyman up the front steps and into the lobby.

A security guard watched him through a glass window. She listened sleepily as he explained his business, then told him to have a seat and make himself comfortable: Investigator Ruiz was very busy today.

He sat down beside a stack of gossip magazines. Walled in white marble, the lobby was dominated by a pair of unmarked doors and a large wooden staircase, the steps of which had been painted black. To the right of his chair, in the gift shop, a clerk was arranging a display of coffee mugs, each printed with the seal of the coroner's office.

Twenty-five minutes went by. Occasionally the unmarked doors opened and someone came out from the interior, letting in a draft of cold air. Despite the coldness Nyman's back was still damp with sweat and an unnatural flush had spread along his cheekbones.

"It's all right," the guard said, watching him through the glass. "Lots of people feel queasy their first time here."

Nyman said that it wasn't his first time. "I was here nine months ago."

"Oh yeah? On business?"

"No. Not on business."

The guard frowned. "You mean—?"

"Personal, yes."

The guard lowered her gaze and became interested in her paperwork. A phone rang, but she ignored it. Nyman was reaching for his cigarettes when he heard the sound of footsteps above him.

A small procession was making its way down the staircase, led by Ruiz. Behind her came a middle-aged woman who could've been mistaken at a distance for Alana Bell. She was moving with difficulty, her arms supported by the two men who walked on either side of her. One man was about her own age and looked like her brother or cousin. The other had a fringe of gray hair and a county nametag.

Looking down from the staircase, Ruiz saw Nyman and made a gesture that told him to stay where he was. Leading the woman to the unmarked doors, she said something in a voice Nyman couldn't hear, nodded to the man with the nametag, and stood aside as he led the little procession through the door.

"Sorry about the delay," Ruiz said, coming over to Nyman. "Looks like we won't need you after all."

"That was Alana's mother?"

"Mother and uncle, yeah. Notifications Unit tracked the mom down at home. She's a schoolteacher in Watts, apparently."

"Do you think she'd be willing to talk to me?"

"To you? Why?"

"I'd just like to talk to her."

For a moment Ruiz looked confused. Then, shaking her head, she told him not to take it personally. "So far this looks like a random hit and run. Accepting the girl as a client wouldn't have made any difference."

He asked her why she thought it was random.

"Because that's what it is, nine times out of ten. Somebody drunk or high."

"But no one witnessed it?"

"Not that we've heard from. Vista Hills P.D. are knocking on doors."

"What about the neighborhood? Did she have any reason to be there?"

Ruiz gave him a chilly smile. "Look, I appreciate you coming down here, but this isn't a collaboration. Any details that need to come out will be released through Public Services. You can take your questions to them."

She said a curt goodbye and walked in the opposite direction, passing through the doors Mrs. Bell had passed through.

Nyman looked at his watch, then went across to the gift shop, where the clerk had finished with the mugs and was breaking down a cardboard box.

"Something I can help you with?"

Nyman picked up a baseball cap that was stitched with the chalk outline of a corpse. "Ever worry about the people who buy this stuff?"

The clerk shrugged. "Depends on why they buy it. Most of them are tourists."

"What about the people who come here to identify a body? Do they always leave by the main doors?"

"Pretty much. Unless the cops are with them. Why do you ask?"

"Just curious."

Nyman went out the main doors and paused on the steps. Across the courtyard, on Mission Road, a city bus was sidling to the curb with a whine of brakes. It let out three or four passengers, closed its doors, rumbled off again, and revealed the Jack-in-the-Box that stood across the street. Nyman strolled down the steps.

The restaurant was filled with a breakfast crowd. He bought coffee and hash-browns and took them to a table by the window, where he had a view of the coroner's office.

"You work over there or something?"

The voice came from the next table, where a man was studying Nyman intently. The man was spare and blond and dirty, with tattered jeans, a heavy wool-lined jacket stained

13

with sweat, a sun-ravaged face that showed the shape of the skull beneath the skin. On his wrist was a tag from the county hospital.

"Work over where?" Nyman said.

"Coroner's place. I seen you come out of there. You one of the doctors that cuts people up?"

"No."

"You're a doctor, though?"

"No."

"You look like a doctor. I can always tell what people look like. Or a scientist, maybe. I knew a guy who was a biologist."

"I'm not even a biologist."

"Look, man, you think you could talk to the other doctors about what they did to me at the hospital? They got no right treating me like that. When a man's sick, don't you think he ought to get some medicine? You know what they did to me over there?"

"Something unpleasant?"

The man pulled his chair closer to Nyman and started telling a story that got more elaborate as it went on. Nyman listened politely until a few minutes after nine o'clock, when Alana Bell's mother and uncle came out of the red-brick building.

With an arm around her shoulders, the uncle led his sister down the steps and over to a Buick that was parked in a visitor's spot.

Wishing the blond man luck, Nyman left the restaurant and jogged to his car.

Chapter 3

He caught up to the Buick at the corner of Mission and Marengo and followed it, at a distance of two or three cars, onto the Santa Ana freeway.

Gold haze hung above the downtown skyline. The Buick drifted into the far left lane and drove toward Civic Center. At the Keene exchange it swung south onto the Harbor freeway and accelerated, as if eager to leave downtown behind.

Gradually the buildings outside Nyman's window got smaller. Office towers gave way to apartment complexes, then to flat stretches of tract housing. The Buick left the freeway and drove east into Watts, winding among residential streets.

He allowed the distance between his car and the Buick to lengthen. When it turned into a driveway he went by without slowing and continued for another few blocks, then parked under a withered palm on 107th.

Hot, sticky air settled over him as he stepped out. The smell of *carnitas* drifted over from a market on the corner, where kids were kicking a ball around on the sidewalk, moving sluggishly in the heat. He picked his way among them and went into the market.

It was a small cluttered room with a meat counter along one wall and a bakery case along the other. Two rattling box fans stood beside the cash register, adding to the noise of a radio playing *banda* music. The woman behind the register was hunched with age and staring at her phone.

Nyman asked if there were flowers for sale.

She raised her head reluctantly. "Flowers?"

"Doesn't matter what kind. Something I could give as a gift."

"For a birthday?"

"For a death in the family."

In that case, the woman said, putting down her phone and lurching out from behind the register, the correct gift was food, not flowers.

She led him over to the bakery case. Snapping a white paper sack down from the glass, she filled it with *conchas* and *polvorones*, tied the sack with a piece of plastic, and told him the price. He paid and went back outside.

The kids with the ball were gone. He made his way north, passing vacant storefronts and small stucco houses separated from each other by iron fences. At 105th the neighborhood changed abruptly; the storefronts disappeared and the houses became more or less identical: lime-green cottages arranged around a grassy common. A city sign said that he was entering the Rancho Village housing project.

The Buick was still parked in front of cottage 26. The man who answered the door was Alana's uncle: taller than Nyman, heavier, twenty years older. He wore a starched khaki shirt with the name of a company written in thread on the breast pocket.

"Something I can do for you, son?"

Nyman told him who he was. "A woman named Alana Bell came to my office yesterday. I think this is where her mother lives."

The man shut the door and came out onto the porch, forcing Nyman to take a step backward.

"No," he said, "this is where I live. Valerie's my sister."

"And Valerie is Alana's mother?"

"That's right." He looked at the sack of food in Nyman's hand but didn't acknowledge it. "What did Allie talk to you about?"

"Nothing very definite. She said she needed help, and asked me to help her."

"And what did you say?"

"I said I couldn't help her, because she couldn't pay me. I turned her away."

The man crossed his arms over his chest. In the window behind him, leaning against the glass, was a sun-faded crucifix. "If you sent her away, why bother to come out here?"

"I wanted to talk to her mother, if that's possible."

"That's not possible," the man said equably. "She's in no mood to talk to anybody right now. And I'm in no mood to pay you."

"You have nothing to pay me for, Mr. Bell. Your niece asked me to help her, and I said no. If I'd said yes, she might still be alive."

The man said: "My name's not Bell. It's Lattimer. Bell was my brother-in-law."

Nyman apologized.

17

"That's all right," Lattimer said, and nodded to the sack. "What's that, anyway?"

"Just some food."

Nyman held it out in a gesture of offering. Lattimer's arms remained crossed over his chest. Without accepting the gift, he nodded to the grass.

"Come on. We'll talk over here."

They walked together to a picnic table that stood in the center of the common, bleached by the sun. Lattimer sat down and leaned forward on his elbows.

"You say Allie didn't tell you what sort of trouble she was in?"

Nyman put the sack on the table between them. "She mentioned something about politics, but only in a vague way. I was hoping you or her mom might be able to tell me more."

"Well, there's not much chance of that. Allie thought that stuff was over our heads. She saved it for her friends at Pacifica."

"Did she say anything about being in danger?"

"Not to me. Not to Val, either. To be honest with you, we didn't see a whole lot of her. She moved out of Val's house last year, when she started her program."

"Did she spend much time in Vista Hills?"

Lattimer lifted his shoulders. "Today was the first time I ever heard about it. I can't imagine she'd have any reason to be in a place like that. Neither can Val."

"You asked your sister about it?"

"The investigator did. Ruiz. She wanted to know if Allie went up there to go to clubs or bars or something."

Nyman asked if such a thing sounded plausible.

"Allie never touched alcohol when she lived down here—I can tell you that. She never cared for that kind of life. Now whether this Freed turned her onto it afterward: that's something I don't know."

"Who's Freed?"

Lattimer's eyes narrowed. "Allie didn't mention her professors to you?"

"She didn't mention anyone at all."

"Well, if you didn't hear it from her, you're not going to hear it from me. I don't tell stories about my own family. That's all there is to say about that."

Nyman nodded and said nothing. The breeze had slackened, making the heat heavier and more oppressive. From the sack on the table came the smell of melting sugar glaze.

"I don't mean to say Allie was a bad person," Lattimer said. "She wasn't that at all. She was a kind-hearted girl. Too kind-hearted, maybe. I never had my own kids, so she was ..."

He let the sentence go unfinished and turned his head away. Nyman, looking down at the tabletop, asked if Ruiz had said anything about Alana's car or apartment.

Lattimer turned back with reddened eyes. "What?"

"I'm assuming she drove herself up to Vista Hills. I was wondering if the car had been found."

"No, I didn't hear anything about that."

"What about the apartment? Did Ruiz say she was going to have it sealed?"

"Look, son, I don't remember every detail. Most of the time I was trying to comfort my sister."

"And you're sure you won't let me talk to her?"

Lattimer straightened his spine and leaned back, laying his hands flat on the table. "I don't see what purpose it would serve."

"It would help me know where to start, for one thing."

"Start what?"

"An investigation."

Lattimer moved a hand dismissively. "Ruiz said there wasn't any need for that. She said it was an accident."

"Maybe it was. The thing about the coroner's office, though, is that they don't have enough investigators to deal with the workload. There's a temptation to call it an accident and move on."

"That's not true of the cops in Vista Hills."

"No, but they have their own priorities. Towns like Vista Hills don't like the publicity of a murder."

Lattimer's expression was skeptical. "You really think she was murdered?"

"I think it's possible. I could tell she was frightened when I talked to her."

"And you think if you find the killer for us, that'll make up for not helping her?"

Nyman shook his head. "No."

A pair of jays had settled on the branch of an oak, chattering at each other and shaking their wet-looking wings. Lattimer glanced at the birds, then turned to Nyman with a half-smile.

"Look, son, I'm sorry Allie came around and wasted your time, but I'm not going to let you upset my sister with a lot of questions. I've left her alone too long as it is."

He rose from the bench, gave Nyman a nod, and walked back across the grass to his house, going through the front door without a glance over his shoulder.

Nyman left the sack of melting food on the table and followed him to the porch. Taking a business card from his wallet, he dropped it in the letterbox, walked back to his car, and drove north to Pacifica.

Chapter 4

The university lay on lush green grounds on the edge of South L.A., separated from the surrounding neighborhoods by thick landscaping and a private police force. Nyman followed a walkway to the bronze doors and marble rotunda of Taylor Hall.

The School of Public Policy occupied the top two floors. A bearded secretary at the front desk told him that Professor Freed had been traveling and probably wasn't in his office.

"You're welcome to check, though. Down that way, on the right."

Nyman went down the hall and knocked on a door with the name Michael Freed posted beside it. The door was opened by a man of early middle age, tall and handsome, with the bulkiness of a former athlete and gray, sensitive eyes. He wore a white Oxford shirt, a loosened tie, and rimless glasses that sat midway down the bridge of his nose.

Nyman said: "Professor Freed?"

"Yes?"

"Tom Nyman. I'd like to ask you a few questions."

Exhaling, Freed took the glasses from his nose and rubbed his eyes. "I hope you're not from the *Business Journal*. I had a guy in here last week, asking about the housing proposal. Took me an hour to get rid of him."

Nyman said that he wasn't from the *Business Journal*. "I work independently. Freelance, you could say."

"Mmm." Freed's smile was cordial but not warm. "Well, I can give you a few minutes, I guess."

Nyman followed him into the office. Freed, sitting down behind a glass-topped desk, said in a conversational tone:

"Not easy to get by as a freelancer, from what I hear. Financially speaking."

"Not easy at all," Nyman said. "And the client I'm working for now isn't paying anything."

"What client is that?"

"Alana Bell."

Freed's cordial smile went away. "What's that supposed to mean?"

Nyman took a card from his wallet and handed it across. Freed read the faded lettering with an expression of distaste.

"You're telling me Alana's hired herself a private investigator?"

Nyman slipped the wallet back into his pocket. "She came to see me yesterday afternoon. Said she was a student in this department and needed help."

"Help with what?"

"Have you seen her recently, professor?"

"Not since she left for Vegas, no. I didn't know she was back in town. What'd she hire you for?"

"Well, for starters," Nyman said, not answering the question, "we talked about politics. The way things get done in L.A. Is that something you know much about?"

Sunshine slanted in through the office window, covering Freed's desk and revealing the sweat that was gathering on his forehead.

"Of course I know about it. My specialty's urban economics."

"And that's her specialty too?"

"She just finished the first year of our master's program; she hasn't had time to develop a specialty."

"But she's been working with you. Her family tells me you've had a strong influence on her."

Freed's distaste seemed to be increasing. "There's no need for innuendo. If you want to accuse me of something, go ahead."

"Are you romantically involved with her, professor?"

"No, I am not. I'm a happily married man." He picked up his phone to check the time. "As a matter of fact, Sarah and I have a lunch reservation in a few minutes."

"Then I'll make this quick," Nyman said. "How long have you been working with Alana?"

"Directly? Not long at all. Just since I asked her to help with the Merchant South research."

"Merchant South?"

Freed seemed happy to change the subject. "It's a development," he said, "in the Merchant District downtown. The city owned four parcels of land that weren't being used, so they leased them to a developer. The idea's to build condos and restaurants and a hotel. Something to revitalize the neighborhood."

"Sounds nice."

"Potentially nice. The city hired me to analyze the pros and cons."

"And you asked Alana to help with the analysis?"

"That's right. We turned in our findings two weeks ago."

"What did you find?"

Freed said nothing for a moment. Then, picking up the card, he glanced at it again and said: "If she's really your client, you should already know the answer."

"Unfortunately I didn't get the chance to ask her. She was murdered last night in Vista Hills."

A carillon was ringing somewhere nearby, in another part of the campus, chiming twelve times to mark the hour. Blood left Freed's face in disconnected patches until the skin was nearly the same color as his shirt.

"What?"

"I'm sorry I didn't tell you up front, but the mention of murder has a way of ending conversations."

Freed rose from his chair and walked to the window. He stood in silence for the better part of a minute, breathing irregularly and looking down at the sun-dappled grounds. His broad muscular back stretched the seams of his shirt and showed wetness under the arms.

"Murdered how?" he said without turning around.

"By a car, most likely. The coroner's still piecing it together. It'll be a while before they release their report."

"And the driver?"

"The driver seems to have gotten away without being seen. Unless you saw him."

Freed turned around. "Me?"

"Were you in Vista Hills late last night?"

"Of course not."

"Mind telling me where you were?"

Anger brought the blood back to Freed's cheeks. "I was on a red-eye from Boston. Coming back from a conference at Tremont College. Would you like to see my boarding pass?"

"Take it easy, professor. You're not on trial. Asking questions is the nature of the job."

Freed stood glaring at him for a time, then exhaled and let his shoulders drop. Sitting down, he made a steeple with his hands and said:

"Of course. I understand that."

"You mentioned a trip to Vegas. Do you remember when Alana left town?"

Freed said that it must've been a week or two ago. "Right after we turned in our analysis. She said she needed to get away for a while."

"For any particular reason?"

"Not that she mentioned."

"Did she go alone?"

"She didn't mention that, either."

"Can you think of anyone, professor, who might've wanted to hurt her?"

Freed hesitated. "I didn't really want go into this," he said, "but Alana wasn't a fan of Merchant South. There were homeless people living on the city's land, and now they're being forced out by the development. She got to know them through her research—came to sympathize with them. She became something of an advocate."

"And you think that might've put her in danger?"

"Possibly. Most of the people living there were harmless. But there were one or two—one in particular—who seemed overly interested in her."

"Interested in a violent way?"

"Potentially violent. Or at least that was my impression. Alana didn't agree."

Nyman took the notebook from his pocket. "Do you remember the name?"

"Eric Trujillo," Freed said at once. "A young kid—probably no more than eighteen. He'd been sleeping in Zamora Park, on the city's land. Alana used him as one of her research subjects. Tried to document how the development was forcing him out of his home."

"What makes you think he was violent?"

"More a feeling than anything else. I only met him once, when I went to the park to see Alana, but he seemed dangerous to me. Following her around, calling her phone."

"And this Trujillo's still in the park? Or has he moved on?"

"No, he's gone now; the city cleared everybody out two days ago. God knows where he ended up."

Before Nyman could ask another question, Freed rose to his feet and stepped out from behind the desk. His tone became brisk and businesslike.

"We'll have to leave it there for now, Tom. The dean has to be told about this, and the other grad students. And I should probably call Alana's family."

With a curt gesture, he got Nyman out of his chair and led him over to the door, steering him with a hand on his shoulder.

Nyman allowed himself to be steered. In the hallway, he put away his notebook and said that he'd come by again later, when Freed had more time. "If that's all right with you, professor."

Freed hesitated, but only for a moment. "Of course. Anytime."

They shook hands and Nyman made his way back to the front desk, where the secretary looked up from his computer.

"Find him?"

"I did, yes," Nyman said. "He was just telling me about a place on campus he likes to go for lunch, but I didn't catch the name. One that takes reservations. Know which one he meant?"

The secretary said: "Probably the Founders' Club. Between the library and Spanner Hall. But they won't let you in if you're not a member."

"That's all right," Nyman said, already moving to the elevator. "I was just curious."

Chapter 5

The lobby of the Founders' Club was hung with black-and-white photos of former Pacifica students. The oldest showed an inaugural class of a dozen young men standing beside a clapboard building on an otherwise empty campus. They wore heavy tweed suits and celluloid collars; in the distance stood rows of orange trees that would soon give way to parking lots and classroom buildings.

"Sorry about that," the hostess said, hanging up her phone and turning to him. "How can I help you?"

He told her his name and occupation. "One of your members is supposed to be meeting her husband here for lunch. Sarah Freed. I'd like to talk to her."

The hostess' smile hardened. "I'm afraid it's against our policy to allow non-members into the dining room."

"One of her husband's students," Nyman said, "was just murdered."

The hardened smile dissolved. Telling Nyman to stay where he was, the hostess left her stand and went into the dining room. Half a minute later she was back in the lobby and beckoning to him.

The dining room was mostly empty. A woman in expensive workout clothes sat alone at a table in the corner, reading something on her phone. She was in her early or middle forties but gave the impression, at first glance, of being twenty years younger. Dark hair was gathered into a knot at the top of her head, accentuating a long neck and broad, well-defined shoulders.

Accepting a menu from the hostess, Nyman sat down across from Sarah Freed and thanked her for meeting with him.

Her gaze was nervous and probing. "Michael said you might want to see me, but I didn't think it would be this soon."

"You already talked to him?"

"He called a few minutes ago. When I was leaving the gym."

"Did he tell you why I went to see him?"

She nodded. "I was sorry to hear it."

A waiter came to the table to give her a glass of sparkling water and a bowl of greens covered with salmon. She ignored the food and said to Nyman:

"But I don't see why you're calling it a murder. The newspaper says it was an accident."

"What newspaper?"

She held up her phone; on the screen was a brief story from the *Conejo Valley Sun*. It said that an unidentified woman had been killed in a traffic accident near the intersection of Lindero and Marine. The police would release further details as they became available.

"That looks like a placeholder," Nyman said. "The story will change as the day goes on."

"Maybe. But isn't it a little reckless to accuse someone of murder when the police are calling it an accident?"

"I didn't accuse your husband of murder, Mrs. Freed."

"You insinuated it," she said in a rising voice. "And you think he did it. Don't you?"

"I don't think anything."

"Yes you do."

"A good investigator," Nyman said, "tries not to speculate until he has enough evidence to speculate with. I don't have enough evidence."

"Don't patronize me. I know how you people work."

Saying nothing, Nyman picked up the menu and began leafing through the pages.

Across the table, Sarah sat up straighter in her chair and took a deep breath. "I'm sorry," she said. "It's just upsetting, having Michael dragged into something like this."

Nyman put down the menu. "I can see how it would be."

"You don't really believe he could do something like that, do you?"

"That's why I'm here, talking to you. So you can help me know what to believe."

The waiter reappeared, this time to take Nyman's order. He asked for a cup of coffee on a separate check. "I won't be taking up much of Mrs. Freed's time."

The waiter nodded and strolled away. Sarah, meanwhile, had leaned back in her chair and was studying Nyman more closely, her gaze moving from the fingers of his left hand to the tie that hung from his narrow neck.

"It must be an unpleasant job," she said. "Prying into the lives of people you don't know."

"Most jobs are unpleasant. Your husband's, for instance. He seems to be under a lot of strain."

"Michael?" She gave the first hint of a smile. "I don't think anyone loves their work as much as Michael does. He could be making twice as much in the private sector, but he'd never consider it."

"You wish he would, though?"

"Make a decent living? Of course I do. Anybody would."

"I would've thought you could make a decent living on a professor's salary."

Her smile widened. "You obviously don't have children. Tuition at a good school in this town is obscene."

"Your husband must think the financial sacrifice is worth it."

"Oh, more than worth it. You wouldn't believe it, just talking to him, but he's a brilliant teacher. His students adore him."

"According to some people, Alana Bell adored him for more than just his teaching."

First surprise, then something like fear showed in her pale green eyes. Glancing sharply at the other tables, she leaned forward and told Nyman to lower his voice.

"Does that mean the rumors are true?"

"That means I don't want to talk about it. Not here, of all places."

"Your husband told me the relationship was purely platonic."

"You asked him outright?"

"Yes. He said she was his student and nothing more."

Flushing, Sarah said: "Then he lied to you. All right? Now can we stop talking about it?"

"How long had the affair been going on?"

"Christ." She put her hands to her temples and shut her eyes. "I have no idea. I never asked him."

"But you found out?"

"Are all these questions really necessary? Or are you just trying to humiliate me?"

"If I wanted to humiliate you, Mrs. Freed, I'd find an easier way. All I'm asking is how you learned about the affair."

Glancing again at the other tables, she said: "I don't remember how I learned about it. It's a feeling more than anything else. After a while you start to recognize the signs."

"Then he's done this before?"

"Yes."

"How many times?"

"That's none of your business."

"Why did he lie to me?"

"Because he panicked, obviously. You have to put yourself in his shoes. An investigator showing up out of the blue, saying that Alana was dead. It's no surprise he lied to you."

"It would've been easier if he'd told the truth."

"Of course it would've. But everybody panics when they're caught off guard. You caught Michael off guard, and I'm trying to correct the mistake."

Taking the wallet from his pocket, Nyman counted out money for the coffee and laid it on the table.

"If you don't mind my saying so, it seems strange that you'd try to protect a man who's been unfaithful to you."

"He also happens to be my husband."

33

"I could see why you might stay for the sake of your children," Nyman said, "but it must be hard. It must make you angry."

"Yes—very angry. That's why I always run the women down with my car. Preferably in the middle of the night, in some suburb I've never been to."

"A lot of people wouldn't blame you if you did."

"I'm not interested in what other people think. We all have choices to make, and I've made mine. Michael's my husband and it's up to me to deal with him."

"Would you say he's a difficult man to deal with?"

"No more than the rest of you."

"Suppose Alana Bell told him she didn't want to see him anymore. Isn't it possible he might've been upset enough to kill her?"

Sarah seemed to find the scenario amusing. "Michael can't stomach the thought of violence, much less the act. He was in tears when he called me just now."

"He cared about her, then?"

"Very much."

"What was your opinion of her?"

"I tried to think about her as little as possible. You won't understand this, Mr. Nyman, but denial can be a healthy thing in certain situations. Ignoring parts of your life can be very therapeutic."

"It sounds like a harsh kind of therapy."

"That's because it is," Sarah said. "Now is this conversation over or not?"

Finishing the last of his coffee, Nyman apologized for interrupting her lunch and said that he had one more question.

"Your husband told me he flew back from Boston last night. Do you remember what time he got home?"

She frowned. "It must've been sometime after two, I guess. Two-fifteen, maybe. I think I looked at the clock when he came into the bedroom."

"And what about yourself? Where were you?"

"While Alana was being killed, you mean? I was at home, asleep. As were our boys, in case you'd like to check their alibis too."

"Was anyone else in the house who can confirm that?"

She looked at him with an incredulous smile. "Yes, actually. Marcella, our nanny. She was spending the night in the bedroom down the hall. Would you like her phone number?"

"Please," Nyman said, taking the notebook from his pocket. "If it's not too much trouble."

"No trouble at all, Tom."

Chapter 6

Heat haze rippled above Figueroa Street as Nyman drove back downtown. He worked his way east into the Merchant District, then parked in a metered spot and used his phone to find the website of Tremont College.

A woman in the Department of Planning and Public Policy told him that Michael Freed had arrived on Tuesday evening to present a paper at a conference the following day. Freed had been on campus till late Wednesday evening, when he'd left to catch his flight at Logan International.

"Do you know what time the flight took off?"

"Well, it couldn't have been much before ten o'clock," the woman said. "He came to the dinner on campus, and that didn't get over till eight."

Nyman thanked her and got out of the car.

He was standing on a street of cinderblock warehouses. The handful of cars and vans parked on the street looked as if they hadn't moved for weeks; they were packed with clothes and food and the belongings of their owners. From the tracks to the east came the rumble of freight trains.

He walked a block and a half to a narrow ribbon of grass enclosed by temporary fencing. A city sign said that Zamora

Park was closed for repurposing and that trespassers would be prosecuted.

He peered through the chain-link. The trees and shrubs had already been torn out, leaving only a weed-littered fountain and a few park benches. Mounted to the tops of the benches were metal bars that divided the sitting area into three small sections, making sleeping on them impossible. People had evidently slept on the ground instead; there were human-size patches of dirt where the grass had been rubbed away.

Halfway down the block, men in orange vests were using jackhammers to break up the asphalt of an empty parking lot. A canvas banner had been hung over the lot's entrance, showing an artist's sketch of the sleek white condo tower that would eventually rise in its place.

Nyman made his way down the block. By the time he reached the lot the workmen had gathered under the shade of a canopy for a water break.

"Looks like you're just getting started," he said as he approached, nodding to the small section of ground that had been broken.

An older man, short and thickly built, with a shaved scalp a few shades paler than his face and neck, acknowledged Nyman with a grunt.

"I'm trying to find a guy who was living in the park across the street," Nyman said. "Kid named Eric Trujillo."

The bald man raised a bottle of water to his lips and said in a bored voice: "Yeah?"

"You guys around when the police cleared everybody out?"

"Some of us, yeah."

"Did it cause a lot of trouble?"

The man took a drink. "You with the paper or something?"

"Just looking for my friend."

The bald man shrugged. "Didn't cause a lot of trouble, no. Cops came in with a bunch of social workers. Told the people they had to leave and where to go to get a bed."

"Did they recommend one place in particular?"

At some unspoken signal, the workmen had begun drifting away from the canopy and back to their equipment. The bald man finished his water and turned to follow.

"They got shelters down here for everything," he said over his shoulder, picking up a hardhat. "If you're looking for a kid, you should check the ones that take kids."

He put the hat over his pale scalp and strolled out into the sunshine.

* * *

Three miles away, Nyman found a Depression-era hotel painted with vivid yellow bees and orange butterflies. A sign above the door said that the purpose of the Hive was to enrich the lives of homeless youth.

Through an intercom in the vestibule he said that he was researching the closing of Zamora Park and had found the Hive on a list of shelters. After a moment, the intercom buzzed and the interior door clicked open.

The intake counselor who met him on the other side was taller and younger than Nyman and elaborately tattooed, with geometric patterns rising up from her wrists to cover her arms and chest and neck. Her long thick hair had been dyed a metallic shade of red.

Looking at him skeptically, she said: "Most people haven't even heard about the park getting closed."

Nyman said that he'd heard about it from a professor at Pacifica. "Michael Freed. One of his students has been working with the people there."

"And you're doing some kind of story about it?"

"At the moment," Nyman said, "I'm just trying to get more information. I thought this might be a good place to start."

"Well, we always did a lot of outreach at Zamora," the counselor said, turning away from the doors and leading him inside. "There were dozens of kids passing through there every day. Now the challenge is finding places for them."

Together they entered a large, cement-floored space filled with second-hand tables and threadbare couches. The hotel's original features had been removed or repurposed; behind the zinc-topped bar stood a line of ping-pong and pool tables. Teenagers were scattered around the room, watching television and eating microwave dinners. The air smelled of food and old furniture and adolescent bodies.

"Reminds me of college," Nyman said.

The counselor smiled. "This is our quietest time—right before school gets out. We're really more of a drop-in center than a traditional shelter."

"And you keep a list of the kids who drop in?"

"For our own files, yeah. But we never share it with anyone."

"Not even to help an investigation?"

Hard white creases appeared around her eyes and mouth. "You said you were doing research for a story."

"I said I was doing research. I didn't say it was for a story."

"So you're a cop, in other words."

Nyman told her what he was. "If you can put me in touch with the boy I'm looking for, you might help me find a murderer."

"I might help you put him in jail, you mean. That's not something I'm going to do."

"His name's Eric Trujillo. He was living in the park until the police shut it down."

One of the kids on the couches—a small, round-bodied girl watching something on her phone—looked up sharply at the mention of Trujillo.

"Look," the counselor said, "we've worked very hard to make this a place where people feel safe. If I start ratting them out, they'll stop coming. And if they stop coming, they'll stop getting the services they need."

"I'm not trying to ruin his life," Nyman said. "I'm asking for information."

"I don't have any to give you."

"Even though an innocent person is dead?"

Rather than answering, the counselor beckoned to a man across the room and asked him to escort Nyman out of the building.

Nyman told him not to bother. Walking back outside to his car, he put the keys in the ignition, lowered the windows, lit a cigarette, and settled back in his seat to wait.

Forty-five minutes passed. People came and went from the coffeehouse and apartment building down the block, but the door of the Hive stayed closed.

Sweat soaked through Nyman's shirt and into the upholstery of the seat. Taking the notebook from his pocket, he found the number of the Freeds' nanny, Marcella. She answered on the third or fourth ring and said in a shy voice that Mrs. Freed had gone to bed last night around ten o'clock and hadn't left the house until late the next morning. Marcella's bedroom was next to the garage, and she would've been woken by the sound of a car engine starting. She'd heard nothing.

Nyman thanked her and hung up. He smoked another cigarette, then called the Vista Hills Police Department to ask if the driver of the hit-and-run had been identified. A man with a courteous voice asked him for his name and put him on hold.

He was still on hold when the door of the Hive opened and the round-bodied girl came out.

Chapter 7

In full daylight she looked older than she had indoors: a woman in her late teens or early twenties, with a heavy layer of makeup and black hair cut just below the ears. She turned away from the Hive and set off down the sidewalk with a backpack hanging from her shoulders.

Nyman got out and followed on foot. She picked her way through the crowd in front of the coffeehouse, then crossed the street and turned east. When she stopped at a bus shelter on 6th Street Nyman was ten feet behind her and slowing to a stroll.

"Eric Trujillo," he said as he drew even. "Any idea where I can find him?"

She turned sharply, the backpack swinging on her shoulders. The surprise of seeing Nyman made her mouth come open; the silver wires of a retainer caught the sunshine.

"You followed me."

"Only because I need to find Eric. It's important."

"Why?"

"You know him, then?"

"I didn't say that," she said, taking a step backward. "I didn't say anything. I don't talk to cops."

"In that case," Nyman said, "it's a good thing I'm not a cop."

"You told them at the Hive you were."

"I told them I was a private investigator. There's a difference. I couldn't put your friend in jail if I wanted to."

A bus had pulled to the curb and opened its door but she didn't seem to notice.

"I don't understand why everybody's always bothering Eric," she said with sudden anger. "He didn't do anything to you. He doesn't deserve this."

Nyman asked her what Eric deserved.

"To be left alone," she said. "With me and Kelsey. That's all he wants."

"Who's Kelsey?"

"You don't know?"

"I don't know anything. That's why I need your help. Is a Kelsey a friend of yours?"

Kelsey was their little girl, the woman said. "Not that it's any of your business."

Nyman asked her how old her daughter was.

"What do you care? It doesn't have anything to do with you."

"I'm just curious."

She looked at him for a moment in indecision. Then, shyly, she took a phone from her backpack and showed him a photo of a prematurely born baby. Its head was narrow and misshapen; its arms were thin and formless and pink, with a layer of soft hair still covering the skin.

"Brown eyes," she said with a note of pride. "Just like Eric's."

Nyman said that she must be a very happy mother. "What's your name, by the way?"

"Marissa."

"I'm Tom."

They shook hands stiffly and formally. Nyman nodded to the photo and asked if the baby was with Eric.

"No, she's with my aunt. My aunt's been letting Kelsey and me stay with her for a while."

"Eric's not living with you?"

Her pride and happiness went away. Pretending not to hear the question, she turned to watch the bus merge back into traffic.

"I'm not trying to pry," Nyman said, "but I need to talk to him. About one of his friends."

She kept her gaze on the bus. "Yeah? What friend?"

"Alana Bell."

The name brought a flush to her cheeks. "Yeah. That's what I thought you'd say."

"You know her?"

"I met her once. At the park."

"I heard that she and Eric are pretty close."

The flush deepened. "I guess so. I don't know. You should ask Eric."

"I'd like to. And I'd like to tell him what happened to Alana last night."

She turned back to him. "What do you mean?"

"Eric should probably be the first one to hear about it. Since he's her friend."

For a time she didn't respond. They stood together in the shade of the bus shelter, watching cars pass in the hazy afternoon heat. Finally, looking down at her phone, she typed three or four sentences with her thumb.

After less than a minute the phone chimed.

"All right," she said after she'd read the text. "He says he'll meet you."

* * *

The 4th Street bridge was a concrete viaduct connecting downtown to Boyle Heights. Beneath its arches ran Burlington Northern railroad tracks and the culverts of the L.A. River.

Leaving his car on Santa Fe Avenue, under the bridge's western end, Nyman made his way along a sidewalk planted with fir trees and bordered on one side by a fence topped with razor wire. Beyond the fence was a short stretch of scrubby grass, then the glinting lines of the railroad tracks.

He came to a section of fencing that had been cut and pulled to one side. Wriggling through, he crossed the scrubby grass to the nearest of the bridge's arches, forty or fifty yards away.

The arch cast a deep, wide shadow. Distributed here and there in the gloom were tents and sleeping bags and encampments, some elaborate enough to have laundry lines. A skeletal woman with brittle gray hair lay on her back beside a shopping cart, smoking the dying end of a cigarette.

"Looking for somebody?" she said.

Nyman nodded. "Eric Trujillo. I was told he lives around here."

"You mean Ricky?" The woman gave a toothless smile. "Like a kid to me, Ricky. A son. You got a problem with him, you better tell me first."

"I don't have a problem with him."

The woman made a courtly gesture with her cigarette, indicating the tent farthest from her cart. "All right. Then you can pass."

He stepped around her and made his way to Trujillo's tent.

It was a pup-tent stained with mold. Nyman said Trujillo's name, got no response, kneeled beside the tent's opening, and lifted the flap: inside were a tangle of dirty clothes, a pack of cigarettes, two empty beer bottles, and a pamphlet from the Mormon church. He lowered the flap and walked to the other end of the arch, where the shadows gave way again to sunlight.

The blow came from his left. It struck him behind the left ear and pitched him forward, sending him sprawling among rocks and gravel and grass. Two kicks—one to his ribs, the other to his head—followed in quick succession.

When he woke up a moment later he was being turned onto his back by strong hands. A young man's face loomed over him: handsome and pocked by acne. The man put his left hand on Nyman's throat and drew back his fist.

Nyman tried to roll away; the punch caught him on the cheek and mouth, driving his bottom lip into his teeth. Blood came first from his lip and then from his nose as the man punched him a second time.

Then the grip on his throat abruptly loosened; the man drew back on his haunches, out of breath. Nyman dragged himself a few feet away and wiped his face with the sleeve of his jacket. The fabric came away wet and dark.

"Come close to me again and I'll kill you," the man said in a quavering, adolescent voice. "You hear what I'm saying?"

Nyman took a handkerchief from a pocket and tried to clean his face. "You're Trujillo?" he said thickly.

"What difference does it make?"

"Need to talk to you about Alana Bell."

Trujillo made a disgusted noise. "You don't want to talk about her. You want to kill her."

Gingerly, Nyman ran his tongue along his swelling lip. "Why would you think that?"

"Because you're security," Trujillo said. "Marissa says you're private security. Just like Fowler."

"Who's Fowler?"

"Come on. I'm not stupid."

"Is Fowler someone who wanted to hurt Alana?"

"Course he is. Who do you think gave her that bruise?"

Nyman was quiet for a time, bleeding and thinking. "On her face," he said at last. "Her cheek. Right?"

"Yeah, you know about it. You know because you were there when he did it. You work with him."

Nyman put the handkerchief back in his pocket. "I don't work with anybody. Alana came to see me in my office."

"Liar."

"She said she was in trouble. She wanted me to help her."

"That doesn't even make sense. Why would she go to you when she could come to me?"

"I don't know. But that's what happened."

"You're lying."

"If you were really her friend, Eric, you should be helping me. It's what she would've wanted."

"Why are you talking like it's the past? None of this is over. Fowler's still trying to kill her."

Nyman sniffed at the blood that was dripping from his nose. "It's too late for that, Eric. She's already dead."

Chapter 8

Traffic whined above their heads as they sat under the 4th Street bridge. From their left came the clanging of a railroad bell. Trujillo put a hand in his jacket and took out a lighter and a half-smoked joint.

His hand on the lighter was trembling. He got it lit on the second try and inhaled hungrily as it started to burn. Without looking at Nyman he said in a shaken voice:

"I don't believe you."

Nyman said he didn't blame him. "You can check for yourself, though. Call the Vista Hills police."

"Vista Hills?"

Nyman told him about driving up to see the body. "The coroner's office thinks it was a hit and run. No witnesses and no suspects."

Blood continued to drip from his nostrils onto his lips and chin, where it was drying in the heat.

Trujillo shook his head and stared down at the joint. He sat hunched forward with an arm around one knee and a foot twitching in the grass. Despite the heat he wore black jeans, a black flannel shirt, workman's boots, and a black-and-silver

Kings jacket. His brown eyes, like his daughter's, were flecked with gold.

"I want to see a license," he said. "What you're saying is true, you should have a license, right? Some kind of badge?"

Nyman took a folded piece of paper from his wallet and handed it across. Trujillo studied it intently, then tossed it onto the grass, rubbed a hand over his eyes, and said in a calmer voice:

"What would she be doing up in Vista Hills?"

"I was hoping you could tell me."

"Why me? How'd you even find out about me?"

Nyman told him what Michael Freed had said about their meeting in Zamora Park.

"That's bullshit," Trujillo said. "I never threatened anybody. Freed showed up one time, acting like he was Allie's dad or something. Telling her they needed to talk. I told him maybe she doesn't want to talk, so why don't you get the hell out of here?"

"What did Freed say to that?"

"I don't know. Said he'd call the cops if I didn't leave him and Allie alone. Said he didn't want Allie working with me anymore."

"How exactly was she working with you?"

Trujillo shrugged. "It wasn't really work. Just talking. The city wanted to build something in the park—told us all we had to leave. Allie wanted to know how it would affect me."

"Why you?"

"She talked to lots of us, not just me. Said the study she was doing needed to take account of our lives, too."

"Did Freed come to the park with her?"

"Only that one time. When he told me to leave her alone."

Nyman's next question was interrupted by Trujillo's phone. He took it from the pocket of his jeans, glanced at the screen, made an irritated noise, and silenced it.

"Call from Marissa?" Nyman said.

"None of your business."

"She seemed like a nice girl to me."

"I don't care what she seemed like to you."

"Were you having a relationship with Alana, Eric?"

Trujillo's glare was cold and angry, but his voice was still calm. "You got it all worked out in your head, don't you? Kid gets a thing for a girl he can't have. Kills her when she tells him no."

"That sounds like the theory Freed was suggesting."

"And you believe it?"

"Not necessarily," Nyman said. "What's your theory?"

"I don't have a theory. I have facts."

"Such as?"

Trujillo held up a finger. "Number one. This Monday. Guy shows up at the park and starts asking where Allie is. Says his name's Fowler and he needs to talk to her."

"Talk to her about what?"

"I don't know—I didn't hear it all. She went over with him to his car and came back after a while. Said he'd told her he worked at the Rexford and wanted her to come there to meet somebody."

"The Rexford?"

"It's a club," Trujillo said. "Real expensive. Models and bottles and shit like that."

"Who did he want her to meet there?"

Trujillo said that he didn't know, then held up another finger. "Number two, though. Allie comes to the park the next day with that bruise on her face. Tells me she hit herself on the bathroom sink. I said it was Fowler, wasn't it, and she just ignored me. Around then was when the cops came in and told us all we had to leave."

"Did she go on ignoring you after you moved out of the park?"

The joint had dwindled to a nub and Trujillo tossed it away into the grass, brushing his hands.

"Pretty much. That was the last time I saw her."

"Is there a number three?"

Trujillo nodded. "Yesterday I called up the Rexford and said I wanted to talk to Mr. Fowler. Made up a story about how he'd offered me a job and I wanted to discuss it with him."

"What'd they say?"

"That I must've made a mistake, because they weren't hiring any bouncers."

Nyman said: "And that's why you think he's some kind of security?"

"One reason, yeah. And the look he had."

"Look?"

"He looked like you," Trujillo said. "Cheap suit. Blank face. All you guys look the same."

Saying that he would have to get a new stylist, Nyman took the notebook and pen from his pocket. In a narrow cursive hand, he wrote a timeline of the events Trujillo had described.

"Fowler came to the park on Monday, then? Two days before she was killed?"

"That's right."

"And you never talked to Alana again after Tuesday morning, when you got forced out of the park?"

Trujillo's foot stopped twitching. He lowered his gaze and inspected the lighter in his hand. "Nope," he said.

"You're sure?"

"Positive."

"You didn't try calling her?"

"What makes you think I even had her number?"

"Freed said you called her quite a bit. He made it sound like harassment."

"Freed's a lying son of a bitch."

Nyman nodded and put away his notebook, then rose to his feet. The movement brought a fresh stream of blood from his nose. Reaching again for the handkerchief, he said:

"Personally, if my friend was being threatened, I would've called to check on her. I might've even gone to see her. Tried to protect her."

"That's nice. I didn't do either one."

Holding the handkerchief to his nose, Nyman said: "I don't believe you, Eric."

"I don't care what you believe."

"Can I give you my card, at least? In case you change your mind?"

"No."

"What about giving me your phone number?"

"No."

"There'll be other people interested in you. The coroner's investigators, for one. And probably the Vista Hills police. If they talk to Freed, he'll tell them about you, and if they talk to me, I'll have to tell them where you're living."

"I'm not sticking around here," Trujillo said.

"That's what I figured."

"And I'm sorry about your face."

He said it in a clipped, pained voice and went on staring at the lighter in his hand.

Nyman told him not to worry about it and walked back to his car.

* * *

The Palm Court was a low stucco building in Little Armenia. Leaving his car in the alley, Nyman walked to the building's street-side entrance, passed through a common room where two or three residents sat sleeping in their chairs, and went down a linoleum-tiled hallway.

At the end was a door on which a small American flag had been taped. The door was open a few inches; from the other side came the sound of a baseball game. Nyman went in without knocking and said in a voice loud enough to be heard above the game:

"Mind if I clean myself up?"

Joseph Moritz sat in an armchair in front of the TV. He was a large, broad-shouldered man in his early eighties, with sparse white hair combed neatly to one side and a somber, aquiline face. He looked at the dried blood on Nyman's face and clothes and said without a change of expression:

"Clean up what?"

"A little mustard on my tie."

"All right. But don't get any mustard on the towels."

The bathroom and was covered in pink tile and smelled of bay rum aftershave. Nyman took off his coat and tie and cleaned himself at the sink.

The game was in the top of the ninth when he came out. The Angels were leading the Red Sox by two runs. He sat down without speaking and watched Joseph watch the game.

The older man's hands—large and thick-veined—lay spread across his thighs, moving occasionally in response to the play on the field. When the half-inning ended, he muted the TV and looked at Nyman questioningly.

"Teenage kid," Nyman said. "Thought I was threatening the woman he had a crush on."

"At the office?"

"Under the 4th Street bridge."

"Odd place to be."

"I've been several odd places today," Nyman said, and started to tell him about Alana Bell. As soon as the game resumed Joseph turned back to the T.V. and Nyman fell silent.

The middle of Boston's order was up to bat. When the last batter popped up to center, Joseph turned off the T.V. with a grunt of satisfaction and said:

"Only five back of Houston now."

They left the room and walked down to the cafeteria. Joseph's spine and shoulders were curved by age and he leaned heavily on his walker, but he was an inch taller than Nyman and thirty pounds heavier.

At the doorway to the cafeteria a smiling woman in scrubs called them by their first names and told them the evening's menu. They put in their orders and sat down by the coffee station.

"So she wanted to hire you," Joseph said, resting his elbows on the table, "but she couldn't pay you. I hope you had the sense to turn her away."

"I did."

"You're learning, then."

"A little bit."

"More than a little. And what happened after that?"

"She was murdered."

For a moment Joseph allowed himself to look surprised. The impassive face became briefly soft and human; the eyes widened; spots of color came into the marble-white cheeks.

"How?"

Nyman took the notebook from his pocket and told him in detail what had happened. While he was talking, the woman in scrubs came to the table to give Joseph a piece of Salisbury steak, roasted potatoes, carrots and peas, and a slice of cherry cobbler. To Nyman she gave a cup of coffee. Joseph had eaten most of the steak by the time Nyman finished talking.

Joseph went on eating. After three or four minutes, saving the cobbler for later, he leaned back in his chair.

"You said she was murdered, Tom. I don't see any evidence of murder."

"The boy said she was being threatened."

"The boy gave you a vague story, most of it second-hand. Anything that wasn't second-hand was conjecture."

"Fine. The bruise on her face, then."

"Look around," Joseph said, sweeping a hand at the other tables. "Everybody's got bruises. That's what life is: getting cuts and bruises. Not something you can build a business on."

"There aren't exactly any other clients demanding my business."

"Not that you know of. They might be standing outside your door this minute, wondering why you're closed."

Irritation showed in Nyman's face. "I admit it's thin. But I have to do it."

Joseph picked up the knife and fork and turned his attention to the cobbler. He ate with an old man's patience, wiping his mouth after every bite. Then he finished his coffee, signaled to the woman in scrubs for a refill, and said to Nyman:

"This isn't rational, Tom. You know how I feel about you, but you're not a rational man. You're an emotional man. You're letting your emotions ruin your business."

"Nobody but you," Nyman said, "has ever called me emotional."

"That's because they don't know you like I do. You went through some bad things; I don't deny that. Most people never have to go through what you went through. But you can't let it control your life."

Nyman, avoiding his gaze, looked down at the untasted coffee in front of him. "You really think the Angels have a shot at Houston?"

"Give up the case, Tom. There's no money and no upside. You've got more important things to worry about."

"I can see them making a run for the wildcard, maybe, but I don't see them catching the Astros."

"How long until you can't pay the rent anymore?" Joseph said.

Nyman got to his feet and left the table.

Chapter 9

He walked back to Joseph's room, went into the bathroom, put on his tie and jacket, started to leave, and then stopped and looked at himself in the mirror.

The skin of his face was patchy. His shoulders rose and fell with shallow, angry breaths. Reaching into his jacket, he took out a small rust-colored bottle, took out one of the blue pills it contained, and swallowed the pill with water from the tap.

He went out of the bathroom. For a time he stood beside Joseph's bed and stared at the blank screen of the T.V., his eyes narrowed in thought. Finally he left the room and walked back to the cafeteria.

Joseph was standing with the woman in scrubs, talking about Salisbury steak. He acknowledged Nyman with a nod and told the woman he'd see her in the morning for breakfast.

Without speaking, the two men walked to the common room and sat down in a pair of wingback chairs. Joseph picked up a copy of the *Times* and said in a sociable voice, as if nothing had happened:

"You talk to Claire's sister anymore? What's her name?"

"Theresa," Nyman said. "She stops by the apartment once in a while."

"She find any work yet?"

"I stopped asking about it."

"Talented kid like that, she should be able to find something. I remember that recital we went to. I'd never heard someone so young play like that."

"Neither had I."

Another silence fell. Nyman said something about getting back to work, but he didn't move from the chair. Joseph leafed through the newspaper, frowning.

"This Rexford place," he said. "It's some kind of restaurant?"

"Trujillo says it's a nightclub."

"A nightclub, then. Probably they were looking to hire a waitress and somebody suggested this Alana Bell."

Nyman opened his mouth to speak, but Joseph was already going on.

"Funny thing is, though, the next morning she turns up with that bruise."

Nyman looked over in surprise, then nodded. "It was still fresh when I saw her."

"And you say she was acting scared?"

"Scared or worried about something—I don't know what. She kept saying she needed help."

Joseph tossed the *Times* onto the table between their chairs and shook his head. "Forty-five years I ran that agency, Tom, and I can count the murder cases on one hand. When somebody dies, it's usually straightforward."

"This time it isn't."

Joseph didn't look at him and showed no sign of pleasure or displeasure. His voice was cool and flat.

"Well, that's for you to decide. It's your agency now."

* * *

The Rexford was an unmarked storefront in West Hollywood, across the street from the Laugh Factory. Its walls were painted a deep carmine red and its door was covered with black-and-gold damask. A man in a shirt marked *Security* stood beside the door.

"Sorry," he said as Nyman approached. "Doors open tonight at eleven."

Nyman looked at his watch. "They pay you to stand out here all day?"

The man smiled. "There's a private event going on right now."

"What kind of event?"

"The private kind. You can come back at eleven."

"Maybe you can help me now. I'm looking for a security officer named Fowler."

"Come back at eleven, I'll be happy to help. Right now I have to ask you to move along."

"You can't answer my question?"

"Move along, sir."

Nyman moved along down the sidewalk.

The club's neighbors were a laundromat on one side and a Coffee Bean on the other. At the end of the block was an auto-body shop specializing in German cars. It was partly enclosed by a chain-link fence and consisted of a three-bay garage and an apron of asphalt crowded with dozens of cars.

Nyman made his way up to the garage. In the nearest bay a silver S-class was up on blocks with its tires removed. A man in coveralls lay on his back underneath it. Nyman smiled at him and nodded and was already past the garage before the man could speak.

Ahead of him was a waist-high, padlocked gate barring access to the alleyway. He lifted himself over it, walked past the service entrance of the Coffee Bean, and came to the back side of the Rexford, where four or five men were unloading trays of food from a catering van. Stenciled on the side of the van was a corporate logo with the word *Koda* in the center.

One of the men, noticing Nyman, said: "Looking for somebody, chief?"

The man had a raw, deeply lined face and a plastic-covered tray in his hand. On his t-shirt was another Koda logo.

Nyman had taken the phone from his pocket and was studying it with a puzzled expression. "I'm looking for something called the Rexford," he said. "A friend of mine invited me to an event there, but I can't seem to find it."

"The Fusion event, you mean?"

"That's right."

"Through that door," the man said, gesturing with the tray. "Then go up to the front and have Dave check you off the list."

"Thanks."

"No problem, chief."

The door opened into a hallway thudding with music. Nyman passed through a second door and came into a small, dimly lit alcove set off from the club's main floor, which was visible through an archway. Here and there were low leather couches and glass-topped tables on which flutes of champagne had been set out. Nyman picked up a flute on his way to the main floor.

The D.J. stood on a raised platform at the back. On the floor were more tables and a few dozen people, all young, all casually dressed.

"You must be from up north," a woman said, appearing at his elbow. She was no more than five feet tall and her eyes, behind thick-framed glasses, were bright with tipsiness.

"Up north?"

"Emeryville, or wherever the hell."

Nyman drank some champagne. "Sorry, I'm just here with a friend."

"Really? I thought you were from the other office. The mother ship. Who's your friend?"

"Guy named Fowler. You know him?"

"Sorry. Afraid not. You should come have a shot, though."

She grabbed his hand and pulled him up to the bar, where a crowd had gathered. She said something to the bartender, shouted something indistinct into Nyman's ear, and after a moment began handing around shots of tequila. The crowd roared with approval; someone slapped Nyman's back and put an arm around his shoulders.

Nyman slid out from under the arm, pretended not to see the shot the tipsy woman was offering him, and moved to the end of the bar. He was standing there a moment later when a man stopped beside him and said:

"Can I have a word with you upstairs?"

The man was solidly built, clean-shaven, fortyish, smiling. Despite the smile his eyes were blank and lifeless and his suit was the same dull gray as Nyman's.

"You're Fowler?"

The man nodded. "Please come with me."

Nyman finished his champagne and followed Fowler through an unmarked door and into a cramped stairwell.

"Fun crowd you have in there," Nyman said.

"Thanks. We try to cater to different types."

"What's Fusion, anyway?"

"FusionStream," Fowler said, motioning for Nyman to walk ahead of him up the stairs. "Some kind of tech start-up with an office in Playa Vista. They sold out last week to another company."

"And this is their celebration?"

"One of their celebrations, yeah. Half of them just became millionaires."

At the top of the stairs were two doors; Fowler unlocked one and beckoned Nyman into what was evidently his office: a square little room with a particle-board desk and monitors showing closed-circuit feeds of the club below.

"Well," he said, sitting down behind the desk, "you asked David about me out front, and then you got Hector to let you in through the back. Obviously you want to see me."

"I wanted to ask you a few questions."

"Well, ask away. Talking to people is the part of my job I like most."

Nyman glanced around the office. "What is your job, exactly?"

"Director of nightlife security. Going on six years now."

"For the Rexford?"

"For the Rexford, yeah, and all the other properties in the Koda portfolio. Which is eight, at the moment. Soon to be nine."

"Where's the ninth going?"

"Downtown," Fowler said, "in the Merchant District. A hotel and condo tower we're very excited about. But I'm sure you know all about that, being from A.B.C."

"A.B.C?"

Fowler smiled and leaned back in his chair. "Alcoholic Beverage Control. Personally I thought we were past the point of these checkups. We're up to date on all the fees and forms."

Nyman said that there'd been a misunderstanding. "I'm here about something else. A friend of mine."

"What friend is that?"

"Alana Bell."

There was no change in Fowler's expression, no dimming of his smile. He opened his mouth to speak, then seemed to notice something on the monitors. Exhaling, he got to his feet and said:

"Can you excuse me?"

"Of course."

After he was gone, Nyman got up from the chair and searched the office.

Chapter 10

Aside from a stack of brochures on the desk, the room was bare and neat and meticulously clean. He tried the drawer of the filing cabinet, found it locked, picked up one of the brochures from the desk, and settled back in the chair.

Inside were photos of expensive hotels and restaurants and nightclubs, all owned by Koda. On the last page was a photo of a handsome, boyish-looking man in a t-shirt and Wayfarers. A caption said that Ethan Kovac was the visionary creator of the west coast's premier luxury lifestyle firm.

Nyman was studying Kovac's photo when Fowler came back in.

"Sorry about that," he said, sliding a phone into his pocket and sitting down. "False alarm. You were saying something about a friend of yours?"

"Alana Bell."

"Alana Bell, right. The name's familiar, but at the moment I can't place it."

"She's a graduate student at Pacifica. You went to see her at Zamora Park this Monday."

Fowler snapped his fingers. "Of course. Nice girl. You're a professor of hers?"

"I'm a private investigator. Alana came to my office yesterday to hire me."

"Ah." Fowler's eyes showed no hint of surprise. "How long've you been in the business?"

"About a decade."

"Really? Former cop?"

"Not exactly. Yourself?"

"No, I came up through the service side. Working the door. It sounds like corporate B.S., but Koda's really a family business. If you work hard, you can distinguish yourself."

Nyman asked if that was why he'd gone to the park to see Alana Bell. "To ask her to join the business?"

Fowler's smile grew wider. "Oh, don't be coy, Tom. She must've told you why I went there."

"She told me a few things. I'd like to hear your version."

Fowler said that there wasn't much to tell. "Ethan wanted to talk to her, and he asked me to arrange a meeting."

Nyman glanced at the brochure. "Ethan Kovac?"

"Right. He said Alana had raised some concerns about one of our developments and he wanted to hear more about it. Wanted to make sure we weren't doing anything wrong."

"What sort of concerns?"

"You'd have to ask Ethan. All I did was convey the invitation."

"And she accepted?"

"As far I know. I told her Ethan would be here at eight and she said she'd try to stop by."

"But you didn't actually see her here that night?"

"No, I was at one of the restaurants. That day in the park was the only time I've seen her."

"You're sure?"

"Of course."

"You didn't give her a bruise on her cheek?"

Fowler stopped smiling and looked startled. "Why would you say something like that?"

"She had a bruise when she came to see me. I've been told you're the one who gave it to her."

"Well, you've been misinformed. I never did anything to her."

"You didn't kill her, Mr. Fowler?"

"Kill her?"

Nyman told him what had happened in Vista Hills. When he finished, Fowler took the phone from his pocket, walked to a corner of the office, spoke to someone for several minutes in a voice too soft for Nyman to distinguish the words, and came back and stood beside the desk.

"Ethan wants to see you," he said. "Right away. He's very upset by the news and he hopes you have time tonight to meet him."

Nyman said he'd like nothing more.

"Terrific," Fowler said, with evident relief. "He'll be happy to hear that. You know the Palisades?"

"I've been there."

"That's where he is now—hosting a fundraiser at one of his houses. I'll give you the address."

* * *

The sun dipped lower as Nyman drove west. He found Ethan Kovac's house at the top of a bluff in Pacific Palisades, overlooking the beach and separated from the street by an ivy-covered wall.

A temporary valet stand had been set up in the street. He parked beside it, gave his keys to a white-jacketed man, went through a door in the center of the wall, and came out on a lawn planted with olive trees.

In the center was a modernist, steel-and-glass house with views of the ocean. He followed a path to the front door, where a woman in a short black dress asked for his name, checked it against a stack of preprinted nametags, frowned, and said:

"Are you donating at the gold level, or the platinum?"

Nyman said that he'd been invited by Mr. Kovac and wasn't donating at any level.

"Give me two seconds," she said, and conferred with someone on a walkie-talkie. Then she wrote Nyman's name on a blank white sticker and attached it to his lapel. "Enjoy the reception. I'm afraid they started without you."

The front door led into a vaulted entryway hung with photos of nightlife scenes, all presumably taken at Kovac's clubs. A man's voice echoed along the hallway, amplified by a microphone.

The hallway opened into a sunken living room filled with rows of folding chairs occupied by people in semi-formal dress. They were facing the far end of the room, where Ethan Kovac was standing with his back to a wall of glass and speaking into a microphone.

He'd aged visibly since the photo in the brochure had been taken. The t-shirt had been replaced by a trimly tailored suit and the boyish face was leaner, with a haze of stubble. His thick black hair was artfully tousled and his eyes were the same shade of glittering blue as the ocean framed behind him.

"But that's what I like most about Roberto," he said, his words softened by a faint accent. "Most of the politicians I meet are trying to get something out of me. A table in one of my clubs, or a room in one of my hotels. All Roberto ever wants is my opinion on a tax proposal or something."

The crowd laughed politely. To Nyman's left, at the makeshift bar that had been erected along one wall, an elderly man rolled his eyes and took a drink of wine.

Kovac said: "Roberto's a politician worth supporting, in other words. Somebody with real solutions. But you're probably sick of hearing me talk about him, so now I'll let you hear from Roberto himself."

He held out the microphone and beckoned to someone in the front row. The crowd applauded; with a show of reluctance a man came forward from his chair and accepted the microphone. He was middle aged and heavyset, with salt-and-pepper hair and a neck that bulged over the collar of his shirt.

"Well," he said, gesturing to the window behind him, "all I can tell you is, we don't have views like this where I come from."

The crowd laughed again and went on applauding. Ethan Kovac slipped off to one side and made his way up the aisle. When he saw Nyman his blue eyes brightened and his pace quickened.

"You're the investigator?" he said as he came closer.

Nyman said that he was.

Kovac put a hand on his shoulder. "Thanks for coming on such short notice. We'll talk outside, if that's okay. These speeches go on forever."

"Fine with me."

Nyman followed him back into the vaulted entryway, through a kitchen and dining room, and finally out into the small backyard that divided the main house from the guest house.

Rather than grass, the yard was covered by a layer of decomposed granite. Beds of sage and desert mallow had been planted at intervals, alternating with olive trees. Kovac led Nyman to a secluded spot at the edge of the yard, where a tall glass barrier provided a windbreak and a view of the sea below.

Standing with his back to the sea, Kovac raised a thumbnail to his mouth and said: "She's really gone?"

"I'm afraid so."

"How?"

Nyman told him how. Kovac chewed his thumbnail and didn't interrupt. Close at hand, he was shorter than he'd looked in the photo and handsomer, with a constant nervous energy.

When Nyman finished talking, Kovac blew out his breath and said, shaking his head: "I can't believe she's dead."

"You knew her well?"

"Not well at all, no. I only met her once, a few days ago. But she was so young. Almost a kid."

Nyman asked him what he and Alana had talked about during their meeting.

"Oh, just about everything, I guess. All the stuff she mentioned in her letter."

"Letter?"

The blue eyes got wider. "You don't know about the letter?"

"No."

"Well, that probably explains a lot. Here—come with me. I'll show you."

Chapter 11

Kovac led him across the yard to the door of the guest house, which he unlocked with his phone. Nyman followed him into a large room filled with minimalist furniture and, running the length of one wall, a strip of corkboard on which blueprints and press clippings and handwritten notes had been pinned.

"My office away from the office," Kovac said.

A teakwood desk was piled with loose papers and a stack of file folders. Picking up a folder and thumbing through it, Kovac found the letter he wanted and handed it to Nyman.

Mr. Kovac,

Recently I was asked by Dr. Michael Freed to assist in the economic analysis of a development proposed by the city's Merchant South Authority.

One of the centerpieces of the proposal is a high-rise luxury hotel and condo tower to be built at 7500 Otis Boulevard, over what is now Zamora Park. Given that the design and operation of the properties will be the responsibility of your company, Koda Entertainment, I hope you'll be willing to meet with me to discuss the impact the development will have on the park's homeless population, a population I work with on a daily basis as part of my graduate research at Pacifica University.

I look forward to your response and have included my contact information below.

Yours sincerely,

Alana Bell

Nyman read through the letter twice, copied down the phone number and address at the bottom of the page, and handed the letter back, saying:

"According to the date, she sent you this last month."

"That's right."

"But you didn't arrange a meeting until three days ago?"

"I get letters like this all the time. Most of them from cranks. You can't really blame my staff for not showing it to me right away."

"But they showed it to you eventually?"

"Of course—and I called her as soon as I saw it. When she didn't answer, I sent Fowler down to the park to look for her."

"Why Fowler? There's no connection to security."

Kovac slid the letter back into the folder. "We're pretty low-key around here. When you need something done, you ask whoever's closest. Fowler happened to be closest."

"Her letter must've made quite an impression on you."

"It made me stop and think, for sure. I didn't even know about the homeless living there. I figured it was worth kicking around some ideas with her. See if we could find a compromise."

"And did you?"

Kovac ran a hand through his hair. "Look. She was a smart girl, but she wasn't exactly realistic. She wanted me to abandon the project then and there, cold turkey. When I told her we'd already invested too much, she said I should use some of the profits to build housing for all the displaced people."

"Nice idea."

"In a perfect world, yeah. But the industry I'm in, the profits are razor-thin. Most of the money I make has to be funneled right back into the properties."

Nyman said that Alana couldn't have liked that answer.

"That's putting it mildly. She thought I was heartless and greedy."

"Which made you angry?"

Kovac grinned. "If I got angry with all the people who think I'm heartless, Tom, I'd never stop being angry."

Beyond the glass walls, the sun was dropping into the sea, leaving purple darkness in the sky above it.

"So how did the conversation end?" Nyman said. "You just agreed to disagree?"

"Essentially. I tried to explain that it's not just about money with me. I can't build shelters for the homeless, maybe, but I can be smart about where I put my properties. Put one in a place like the Merchant District, and you start generating jobs and more development. Construction, restaurants—all that. You take a neighborhood that's kind of a slum and in a few years people are making a living wage."

"A rising tide lifts all boats."

"Exactly."

"What did Alana think of that?"

"She thought it was bullshit," Kovac said, laughing. "Which it is, you know, on one level. To really spread that new income around, you have to have politicians in place who are on board with the idea. Which is why I try to help people like Roberto Reyes."

"The man you're raising money for?"

Kovac nodded. "Tonight's sort of a kickoff for the general election. Roberto's a good guy. First generation, like me. You put a guy like him in office, he knows what it's like to struggle. He's trying to make a real difference."

"In L.A.?"

"No, in Riverside County." Kovac turned away from the desk and gestured for Nyman to follow him back outside. "He's running for the State Senate. That's one thing I've learned about politics. If you want your money to make an impact, you have to spend it at the local level, and you can't just stay in your own neighborhood."

They crossed the checkerboard yard and came into the main house just after Reyes had finished his speech. The guests had left their chairs and were milling around the makeshift bar. Along the opposite wall, a string quartet was playing.

"You're welcome to stay and mingle," Kovac said, "but it won't be very exciting. Just me trying to get people to open their checkbooks."

Nyman asked him if he would have time after the fundraiser for more questions.

"Not tonight, no. I'm booked pretty solid for the next few days."

"What about suspects?" Nyman said. "Can you think of anyone who might've wanted to hurt Alana? Someone at Koda, for instance?"

Kovac shook his head. "Wish I could help, Tom, but I don't make a habit of hiring murderers. I'd vouch for every single person in my organization."

A tall, long-limbed woman in her late teens or early twenties detached herself from the crowd and came forward to talk to Kovac, moving slowly and with self-conscious poise, as if she were aware of her own beauty. Jewelry rattled at her wrists as she looped an arm around Kovac's neck.

"Tom, I'd like you to meet Rhea, my wife. Rhea, this is Tom. We just wrapped up a little business."

"Pleased to meet you," Nyman said.

The woman gave him a brief nod and started to talk earnestly to Kovac in a low voice, her lips turned downward in displeasure. Kovac listened with an annoyed look and responded in the same low tones, taking her by the elbow and turning away from Nyman and the other guests.

At the front of the room, the woman in the short black dress announced that everyone who'd donated at the platinum level should proceed to the lanai, where there would be a private champagne reception with Mr. Reyes and Mr. Kovac.

Guests started drifting out of the room. Soon Nyman was one of a dozen people still grouped around the bar. He was pouring club soda into a glass when someone leaned toward him and said in a confidential tone:

"Don't blame you for not paying for the meet-and-greet. Waste of money, if you ask me."

It was the man who'd rolled his eyes at Kovac's speech. He was short and expensively dressed, with a diamond tiepin that matched his cufflinks and polished brown brogues that reflected the lights overhead.

"Chances of Reyes getting elected are slim to none," he said, splashing more wine into his glass.

Nyman said: "You keep up with the state races?"

"Enough to know that Aldridge has twice as much cash on hand. Tried to explain that to my wife, but she doesn't care. She'll donate to anything Kovac puts in front of her."

"Who's Aldridge?"

The man seemed surprised by Nyman's ignorance. "The Republican running against Reyes. The one Kovac held a fundraiser for last month."

Nyman frowned. "Kovac's raising money for both candidates?"

"Of course he is. They're both running for the 28th District. Palm Springs and Rancho Mirage. Right where Kovac wants to build a new resort."

"And he thinks giving money to Reyes and Aldridge will help the deal?"

The man looked at Nyman again in surprise, then gave him a wine-reddened smile and patted him on the shoulder.

"What I wouldn't give to be your age again," he said. "So innocent."

Chapter 12

Mail lay piled in the entryway when Nyman got back to his office. From the restaurant next door came the murmuring clatter of the dinner crowd. He tossed the mail onto the desk and walked to the filing cabinet. From the top drawer he took a bowl, a can of soup, and a plastic bottle of Ballantine's.

While the soup was microwaving he poured an inch of scotch into a cup and sat down in his chair, not looking at the cup he'd given to Alana Bell, which still stood half-empty on the edge of the desk. He drank the scotch and drew an envelope—smaller than the others and hand-addressed—from the pile of letters.

Inside was a personal check for eighty dollars. He frowned at the number, then took a metal box from the desk and unlocked it with a key from his keyring. Inside were two other checks and a small pile of bills. Behind him the microwave beeped.

He was carrying the soup to his desk when a knock came at the door. Through the glass he could see a young woman, tall and thin and blonde.

Nyman opened the door with a smile and waved her inside, saying: "Joseph was just asking about you. Drink?"

"What are you having?"

"Scotch."

"No thanks. Just coffee."

She spoke in a hoarse mumble and her face was a dull, waxy gray. Despite the heat she wore a long-sleeve shirt with frayed cuffs. Sitting down in the same chair Alana Bell had used, she glanced sleepily around the office.

"I tried your apartment first," she said, "but nobody was there."

Nyman gave her a cup of cold coffee. "It's been a busy day."

"New client?"

"In a manner of speaking," he said, and told her about the case, including his encounter with Ethan Kovac.

The mention of Kovac brought a brief flicker of curiosity to her eyes. "What's he like?"

"Kovac?" Nyman shrugged. "All right, I guess. Why? You've heard of him?"

"Of his clubs, yeah. I thought everybody knew about them."

"I'm unhip, Theresa. You forget that."

"You're not unhip. Just uninterested. Claire was the unhip one."

Lowering his eyes, Nyman poured more scotch into his cup. "Anyway, it's good to see you. I was down at your old school today. At the Founders' Club."

Theresa nodded but didn't seem to be listening. She stared dully into the cup, as if seeing the coffee from a distance.

"When you were there," Nyman said, "did you ever take a class with Michael Freed?"

"Hmm?"

"At Pacifica. He's a professor of public policy."

"Oh." She roused herself and took a drink. "No, I don't think so."

"What about a grad student named Alana Bell? Ever heard of her?"

"Afraid not. I was only there a semester, anyway. College didn't agree with me."

"Your sister thought you had a lot of talent," Nyman said. "For music, especially. Ever think of going back?"

She gave him a bleak smile. "Claire overestimated my talent. And I'm too old for college."

"You're only twenty-nine."

"Twenty-eight," Theresa said, "and it didn't agree with me, like I said."

Nyman said that never finishing college was something he regretted. "For a while I had an idea of becoming an architect. Or an anthropologist. Basically I never got past the A's."

There was boredom in her voice as she said: "That kind of thing never interested me."

"Maybe it would if you went back."

"Maybe. But I wanted to ask you something, Tom."

Without a show of surprise, Nyman nodded. "How much?"

She licked her lips. "Would a hundred be too much?"

"I don't have a hundred. The most I could do is fifty."

"What about seventy-five?"

"If I had seventy-five, I'd give it to you," Nyman said. "Fifty is all I can do."

"You've got a check there for eighty."

"That check," Nyman said, "is from Mr. Brand."

"Who's Mr. Brand?"

"An old man who told me his brother was trying to kill him. I spent a week guarding his house, and now he's paying me back in installments."

"Did the brother try to kill him?"

"The brother didn't exist. Mr. Brand was just lonely."

Theresa nodded and finished her coffee. Her eyes shifted restlessly around the room. The fingers of one hand plucked at the sleeve of the shirt.

"All right," she said. "Fifty's fine, I guess. I appreciate it."

Nyman reached for the metal box. He counted out the bills and handed them to Theresa, saying: "It's fifty-four."

"Okay. Thanks."

When she stood to leave, Nyman said: "I could help you, you know."

She blinked at him. "What?"

"Going back to school. Or getting back into music, at least. There's a guy who plays at the Green Door. He might be willing to help. Show you the ropes and help you get some work."

"It's too late for something like that, Tom."

"Claire didn't think it was too late. She believed in you."

"I know she did," Theresa said, turning her back on Nyman and opening the door. "But she's not around, is she?"

* * *

Alone again in the office, he ate the soup, read the mail, locked up for the night, and drove down to Jefferson Park.

Wind blew trash along the pavement and rattled the leaves of the palms. According to the address she'd given Kovac, Alana Bell had lived on a side street just below West Adams

Boulevard. Nyman drove past dollar stores and darkened churches and came eventually to a squat concrete building with cracks rising up from the foundation.

Her apartment was on the second floor. An unlocked street-door led him up a flight of steps and onto a landing exposed to the open air. A strip of light showed under the door of the apartment; from the interior came the sound of footsteps on a creaking floor.

He knocked twice, loudly, and the footsteps went on as before, without stopping. He touched the doorknob, felt it turn, and a moment later was inside the apartment and closing the door behind him.

It was a single small room with a kitchen at the far end, a T.V. and futon by the door, and a bathroom slotted into a corner. Alana's mother, Valerie, was standing in the kitchen with a cardboard box cradled in her arm.

She glanced at Nyman with red-veined, exhausted eyes and went on packing cups and dishes into the box. She looked smaller and frailer than she had that morning at the coroner's office; her face was swollen from crying and her expression was blank and lifeless.

"Which one are you with?" she said hoarsely. "The coroner or Vista Hills?"

Nyman told her who he was. She listened without any sign of interest or comprehension and said nothing in response, turning her attention back to her packing. Nyman stood awkwardly in the same spot, not coming any farther into the room. His hand was still on the doorknob when Valerie Bell said:

"I've talked to so many people today I can't keep it straight. From the university, too. Are you from the university?"

He told her again who he was. She nodded as if she'd understood and said in a monotone:

"I told Allie she ought to live in university housing, but she wouldn't hear it. She said she wanted to be on her own, in a real neighborhood. She's always been like that, you know. Always has to have her own way."

She closed her eyes and took a step backward. A plate slipped from her hand and shattered on the floor. The cardboard box followed it, landing on its side and scattering cups and dishes. She sagged back against the refrigerator and put her hands over her face. She cried in racking sobs, sliding down against the refrigerator until she was sitting on the floor beside the dishes and cups and broken ceramic.

Nyman took a step toward the kitchen, then stopped. A neighbor banged on the wall and shouted at them to be quiet. Nyman's face as he watched the woman cry was creased and bloodless and uncertain.

Tentatively, he went into the kitchen and picked up the scattered dishes. He put them back in the box, then started taking plates and cups down from the cabinets and stacking them on the countertop, as if to help her in her packing.

Gradually her sobs became quieter. She took the hands away from her face and rubbed them on her shirt. With her back against the refrigerator, she sat motionless on the floor and watched him stack dishes.

After a time, she said: "You're the private investigator. Nyman."

He paused with a dish in his hand. "Tom Nyman, right. I talked to your brother this morning. After he brought you back from the coroner's office."

"I know. Paul told me."

"Does Paul know you're here, Mrs. Bell?"

"No." Her voice was weak but more human. "No, I told him I was going home to bed. He didn't want me to leave, but I insisted."

"Getting some sleep might be a good idea."

She turned to look at the rest of the apartment. Her gaze moved over the futon, the small bookcase beside it, the framed photos on the walls.

"I won't be doing any sleeping tonight," she said.

Nyman said that in that case she shouldn't be alone. "Why don't you let your brother know where you are?"

She said nothing in response and went on staring at the photos, absorbed in thought or memory.

Leaving the kitchen, Nyman walked to the bookcase and took out his phone. He searched online until he found a listing for a Paul Lattimer with an address in Watts.

Lattimer answered in a voice slurred by sleep. He listened to what Nyman had to say, cursed, said he would be there in ten minutes, and hung up without saying goodbye.

Chapter 13

Nyman put away his phone. Valerie was sitting in the same place on the floor, her hands over her face, her shoulders rising and falling as she cried. He looked at her for a moment in indecision, then checked the time on his watch and kneeled down beside the bookcase.

Taking the books out one by and one, he glanced at the titles and ran his fingers along the pages, finding nothing more interesting than a bookmark. He got to his feet and moved to the closet, where he found nothing apart from clothes and shoes and more books.

On a shelf beside the door was a bowl filled with junk mail and unopened letters. Under the letters was an address book with names and numbers written in pencil. He was studying the names when he heard footsteps on the outer stairs.

Paul Lattimer came in a moment later, out of breath from the climb. His eyes had the same scratchy redness as his sister's and his broad shoulders sagged with exhaustion.

Without acknowledging Nyman, he went into the kitchen and kneeled down beside Valerie. Taking her hands into his own, he said something in a voice Nyman couldn't hear. With a sob she fell forward and put her face against his shoulder. Lattimer's arms came forward to hold her as she cried.

Nyman left the apartment and waited outside the door.

* * *

Leaning against the waist-high wall at the edge of the landing, he took the cigarettes from his pocket and found his lighter. He'd smoked two in slow succession before the door opened and Lattimer came out.

With a wordless gesture he asked for a cigarette. Nyman gave him one along with the lighter and the two men stood at the wall and looked up at the thinly scattered stars. After a time Lattimer said in a quiet voice:

"Finally got her to lie down on the couch. Gave her one of my sleeping pills."

Nyman nodded and said nothing.

"I guess I ought to thank you for calling me," Lattimer went on. "A lot of people wouldn't have gone to the trouble."

Nyman said that it hadn't been any trouble. "I've learned some things, incidentally. About what happened to your niece."

Lattimer looked at him with heavy-lidded eyes. "What kind of things?"

Nyman told him about the people he'd met and the facts he'd pieced together. Lattimer listened with a frown that got deeper as Nyman went on. His eyes lost some of their tiredness and his voice, when he spoke, was more urgent.

"If these nightclub people didn't do anything but talk to her, why'd she come away with that bruise?"

"That's what I'm trying to figure out," Nyman said.

"And why would Freed say she went to Vegas? I never heard anything about Allie going to Vegas."

"She didn't take a lot of trips?"

"She didn't have the money for trips. Not unless she was getting it from somewhere we didn't know about. But it sounds like there were lots of things we didn't know about."

He flicked his cigarette into the alley below and thrust his hands into his pockets. He turned away and stood leaning with his back against the wall, his eyes dark and thoughtful.

After a silence, Nyman asked him if the family had been contacted by the Vista Hills police.

Lattimer shrugged. "Couple of men came by the house. Said they found Allie's car parked on the same street she was killed on. No sign of a break in."

"Did they find anything inside?"

"Not that they told us about."

"Which side of the street was the car parked on?"

"I don't know. I don't think they mentioned it."

"What about witnesses?"

"Haven't found any, apparently. A few of the houses on the block had cameras, but nobody had the right angle to catch the accident. Department's putting up a reward for anybody who comes forward."

"And the coroner's office?"

Ruiz had advised them not to expect anything till morning, Lattimer said. "She told us she'd be working through the night."

Nyman ground out his cigarette. Nodding to the apartment, he said: "There's an address book in there with the mail."

Lattimer looked at him in surprise. "Allie's address book?"

"Seems to be. I was wondering if you'd go through it and tell me who the names belong to."

"I doubt I'd recognize any. Allie kept her social life to herself."

"Anything would help."

Lattimer nodded and led Nyman back inside. They found Valerie lying on the futon in an awkward, propped-up position and gazing intently at one of the photos on the wall.

Taking the address book into the kitchen, Lattimer leafed slowly through the pages, pausing over each name. After he'd been through the book two or three times he tapped one of the entries.

"This guy. Patrick Choi. I think he might've been one of her friends at Pacifica. Seems like I remember her talking about him."

Beside Patrick Choi's name was a phone number with an L.A. area code. Nyman was copying the number into his notebook when Lattimer said:

"You intend to keep working on this, I take it? On what happened to Allie?"

"Yes. Unless your family has any objection."

Lattimer leaned back against the counter and shook his head, looking down at his feet. "It doesn't seem right, though. You working on this and not getting paid."

"I didn't come here to ask for money, Mr. Lattimer."

"I know you didn't. My sister and I didn't ask for your charity, either."

"It wasn't intended as charity."

"Let's forget what you intended. I'm asking what kind of fee you'd charge for a job like this."

"Working full time, you mean?"

"Working as much you need to."

Nyman told him his hourly rate and the amount of a typical retainer.

Lattimer nodded. "I can give you a check for the retainer tonight. The rest might take a while."

Nyman eyed him carefully. "Would I be working for you personally, or for the whole family?"

"Does it make a difference?"

"Not to me, but to other people it might. It helps to be able to say exactly who's paying me."

Lattimer's response was cut short by Valerie Bell, who looked over from the futon and said:

"Whatever you're whispering about, you might as well say it out loud. I'm not a child."

Lattimer, handing Nyman the address book, went back into the living room and kneeled beside her. They talked in hushed voices while Nyman paged through the book and copied down names and numbers. Then Lattimer got to his feet and left the apartment; from the street below came the sound of a car door opening and closing.

When he came back in he was carrying a checkbook. He took a pen from a drawer, filled out the check, and put it on the counter in front of Nyman.

"You'll be working for all of us."

Chapter 14

The coroner's office, late at night, was a black shape against the gray darkness that hung above Mission Road. Nyman climbed the front steps and went into the lobby, where he told the overnight guard that he needed to see Ruiz.

"Name?"

"Tom Nyman."

The guard picked up his phone and had a brief, murmuring conversation. Then he put a hand on the mouthpiece and said: "Unless this is an emergency, she says you can come back tomorrow during normal hours."

"Tell her I'm here at the request of Alana Bell's family. They hired me to investigate her death."

The guard murmured into the phone, nodded, hung up, and rose from his chair. "She's on the security floor. I'll take you down."

The elevator took them to an anteroom that ended in a pair of locked steel doors. Ruiz was waiting at the doors, wearing a white mask over her nose and mouth. Her makeup had been sweated or scrubbed away; lines of age and exhaustion made her look older than she had that morning.

"I told the family not to expect anything until tomorrow," she said.

"They're not doing very well at the moment. I thought some news might help them through the night."

"I don't have much news to give them."

"But you have some."

Ruiz glared at him, then looked at the clock beside the elevator. Saying that she could only give him a few minutes, she handed Nyman a mask like her own, told him not to touch anything, and led him through the doors into a wide, brightly lit hallway.

Here and there along the walls were gurneys on which corpses lay, most of them naked and wrapped in clear plastic sheeting. Plexiglass windows gave views of the autopsy suites that ran along either side of the hall.

Most of the suites were darkened for the night. In the suite nearest Nyman, a woman in scrubs stood beside a slab on which a naked dead man lay. Deep incisions ran from the man's shoulders to the center of his chest and on down to his pelvis; the skin had been pulled aside and the breastbone removed, revealing the crimson interior. Buzzing in the woman's hands was the Stryker saw she was using to open the man's skull.

Following Ruiz, Nyman went past the autopsy suites and through another locked door, coming at last into a series of interconnected rooms filled from floor to ceiling with sheeted corpses on steel shelves.

"Here you go," Ruiz said, stopping at a shelf and pulling aside the layers of sheeting that covered the body of Alana Bell.

Nyman stepped forward. Alana's eyes and mouth were open. A blow of some kind had left the side of her head pulpy and misshapen, with dried blood running in a jagged seam above her ear. Bruises and livor mortis made her skin a patchwork of green and purple.

"We did the photographs and x-rays a few hours ago," Ruiz said. "Clothes are bagged up and waiting for chemical analysis."

"What did the x-rays show?"

"About what you'd expect. Skull fracture, broken pelvis, bumper injuries to the right leg. Car hit her from behind— probably as she was walking along the side of the road. No signs that the car tried to brake."

"Which means she was hit intentionally," Nyman said.

"Or that the driver didn't see her. There aren't any street lamps on that road."

"But if you hit something, your first instinct is to stop. At least for a moment."

"Assuming you're sober enough to realize what you've done. I've seen guys so drunk they drive through buildings without noticing."

Nyman said that an intentional hit-and-run seemed like the simplest explanation.

Ruiz smiled and folded the plastic sheeting back over the body. "With all due respect, you don't have the training to make a judgment like that. Or the information. We've hardly started our analysis."

"The D.M.E.'s planning a full autopsy?"

"And toxicology. Results will take over a month to get back. I suggest you go home and let Vista Hills handle things. This isn't the kind of work you're used to."

Nyman's gaze remained on the sheeted corpse. "How would you know anything about my work?"

"I'm an investigator, Tom. Your business card was in the decedent's pocket. It's my job to check up on you."

Nyman turned to look at her. "Find anything interesting?"

"Nothing I wouldn't expect from someone who worked for Moritz. The coroner's always had a good relationship with your agency."

"I'm glad to hear it."

"And as a matter of fact I remember you from your visit last year."

The skin of Nyman's face, already pale, turned a sickly shade of yellow.

"It was O'Bannon's case," Ruiz went on, "but I helped him out. He said you handled it as well as anybody could've."

From the autopsy suites came the shrill, buzzing whine of the Stryker saw. The whine was accompanied by the blast of air conditioners and the sudden pounding of blood in Nyman's ears. Turning to one side, he put a hand on the wall to steady himself.

"I see," he said.

Above her mask, Ruiz's eyes narrowed. "Sorry," she said. "It was stupid of me to bring that up."

Nyman said: "No, it's all right. It's time for me to be going, anyway."

"You're sure?"

"Yes. I've taken up too much of your time."

Without waiting for Ruiz to lead him, he turned and made his way back through the columns of bodies. Half-numb, unwieldy legs carried him into the main hallway, where the bulbs above his head burned with painful brightness.

Ruiz caught up to him and asked if he was all right. He ignored the question and looked into the lighted autopsy suite as he went past. The Stryker saw was quiet now and resting on a table; its blade was bright and wet and dripping.

He didn't say goodbye to Ruiz and didn't speak to the guard who rode with him in the elevator. In the darkened parking lot he stumbled over a curb, then kneeled for a time on the pavement, as if he were going to be sick.

Then he rose to his feet and climbed into the car.

* * *

Glass tubes glowing green with neon gas outlined the door of a small building on Culver Boulevard. Nyman passed through the doorway into a dark, low-ceilinged room crowded with tables, red-leather banquettes, a stage, and a bar at which a dozen or more people were sitting. On the stage a man was playing "Alfie" on a keyboard.

Sliding into an open space at the end of the bar, Nyman made eye contact with the bartender and smiled. His face was still yellow; the smile failed to extend upward to his eyes. The bartender returned the smile, reached for a bottle, and poured gin into a shaker.

Nyman took the notebook from his pocket. He was staring absently at one of the pages when the bartender set the Gibson in front of him and said:

"You didn't come in earlier, I said to the guys: 'He finally got a client.'"

Nyman took a long drink. "A dead client."

"Well, better dead than none at all."

"Maybe."

The bartender's face—a dark brown reddened to maroon at the nose and cheeks—lost its smile and became serious. "Not so good night, Tom?"

"A night is a night."

At the middle of the bar, a woman detached herself from a group of drinkers and made her way over with steps that were carefully controlled. She was a decade older than Nyman and elaborately made up, with a tight white blouse and tanned skin just starting to be discolored by liver spots. Her nails were long and artificial and she pressed them into Nyman's back as she put an arm around his shoulder.

"You missed the dancing, Tom, but maybe we can get it started again."

Nyman finished the gin in his glass and said that he couldn't dance.

"Course you can," the woman said thickly. "Anybody can."

"Having a nice time, Laura?"

"Well," the woman said, tilting her head at a thoughtful angle, "it was a little boring, to be honest, before you got here. But now you're here and we're going to dance."

"Let's have another drink first."

"All right," Laura said, squeezing in beside him at the bar. "But only one."

They had another round of Gibsons, then switched to Irish Coffees. At Nyman's request the man at the keyboard played "My Funny Valentine." Nyman gave Laura a dollar to put in the fishbowl beside the keyboard.

When she came back along the bar a small man climbed off his stool and told her he was going home. She said she was going to stay. He said she was his wife and she ought to come home with him. She patted him affectionately on the cheek and said she'd be there soon enough. The man shrugged and rubbed a hand over the spot where she'd touched him and, walking past Nyman on his way to the door, said in a friendly voice:

"Nice to see you again, Tom. Sorry you missed the dancing."

After the Irish Coffees Nyman and Laura drank scotch. Customers drifted away from the bar and went out the green-lighted door. The piano player, packing up his keyboard, paused beside the bar to say goodnight to the bartender. When he turned away, Nyman stopped him with a hand and asked if he ever gave private lessons.

"For you?"

"For my sister-in-law," Nyman said. "She's got a lot of talent."

"How old?"

"Twenty-eight."

The piano player frowned. "Come by my place sometime and we'll talk about it. I have Sundays off."

Taking a napkin from the bar, he wrote down a Burbank address, handed the napkin to Nyman, and followed the rest of the customers out into the street.

Behind the bar, the bartender moved more slowly than before and looked more frequently at the clock. Nyman had long since put away the notebook and was talking to Laura in a low, serious voice that was only occasionally slurred. At exactly ten minutes to two the bartender said:

"Sorry, guys, but I gotta close up."

Nyman and Laura left the bar together, their arms around each other's waists. The night was still hot; the thin scattering of stars had become thicker since he'd left Alana Bell's apartment. He led the woman to the end of the block, where an apartment building stood behind a pair of sun-browned palms.

The paint on the building's façade was chipped and faded; crooked metal letters identified it as the Monte Carlo Arms. He led Laura up a wooden staircase and unlocked the door of apartment 2C.

The living room was small and bare; in one corner stood a pile of empty cardboard boxes. A hallway led to a bathroom and two bedrooms. The door of the larger bedroom was closed.

"You moving out or something?" Laura said, shuffling unsteadily to the couch.

Nyman didn't answer. He went into the kitchen to put on a pot of coffee. Then, taking off his tie and jacket as he walked, he came back into the living room and sat down on the couch, where Laura was lying with her legs pulled up to her chest, already asleep.

He said her name and shook her by the shoulder, but her mouth had fallen open and she was snoring. He watched her for a time, frowning, and then went back into the kitchen.

He poured coffee into a mug, added an inch of Bacardi from the row of bottles beside the sink, and carried the mug into the smaller of the two bedrooms. He sat down in the chair beside his bed and took a book from the nightstand.

When he woke four hours later the mug was empty, the book was still in his hand, and Laura was gone.

Chapter 15

The day dawned hot and windy. Nyman, still in the same clothes, went into the kitchen and filled a clean mug with the rest of the coffee. Then he walked to a window and looked down at the palm trees and brown yard below.

A small, shirtless boy from another apartment was standing at the edge of the yard and throwing peanuts from a can into the grass. Birds—first jays, then crows—drifted down from the trees and picked the peanuts out of the grass, lifting their glossy wings as they bent forward.

Nyman watched them with eyes that were swollen and discolored. The hand holding the mug was shaking. After five or ten minutes he turned away and walked to the kitchen table, where his notebook was lying open at the page with Patrick Choi's phone number.

He took the phone from his pocket and dialed. After a short conversation he hung up and went into the bathroom to brush his teeth and wash his face. When he left the apartment it was eight o'clock and the yard was black with crows.

* * *

In Echo Park, a few blocks from Angelus Temple, Nyman found Patrick Choi at a table on the patio of a diner. He was in his early twenties, wiry, shy, with black hair shaved at the sides and worn long at the top, so that his bangs came down in a crest to cover part of his face.

Nyman thanked him for coming and apologized for calling so early. Choi ignored the apology and said:

"You think she was murdered, don't you?"

Nyman sat down at the table and reached for the menu. His hands were no longer shaking and his tone was mild and friendly.

"Is that what Professor Freed told you?"

"I haven't talked to Freed. All I got was an email from the dean saying Allie had been killed in a car accident."

"Then why mention murder?"

"Because you're a private investigator. Allie's family wouldn't have hired you to investigate an accident."

Nyman admitted as much. "And yes, I do think she was murdered."

"Why?"

Nyman told him his reasons. Choi stopped him more than once to ask a question or clarify a point; despite his shyness, he met Nyman's gaze directly and intently.

When Nyman was finished, Choi nodded and sat back in his chair. "That's why you wanted to see me, then. Because of my connection to Merchant South."

"I wasn't aware you had a connection."

"Allie didn't tell you?"

"She didn't have time to tell me very much."

"What about Freed?"

"He told me even less, in some ways."

Choi gave a small smile. "Yeah. There are probably lots of things he didn't tell you. He and Allie spent a lot of time together."

"I've heard they were romantically involved."

"Physically involved, at least. Allie never struck me as a romantic kind of person."

"What kind of person was she?"

Choi let his gaze wander to the next table, where a dog was lying at its owner's feet, panting.

"I'm not really the one to ask," Choi said. "I hardly knew her."

"Her uncle seemed to think you two were pretty close."

"Her uncle's wrong, then. We weren't close at all."

"You never talked to her?"

"Only in class and around the department. Everybody talks to everybody."

"You must've gotten some kind of impression of her, then."

A waitress came to the table to fill their water glasses and take their orders. After she'd gone away, Choi said that Alana had been no different from any of the other students in the program.

"Just a little more ambitious, maybe. She knew what she wanted and she knew how to get it."

"What did she want?"

"Different things from different people," Choi said. "From me it was access. A way into the councilmember's office."

"Councilmember?"

"The L.A. city council. I did an internship last semester with Grace Salas."

Nyman said that the name sounded familiar.

"It should. The Merchant South development was basically her idea."

"How so?"

A busboy came over to put two cups of coffee on the table. Choi's eyes, looking up at Nyman as he reached for his cup, were wary.

"You really don't know about any of this?"

"I don't anything," Nyman said. "Why was Alana so interested in Salas?"

"It wasn't just Salas; she was interested in everybody. The council. The mayor. The developers. She thought the whole thing was a scam. That Merchant South was just a way for everybody to get rich."

"Get rich how?"

Choi shrugged and drank. "I don't know where she got the idea. She thought I'd be able to give her some kind of inside dirt on Merchant South. As if they'd give anything important to an intern."

Nyman asked if that was why she'd wanted to work with Freed on his analysis.

"She never said it outright, but that's what I figured. I got the sense she wanted to blow up the whole development, either through Freed's report or her own pressure."

"She cared about it that much?"

"She seemed to. With any kind of big development, somebody's going to get hurt; but Allie didn't want to see anybody get hurt. She wanted the world to be perfect. All roses and rainbows."

They were interrupted by the arrival of some of their food and the small talk of the waitress. When she'd gone away, Nyman said:

"It sounds like you didn't think very highly of Alana."

Choi turned his attention to his food. "I didn't think much about her one way or the other. I hardly knew her."

"You seem to know how her mind worked."

"I'm good at reading people, I guess."

"You're sure you never saw her socially?"

"Not that I remember. Once or twice, maybe, at the most."

"Did she ever go to any bars or clubs in Vista Hills?"

"Allie? She never went to bars or clubs, period. The only thing she cared about was her work. That's why it was so bizarre when she sent me the text from Vegas."

Nyman paused with the fork in his hand. "Vegas?"

Choi nodded. "She kept begging me to get her a meeting with Salas. I finally set one up a couple weeks ago—for the Friday before last—but Allie sent a text saying she couldn't make it, because she was in Vegas. Sent a picture to prove it."

He took a phone from his pocket, found the photo he was looking for, and put the phone on the table.

It was a picture of Alana Bell, evidently taken by Alana herself. She was standing in front of a wall of glass and smiling at the camera, her chin slightly raised. Framed in the window behind her was a section of the Las Vegas Strip in full daylight, the outlines of the casinos blurred by the glass. Visible in the lower right-hand corner was the façade of a building encased in stainless steel. A sign had been attached to the façade, a two-letter symbol comprised of an overlapping L and V.

Nyman said: "Did she tell you what she was doing there?"

Choi shook his head. "Not a word. That was the last time I heard from her."

"She didn't get in touch when she came home?"

"No. A friend of mine saw her in City Hall last week, though. Apparently she got an appointment with Salas on her own. Spent an hour in her office, just the two of them."

"Talking about what?"

"You'd have to ask the councilmember."

Nyman looked again at the picture. There was no bruise on Alana's face, no sign of anxiety or fear.

"Want me to send it to you?" Choi said. "The picture?"

"If you wouldn't mind."

"No problem."

While Choi sent him the photo, Nyman looked at his watch. "The council has a meeting this morning, doesn't it?"

"Every Friday at ten."

"Usually lasts about an hour?"

"More like an hour and a half."

Nyman nodded to the phone in Choi's hand. "Was that the only picture you kept of her?"

Choi's eyes were party hidden by the fringe of black hair. He put the phone back on the table and reached for his coffee. "I don't know. I might've kept some others."

"How many?"

"I couldn't tell you."

"You took a lot of pictures of her?"

"We all took pictures together—in class and stuff. I didn't follow her around taking pictures, if that's what you're implying."

"There's no reason to get angry, Patrick."

"I'm not angry."

"You cared about her, didn't you?"

Dark blood, as if from a fresh wound, rose in Choi's neck and face. He put down the coffee, took the wallet from his pocket, and counted out money for the bill.

"It must've been hard," Nyman said, "seeing her spend time with someone like Freed. You must've been upset."

Arranging his money on the table, Choi shook his head. "I didn't get upset, and I didn't kill her."

"I'm not saying you did. Where were you Wednesday night, though, just for the record?"

He'd been on campus, he said. "In the library. You can ask the guy at the checkout desk."

"You know the guy's name?"

"No. But he's always there on weeknights."

Nyman took out his notebook and made a note.

Choi, watching him, said: "You think I did it, don't you?"

"I don't think anything. I'm just asking questions."

"I never would've done anything to her. You can ask anybody."

"I'm not accusing you, Patrick."

"If you knew how I felt about her, you'd know I couldn't have done it."

"How did you feel about her?"

Choi put the wallet in his pocket and stood up. "That's none of your business."

"What about Alana? Did she know how you felt?"

Choi gave a sharp, bitter laugh. "I don't think the idea ever occurred to her," he said, and left the restaurant.

Chapter 16

Nyman passed under the shaded portico of City Hall and came into the air-conditioned dimness of the lobby. Telling his name and business to a security guard, he accepted a nametag and walked with echoing footsteps to a bank of elevators covered in cast bronze. He left the elevator at the twenty-fourth floor and went through a door marked *Ethics Commission.*

He told the man at the receptionist's desk what he was looking for. The man led him to a workstation and showed him how to search the Commission's public files. Half an hour later, having filled a page of his notebook with names and figures, Nyman thanked the man, took the elevator to the third floor, and made his way into a large ornate room with rows of marble columns flanking a central gallery.

The members of the City Council were sitting in a half-circle behind broad oak desks. Nyman sat down on a bench that gave him a view of Grace Salas.

In her middle or late sixties, dressed in a black suit with silver piping at the collar, she'd risen from her chair and was reading from a piece of paper.

"—that we adjourn today in memory of Alberto Aguilar, who passed away last week after a twenty-nine-year career in the Department of Water and Power. Alberto was a resident of my district, a kind-hearted man who could always be counted on to support his neighbors. He's survived by his wife Julia, four children, and six grandchildren."

She sat down and slid the paper into a manila folder. There was no clapping or show of approval; the other members gave no indication of having listened. A man at the center of the half-circle said:

"Seeing that there are no other adjourning motions, that concludes the agenda. The meeting is adjourned. Have a safe weekend, everybody."

The chamber filled with noise as people shuffled to the door. Assistants and aides came in to talk to the councilmembers; the noise grew louder with a dozen conversations. Nyman, following the crowd, made his way out of the chamber.

Salas emerged a few minutes later, flanked by two aides who talked to her in low, imploring voices. Nyman followed them at a distance, his hands in his pockets.

They went up to the fourth floor. Passing between walls covered in black-and-white photos of L.A., they came to a door painted with Salas' name and the number of the district she represented. The aides said their goodbyes and moved away toward the elevator. Salas was opening the office door when Nyman said:

"Mind if we talk for a minute?"

She turned. Her gaze, moving over his face and clothes and returning to his eyes, was brisk and curious. Her smile was friendly.

"Sorry," she said, "but I have to leave early today."

"This will only take a second."

"Call my office on Monday. They'll be happy to set up a time."

"It's about Alana Bell," Nyman said. "Her family hired me to investigate her murder."

The smile went away. "In that case," she said, "you'd better come in."

The office was large and well appointed. Its walls were covered with diplomas and newspaper clippings and letters from constituents. On the desk was a photo of a younger Grace Salas marching with a crowd of people down what had once been Brooklyn Avenue.

"Your name's Nyman, isn't it?" she said, sitting down behind the desk.

"You've heard about me?"

"From Michael Freed, yes. He told me you've already talked to him and his wife."

"Did he tell you anything else?"

"Only that you have a very active imagination."

On the contrary, Nyman said, he had a feeble imagination. "But I've learned a few things about Alana's death. Things I'd like to ask you about, if it's not too much trouble."

"Trouble?" Salas leaned forward. "Mr. Nyman, we're talking about a brilliant young woman who died for no reason. If her murderer's out there somewhere, I'll do anything I can to help you find them."

The words came out smoothly and without any note of falseness. Nyman asked her why she thought Alana was brilliant.

"Because it was obvious. She came to see me last Friday—sat in the same chair you're sitting in. We talked for an hour, maybe. Two hours. I meet lots of people in this job, but I don't meet many who are as sharp as she was."

"What did you talk about?"

Salas shrugged. "Anything and everything. It was like talking to my younger self. So much idealism. I got started even earlier than she did: the East L.A. walkouts in sixty-eight. Seventeen years old and ready to take on the world."

"And you thought Alana had the same kind of passion?"

"Yes, but she had something even better—or something equally good, I guess. She had discipline. I saw that in the work she did with Freed. She had a plan for what she wanted to do and she was getting herself the skills to make it happen."

"At Pacifica?"

"At Pacifica, sure, but on the street, too. The work she did in Zamora Park: that was all on her own initiative. She got academic credit for it, probably, but it wasn't necessary for the review Freed was doing. Her work with the homeless was her passion."

Nyman said that he'd like to know more about Freed's review. "This was for the Merchant South development?"

"Right. Which is all being built on the city's land. The taxpayers' land, to put it another way. So what we wanted from Dr. Freed was an analysis—an independent economic analysis—to make sure the city was using the land in the best possible way for the taxpayers."

"And how is it being used?"

"Right now it's not being used at all. When the construction's finished, three of the parcels will be covered by shops and restaurants. We're putting a hotel and mixed-used condo tower on the fourth."

"All built by Ethan Kovac?"

"Ethan?" Salas blinked in surprise. "No, his company's only involved with the tower."

"But you think he's the right man for the job?"

"Of course. Everyone knows what he's done in L.A. with his properties. Koda's the obvious pick."

"And you're not saying that out of gratitude?"

Salas's friendly expression stiffened. "Gratitude?"

Nyman took the notebook from his pocket. "You ran for reelection last year. According to the Ethics Commission, both Kovac and his company contributed very generously to your campaign."

"Yes, and we got contributions from a few hundred other people. You might not know this, Mr. Nyman, but Ethan Kovac happens to be a major supporter of progressive candidates. He's helped a lot of people."

"He's also helping the Republican candidate in the 28th State Senate district," Nyman said. "As well as the Democratic candidate. The same district where Kovac wants to build a new resort."

The stiffness had extended to Salas' jaw and neck. "You're suggesting that my support for Merchant South was some kind of quid pro quo?"

"I'm not suggesting anything. But you also got contributions," Nyman said, glancing at the notebook, "from

Kovac's sister, brother-in-law, and the vice president of his company. All equally generous."

Salas rose from her chair. Her voice was cold. "Like I said, I'm leaving early today, so I'm afraid we'll have to continue this another time."

Nyman rose with her. "My guess is that Alana knew about Kovac's contributions. My guess is she thought Merchant South was a dirty deal. And that's probably why she came here to see you last week."

Salas walked to the door and held it open. "If she thought it was so terrible, why did Freed's analysis say it was a win-win?"

Nyman said that he didn't know. "But then I haven't had a chance to read the analysis."

"Well, I'm sure you can find it somewhere. A man in your profession shouldn't have trouble digging up dirt."

Nyman, saying that she was probably right, made his way to the door. Pausing under the lintel, he turned back to her with a frown.

"If Kovac's company is only handling part of the development, who's in charge of the rest?"

"Does it really matter?"

"I don't know. It might."

She said: "Our primary contract for Merchant South went to Savannah Group. They're the ones who brought Koda on as a partner."

"And where's Savannah Group located? In L.A.?"

Salas's eyes, gazing into Nyman's, were hard and black and calculating. "As a matter of fact," she said, "they're based in Las Vegas."

Chapter 17

Nyman drove back to his apartment. In the smaller of the two bedrooms, he took a cracked leather valise down from a shelf in the closet. Into the valise he put a change of clothes, a bag of toiletries, and a mostly full bottle of Gordon's.

Moving into the kitchen, he added pieces of fruit from a bowl on the counter and a loaf of bread from the cupboard. Then, glancing at the door of the other bedroom, which had remained closed, he turned off the lights and went down to his car.

Three hours later he stopped for gas in Barstow. Hot wind blew in off the creosote scrubland, rattling the sign of the service station. While the gas was pumping, he took a stack of business cards from the glovebox and found a card printed with the name Lawrence Sutter.

He called the number on the card, talked to an answering machine, hung up, paid for the gas, and continued east on the Mojave freeway.

* * *

The Lady Luck Inn was a sun-bleached motel on Paradise Road, more than a mile off the Las Vegas Strip. Nyman left his car beside an empty swimming pool and went into the manager's office, where a teenage clerk sat behind a plexiglass wall.

"Room?"

"For tonight, yes. And maybe a few nights after that."

"Smoking or non?"

"Is there any difference?"

"With smoking you get an ash tray."

"Better make it smoking, then."

"Thirty-five dollars."

Nyman paid, accepted his key, took a tourist brochure from a rack beside the door, and followed a concrete path to his room.

Taking the bottle of Gordon's from his valise, he poured gin into a plastic cup from the bathroom and sat down on the bed, unfolding the brochure so that its map of the Strip lay spread across the bed. Then he took the phone from his pocket and found the photo Patrick Choi had sent him.

He drank the gin and studied the map and photo. More than once he enlarged the photo and tried to read the lettering on the signs that were blurred in the window behind Alana Bell's smiling face. Apart from the overlapping L and V, nothing was legible.

At a quarter to six he circled a spot on the map, showered, shaved, dressed, and left the motel.

A twenty-minute walk brought him to Las Vegas Boulevard and the casinos of the Strip. A crowd of tourists, sweat-soaked and clutching glasses and bottles, shuffled slowly along the sidewalk, ignoring the panhandlers at their feet.

Nyman followed the crowd north, passing New York-New York and the MGM Grand and coming eventually to Kasbah, a glittering tower of paneled glass, where he stopped and looked across the street.

There, at the base of another casino tower, stood a collection of luxury stores. Riveted to the façade of the Luis Vuitton store was its logo: an overlapping L and V.

He turned and went into Kasbah.

The casino's theme was vaguely North African. In the center of the lobby a pair of escalators rose and intertwined to form a kind of minaret, disappearing into the billows of Berber-like cloth that hung from the ceiling.

He rode the escalator up through the billows to the mezzanine, where a glass wall looked out on the Strip. Standing at the glass and looking down on the boulevard, he was more or less level with the Vuitton store's logo.

"Looking for someplace to go tonight?"

A woman in a cocktail dress had stopped beside him. One hand was on her hip; the other was holding out a piece of glossy cardboard with a picture of a martini glass on it.

"Two-for-one happy-hour drinks at Souk," she said, winking.

Nyman accepted the coupon and looked at the other side, which showed a paragraph of fine print.

"Souk is a club here?"

The woman nodded. "On the main floor, next to the sportsbook. Maybe I'll see you there."

She winked again and started to move away to the next customer, but Nyman touched her arm.

"Sorry, but maybe you can help me. I'm looking for a friend of mine. She was here two weeks ago."

He showed her the picture of Alana Bell. The woman's seductiveness went away and she took the phone in both hands, studying the picture.

"Wow, she was standing right here, wasn't she?"

"This would've been sometime on Friday, July first," Nyman said.

"Sorry, I don't recognize her. We get people coming through here all the time. Tons and tons."

"You were working that day?"

She frowned, calculating. "Two Fridays ago? No, that would've been Jordan's shift, I think."

"Is there a way I could talk to Jordan?"

"Not really. They don't let us give out contact info. Which makes sense, when you think about it."

"What about someone who could tell me if my friend had a room here?"

She shook her head. "Sorry—that's the hotel side of things. Good luck finding her, though. She looks nice."

She smiled and moved away with her stack of coupons.

Nyman stayed for a time beside the glass, looking down on the Strip. The sun was edging behind the towers, leaving parts of the boulevard in shadow and bringing out the lights that shone on the Bellagio's fountains. As he stood watching the fountains his phone rang.

He took it from his pocket. "Hello? ... Lawrence, yes, thanks for calling back ... No, just five minutes ... Right. I have one more thing to do here, then I'll be there ... Perfect. Thanks."

He rode the escalator back down to the lobby. People with luggage were lined up at the marble-topped registration desks, waiting to check in. Nyman took up his place at the end of the line. After ten or fifteen minutes a smiling clerk beckoned him forward.

"How can I help you?"

Taking the phone from his pocket, he laid it on the marble and said in a sheepish voice: "A colleague of mine is in town, and I just realized she left her phone in my office. I was hoping to return it."

"Your colleague is a guest here?"

"I think so, yes. Her name's Alana Bell. A-l-a-n-a."

"I'm sorry, sir, but we're not allowed to give out information on who's staying with us."

Nyman said that he didn't need any information. "I just want to make sure I'm returning the phone to the right place. If she's staying here, I'll leave it with you and you can give it to her."

The clerk hesitated, looking from Nyman's face to his dull gray suit and navy tie. Then she turned to her computer, tapped out something on the keyboard, and a moment later shook her head.

"I wouldn't advise you to leave the phone with us, sir."

"You're saying she's not listed as a guest?"

"I'm saying our records indicate that you'd be better off looking for her somewhere else."

"And your records would include someone who checked in as long as two weeks ago?"

"Yes, sir. They include everyone. Now is there anything else I can do for you?"

Picking up the phone, Nyman thanked her for her help and moved away toward the main doors.

He was nearly out of the building when he glanced back over his shoulder and saw the woman in the cocktail dress riding down the escalator. She'd put away her coupons and was talking to a tall, heavily built man with pale blond hair and a plastic cord wrapped around one ear.

At a gesture from the woman, the man turned to look in Nyman's direction. Their gazes met momentarily; then the doors swung shut and Nyman was back among the tourists on the Strip.

Chapter 18

Long rays of evening sunshine came in through the entrance of the Flamingo, filling the gaming floor with light. The noise of slot machines and roulette wheels followed Nyman across the floor and over to the Garden Bar, where drinkers sat on stools overlooking an imitation nature preserve.

At the end of the bar, hunched over a video-poker screen, was a thick-bellied man in his late fifties. He drank steadily from a can of Diet Coke, tapping the screen to manipulate his animated cards. The skin of his face hung in loose folds; his eyes were partly covered by bifocals.

Nyman sat down on the stool beside him and asked if he was having any luck.

Without looking up from the game, Lawrence Sutter said: "Been in this town thirty years, Tom, and I never had any luck. Never worked a murder case, either."

"There's always a first time."

"For you, maybe. Want to tell me the details?"

Nyman told him. While he listened, Sutter signaled the bartender for another Diet Coke and a bowl of pretzels. When

Nyman finished, Sutter reset the game and leaned back on the stool, finally looking at him.

"You tell Joseph any of this?"

"Most of it."

"What did he think?"

"That I was wasting my time."

The new soda and pretzels arrived. "As long as you've got a paying client," Sutter said, "nothing's a waste of time. But it does sound a little iffy."

"That's why I called you. To fill in some of the gaps."

The eyes behind the bifocals became apprehensive. "Which gaps?"

"The development company that's based here, for one thing. Savannah Group. Anything you can tell me about them?"

"Real estate's not exactly my specialty, Tom."

"Surely you've heard something."

Sutter took another drink, then shrugged. "Little things in the paper, maybe. They started out here in the eighties or nineties—building apartments, I think. Made enough money to start doing bigger projects around the country."

"And their critics?"

"What about their critics?"

"Suppose Alana Bell came here to try to stop Savannah from going forward with Merchant South. How do you think they'd react?"

Sutter shook his head. "Not with murder, if that's what you're thinking."

"Why not?"

"Because there's no sense in it. Any firm their size is going to have plenty of critics, most of which are a lot more dangerous than some grad student. What kind of threat could she be?"

"She was helping her professor analyze one of their developments."

"An analysis that came out positive, from what you just said. And anyway, you don't kill somebody because of a bad report. Developers deal with that kind of thing all the time."

Nyman conceded the point. "What about Ethan Kovac, then?"

"He's the nightclub guy?"

"Among other things," Nyman said. "Savannah contracted with him to operate the hotel for Merchant South."

Sutter's response was interrupted by a ringing in his pocket. Apologizing, he took out his phone and had a terse, profane conversation with someone on the other end. When he hung up his jaw was clenched and he was signaling the bartender for his check.

"I'm going to have to run out on you, Tom. Got a new kid working surveillance that can't go an hour without some kind of disaster."

Nyman said he was sorry to hear it. "Nothing too serious?"

"Nothing more than incompetence."

Rising from his stool, Sutter squinted at the receipt the bartender had handed him.

Nyman, watching him, said: "Before you go, there was one other favor I was going to ask."

Sutter signed the receipt. "Yeah? What's that?"

"Joseph says you do contract work for some of the big casinos. I'm guessing they keep a database of the names of their recent guests."

EDGE OF THE KNIFE

"Some do, yeah."

"Which means they might be able to tell us where Alana Bell stayed while she was here."

Sutter put away his wallet and exhaled. "Look, Tom, the more favors I ask of these guys, the less likely they are to answer my calls."

"I know it's an imposition. I wouldn't ask if it wasn't important."

Sutter didn't try to hide his annoyance. Reaching again for his phone, he told Nyman to stay where he was and walked toward the nature preserve, putting the phone to his ear.

Nyman ate a pretzel and watched the ducks swim in circles in the pools beside the Paradise Buffet. When Sutter came back he was shaking his head.

"Talked to a guy at Crown Gaming. They've got no record of any Alana Bells at any of their hotels in the last month."

Nyman took out his notebook. "Which casinos does Crown own?"

Sutter told him.

Nyman wrote down the names and nodded. "Thanks. That narrows it down, at least."

"You're going to try your lost-phone story at more places?"

"As many as I can."

Sutter made a clicking noise with his tongue. "I see now why Joseph likes you. You got the same lust for punishment."

* * *

Leaving the Flamingo, Nyman made his way across the pedestrian overpass to Caesars Palace, where he repeated his lost-phone story at the reservation desk. He did the same at the other casinos on the northwest side of the Strip, then moved to the northeast side. Each time the answer was the same.

At ten o'clock he left the Strip and tried hotels and motels on quieter streets. The desert air, still well above a hundred degrees, had the sharp dry smell of gunpowder. He walked more slowly than before and related his story with less enthusiasm.

A few minutes before midnight, a tall, thickly bearded clerk nodded and said: "She was here, yeah, but it looks like she left about two weeks ago."

Nyman was at a small hotel off Desert Inn Road. The walls were covered in wallpaper made to resemble black crepe. Arranged around the lobby were chairs in white leather. The color scheme extended to the tuxedo the clerk was wearing and the flowers—black orchids and white roses—that floated in a bowl beside his computer. According to its sign, the hotel was called Tryst.

"Checked in on Friday, July first," the clerk said, looking at his computer, "and left at some point after that."

"What do you mean, at some point?"

"She paid for three nights, but she never bothered to check out, so we're not sure when she left."

"Why didn't she check out?"

The clerk smiled coldly. "If all you want to do is return her phone, it shouldn't matter either way."

"She's a friend of mine. I'm worried about her."

"Then you should've told her you've been hanging on to her phone for two weeks."

Nyman, after a pause, took a business card from his wallet and put it on the desk. "The woman we're talking about was murdered two nights ago."

"We're under no obligation to talk to private investigators," the clerk said.

"Maybe not, but it would be the decent thing to do."

"Assuming this card is real, and your story is real."

Nyman took a twenty-dollar bill from his wallet and put it on top of the card.

The clerk nodded. "All right. Let's see what we can do."

Chapter 19

The pulse of dance music seeped through the crepe-covered walls as Nyman watched the clerk consult his records. Occasionally the street-door opened and people came in: women in short metallic dresses and men in untucked collared shirts. Without glancing at the registration desk, they crossed the lobby and disappeared behind a curtain of red brocade.

"Looks like she stayed in the fourth-floor suite," the clerk said. "And she upgraded to the Indulgence package."

"Which means what?"

He shrugged. "Bottle of champagne and some restaurant vouchers."

"Not exactly the height of indulgence."

"Depends what you're used to. Usually it's something couples buy."

"Was she here with someone else?"

"She booked at the two-person rate, at least. But we never ask for the name of the other guest."

"Who paid the bill?"

The clerk squinted at the screen. "Could've been anybody. It was a cash payment. All three nights in advance."

Nyman found the photo of Alana on his phone and showed it to him. "Do you remember checking her in?"

"Nope. Sorry."

"You're sure? Take a closer look."

"I don't need a closer look. She checked in at four in the afternoon. My shift doesn't start until ten."

Nyman asked if he could talk to the employees who were working that day.

"If you go away and let me start the night audit," the clerk said, "you can talk to anyone you want. The break room's through there, at the end of the hall. Knock and someone'll let you in."

Nyman crossed the lobby to the red brocade curtain. On the other side he found a tufted-leather door through which the dance music could be heard more clearly. Moving past it, he came to a plain metal door at the end of the hall.

The woman who answered his knock was only a year or two out of her teens. Her brown hair was pulled back into a lank, stringy ponytail; the thinness of her body was partly obscured by a maid's uniform.

She nodded to the tufted-leather door. "The club's through there."

Nyman told her who he was and what he was doing. With no sign of surprise or curiosity, she stepped back from the door and waved him into a brightly lit room with a sink and refrigerator and a row of lockers. Through an open doorway he could see part of a laundry room.

An older maid was eating a meal of *machaca* and eggs at one of the tables. She leaned low over the food and ate slowly, watching Nyman in her peripheral vision. A sign on the wall said that employees were required to report injuries to the management.

He sat down and took the cigarettes from his pocket, wordlessly offering the pack to each woman in turn. The younger maid's face became friendlier as she took one.

"You really think this girl was murdered?"

"I think it's possible."

"You have a picture of her?"

He showed her the picture on his phone. She looked at it intently, then shook her head. "Sorry. Don't remember her."

He held the phone out to the older maid. She glanced at it, then looked directly at Nyman for the first time.

"No," she in a voice that was hardly audible.

Nyman asked if he could have a look at the room Alana had stayed in. "Assuming it's empty."

The younger maid said: "It's been cleaned a bunch of times since she left. If there was anything in there, we would've found it already."

He said she was probably right. "But I'd still like to see it, if you don't mind showing me."

She looked questioningly at the older woman, who shrugged and went on eating. Rising from her chair, the younger maid said:

"Well, I guess it wouldn't hurt."

She led him through the laundry room and into the hallway beyond. During the elevator ride he learned that her name was Alicia and that she'd been working at Tryst for two years.

"I won't be staying here much longer, though."

"You have a new job lined up?"

"Pretty much. The shows on the Strip are always holding auditions for singers and dancers. It's only a matter of time before something works out."

"You're a performer?"

She nodded. "I've heard there's lots of openings in L.A., too. Sometimes I think about going out there if I can't find anything here."

Nyman said he'd met people who'd moved to L.A. for that reason.

"Did they make a living out of it?"

"Some did."

"You don't think it's just a pipe-dream, then? People are always telling me it's a pipe-dream and nobody ever really makes it."

Nyman said: "I wouldn't listen to other people."

At the fourth floor, Alicia unlocked the door of suite 410 and led him inside.

It consisted of two small rooms and a kitchenette. Beyond the ordinary furnishings, it had a circular bed, a partially mirrored ceiling, and framed reproductions of Mapplethorpe nudes. A bar cart was stocked with vodka and tequila and mixers.

"Mind if I look around?"

"Go ahead."

Working slowly and methodically, Nyman searched the suite, starting with the bed. From the bed he moved to the living room, bathroom, kitchenette, entryway. He found nothing.

"Sorry," Alicia said. "Told you it'd been cleaned, though."

He nodded and walked to the window, where he looked down on the headlights moving on Desert Inn Road. He was checking the time on his watch when the door opened and the older maid came in.

Her face was shy and uncertain. Looking first at Alicia, then at the nudes on the walls, she met Nyman's gaze and said in her quiet voice:

"The girl who stayed here. She was really a friend of yours?"

"We didn't have a chance to become friends. But she came to me for help."

"And now you're trying to help her?"

"Something like that. Her family hired me to find her murderer."

"They trust you?"

"They seem to. Why?"

Hesitantly, she reached into the pocket of her uniform and brought out something small and round, then held it out to Nyman.

He moved away from the window. In her palm was a fifty-dollar chip with a picture of what looked like a minaret in the center.

"She gave it to me," the maid said, passing it to Nyman. "As a tip."

The chip was new and unblemished. Holding it up to the light, he saw that the minaret was a stylized sketch of the Kasbah casino tower.

"They had lots of them," the maid said. "Chips like that, and money."

"They?"

"Your friend and the man. The one staying here with her. One day they came in when I was cleaning. He told me he'd just won a jackpot."

"At Kasbah?"

She nodded. "He said he never had any luck before, but maybe Vegas was a lucky town for him. I said I was happy for them, and then the girl gave me the chip. She said they had plenty more."

"Do you remember the man's name?"

"He never told me."

"What about how he looked?"

She shrugged. "I don't know. Average."

Nyman opened his mouth to ask another question, then closed it. Taking out his phone, he found a photo of Michael Freed on the Pacifica website and showed it to her.

"Was that him?"

She squinted at the photo, then nodded. "Could be. Probably."

"Did they tell you why they came to Vegas?"

"They didn't need to tell me. They were here to be together."

Nyman asked her if she'd had any other interactions with them.

"No, just when she gave me the chip. I've been here eight years and no one ever gave me more than a couple dollars."

"It was generous of her."

"Very generous. That's why, when you showed me the picture, I thought you were after her money."

"I didn't know she had any money. She told me she didn't have any at all."

The maid nodded sadly and took the chip from his hand. "Maybe she didn't. The way the man looked at her when she gave it to me—I thought maybe he wouldn't let her keep any for herself."

"He was upset that she gave it to you?"

"He didn't say it, but you could see it in his eyes. You see it all the time. Somebody gets a little something, they don't want to share anymore."

"You think he was greedy?"

She shrugged and put the chip back in her pocket. "No more than the rest of us."

Chapter 20

Nyman took a cab from Tryst to Kasbah. It was one o'clock in the morning, but the clerks at the registration desk were bright-eyed and smiling. At the elevators, security guards were checking the keycards of anyone trying to ride upstairs.

He made his way past slot machines and roulette wheels, past the smoke-clouded sportsbook and the roped-off entrance of Souk, and crossed to a side-bar where a graying woman was pouring shots for two young men.

Nyman waited for her to make eye contact with him, then said: "If I wanted to ask about someone who won a jackpot here, who would I talk to?"

Ignoring him, she tore a receipt from the credit-card machine and put it in front of the smaller of the men, who didn't seem to notice it.

He was looking at a woman at the end of the bar. She sat alone on a stool in a strapless black dress that accentuated her figure. Her face, catching the light off the mirrored bar, was pale and angular, with heavily shadowed eyes and lips painted a dark glossy red.

The bartender turned to Nyman. "Sorry, we're not supposed to discuss our guests' winnings."

"Not even with the police?"

"You're a policeman?"

"I've been working with the L.A. coroner's office."

Holding up a forefinger, she turned back to the young man, grabbed his wrist, and forced a pen into his hand. He looked down at the pen in surprise, noticed the receipt, signed it with a flourish, picked up the shot glasses, and handed one to his friend. They toasted and drank and moved to the end of the bar to talk to the woman.

"Well," the bartender said to Nyman, "if you're here on coroner's business, you should probably talk to Stephen."

"Stephen?"

"Mr. Emmler. The casino manager."

"Know where I can find him?"

She looked at a clock on the cashier's terminal. "This time of night, he'll be in the high-limit room. It's back that way and under the awning."

Following her directions, he found an awning of green silk and came into a high-ceilinged room with gaming tables arranged around a pool of water lined with *zillij* tile. Moorish arches and potted lemon trees gave the illusion of an open-air atrium.

The illusion was belied by the room's quietness. Cards ruffled in the hands of the dealers. Chips dropped softly on cushioned green felt.

Behind the nearest table stood the same man he'd seen earlier on the escalator: tall and heavyset, with boyish features and blond hair cut so close to the skull that it was almost translucent.

Nyman went past the pool of water and stopped beside the man. Without speaking, they stood together and watched an older, well-dressed woman play a hand of mini-baccarat.

With fingers lengthened by false nails, she put two chips on the square of felt labelled *Banker*. The croupier plucked four cards from the shoe, put the first pair on the right half of the table, and said: "Three."

He put the second pair on the left half of the table—"Eight"—and dealt a third card to each pair. After a pause, he pushed the right-hand cards forward and said: "Player. Nine over eight."

Then he swept away the cards and chips and looked at the woman expectantly.

While she considered her bet, the blond man leaned toward Nyman and whispered: "Anything I can do for you, sir?"

"Are you Stephen Emmler?"

The man nodded. "And your name?"

"Tom Nyman."

"Pleased to meet you, Mr. Nyman. Why don't we go where we can talk without bothering the players?"

Nyman followed him out of the high-limit room and onto the gaming floor. Emmler cast a proprietary glance over the floor, then looked at Nyman with a smile. His face was smooth and entirely hairless.

"You were here earlier, weren't you? One of our floor ambassadors pointed you out to me."

"I was asking about a friend of mine."

"That's what she said. Your friend's not in any trouble, I hope?"

"A lot of trouble. And I think it might've started here."

133

"At Kasbah?"

"In the casino, at least. She was involved with a man who won a jackpot here two weeks ago. Michael Freed."

Emmler's face was composed but his eyes were moving quickly, as if trying to look at Nyman from different angles at once.

"What kind of jackpot?"

"I'm not sure. He came away with a lot of cash and chips. Do you keep a record of your big winners?"

Ignoring the question, Emmler said: "I'm sorry, but I don't see what you mean by being in trouble. Most of our guests think winning money is a good thing."

Nyman told him what had happened to Alana Bell.

Emmler's eyes stopped moving; the hairless face flushed pink. Glancing at the people on the gaming floor, he touched Nyman's arm and said:

"We'd better go to my office."

He led him off the floor and into a windowless room hardly big enough to hold a desk and two chairs. On top of the desk was a photo of a woman and two young girls.

Emmler took a pen and sheet of paper from his desk and said, sitting down: "All right, start at the beginning."

Nyman started with Alana's arrival at Tryst. Emmler listened attentively and made notes on the paper in large block letters, biting his lip as he wrote. Then he sat back in the chair and tipped his head to one side.

"So she came to Vegas with Freed. Then Freed won some money at our casino. Then she died two weeks later. Correct?"

"Correct."

"Well, I don't mean to be stupid, but I don't see the connection between Freed's winnings and her death."

"I'm not saying there is a connection. I don't have enough information to know either way."

"So that's why you're here? To get more information?"

"Right."

Despite the chilliness of the room Emmler was sweating. "That's where the trouble comes in, unfortunately. Our business is all about giving guests the highest level of service. A key part of that is discretion."

"I'd think a casino would be eager to advertise its big winners."

"Most of the time, sure, but you need the winner's permission. Some people don't like the publicity."

"People like Freed?"

"I don't remember Freed offhand, assuming he was even here."

"I'm sure you have records you could check. And some of your employees might remember him."

"Again, though, protecting our guests has to be our top priority."

Nyman nodded to the photo on the desk. "If it was one of your daughters, you might have different priorities."

The sweat had descended to level of Emmler's eyes. At the mention of his daughters, he picked up the pen and looked down at the paper.

"Maybe you're right about that. If you're willing to give me a little time, I'll see what I can find out."

"Thanks. I'd appreciate it."

"Of course it might take me a while to get back to you. You're staying here in town?"

"At the Lady Luck on Paradise. But you can just call my phone."

"Always a good idea to know where to find you, though. You remember your room number there?"

Nyman frowned. "One-eleven, I think."

"And you'll be going there now?"

Nyman's frown went away and he looked at the man's bowed head with new interest. "Not right away, no. You know of a good place to get a drink at this time of night?"

Still not looking at Nyman, Emmler said: "The Aloha Lounge is pretty good, if you want to avoid the crowds. It's around the corner on Harmon."

"Sounds perfect."

Emmler put down his pen and finally looked up. "Well, I can't promise anything, but I'll do what I can. The security guard outside will walk you back to the casino floor."

Nyman thanked him for his help, went to the door, and paused there with his hand on the knob. "It's private investigating, by the way," he said.

"What?"

"My profession. You never asked what it was."

The pen in Emmler's hand was trembling. "Didn't I?"

"No."

"Well—I must've just assumed it, then."

Nyman smiled. "I guess you must've."

Chapter 21

The Aloha Lounge was a dark room with rattan-covered walls and a bar made of lava stone. The only light came from imitation torches hanging from the ceiling and slot machines lining the back wall. Nyman sat down at the mostly deserted bar and asked for a gin and soda.

"Lime?"

"No thanks."

Lying in a puddle on the bar was a discarded copy of the *Review-Journal*. He opened the paper to the front page and glanced over the headlines, his expression dull and incurious.

He read a pair of stories about local politics, started to turn the page, then stopped, frowning. He took the phone from his pocket and opened the website of the L.A. *Times*. In the archives he found a list of articles about Merchant South; the most recent was dated July fifth.

> *Under fire from critics, the Los Angeles city council today released a report claiming that the proposed $900 million redevelopment of downtown's Merchant District will bring jobs and housing to the moribund neighborhood.*

Michael L. Freed, a frequent adviser to the city on real estate proposals, found after a months-long analysis that the city's plan represents the best possible use of the four parcels of land earmarked for the project.

"In terms of maximizing revenue," Freed wrote, "the mixed-use complex outlined by the developer will create much needed benefits not only for the district, but for the city and county as a whole."

The project's lead developer, Savannah Group, recently broke ground on the 22-acre site, which will feature restaurants, retail space, a hotel, and an eighteen-story luxury apartment tower. Critics have charged that the project represents a giveaway to the Las Vegas-based developer, which will receive tax breaks totaling nearly $50 million for the first phase of construction.

"If the council really wanted to help the district, they would've sold the land to the highest bidder and used the money for programs for the residents," said Jeff Geller, director of the Downtown Homeless Alliance. "Instead they leased it on favorable terms to a developer who'll take all the profits out of state."

Councilmember Grace Salas, who serves as head of the committee overseeing the project, disagrees.

"Michael Freed's impartial analysis proves that we've worked from the beginning to put the taxpayers' needs ahead of any other concern," she said. "The economic activity created by this development will generate revenue far exceeding the city's initial investment."

Scrolling back to the top of the page, Nyman found the story's byline and was writing down the reporter's name when someone sat down on the stool beside him.

"What's that you're drinking? Vodka?"

The voice was soft and throaty. Looking up, he saw that it belonged to the pale, sharp-featured woman he'd seen in Kasbah. Her glossy red lips were curved in a playful half-smile; her slender hands were wrapped around a black-and-silver purse.

Nyman said he was drinking gin.

The woman turned to the bartender. "Gin and rocks."

The bartender gave her a long look of distaste, then reached for a bottle of Tanqueray. The woman pretended not to notice the look and said to Nyman:

"You were over at Kasbah, weren't you? By the slots?"

Nyman nodded. "You were attracting a crowd at the bar."

"A crowd of boys. Drunken boys."

"There seem to be a lot of them around."

"Oh, they're always around. You can't get away from them."

Close at hand, despite her thick makeup and the dim lighting, he could see the dark smudges under her eyes and the deep, narrow clefts on either side of her mouth.

"You live here in Vegas?" he said.

"Most of the time. What about you?"

"Los Angeles."

"Mmm. Let me guess. You're a businessman in town for a conference."

"Something like that."

"I knew it." She smiled and sipped her drink. "I could tell by the clothes. Nobody wears clothes like that unless they're here on business."

"Someone told me yesterday I look like a cop."

"No," the woman said, leaning playfully to one side so that her shoulder bumped against Nyman's. "You look like an accountant."

"Thanks."

"I bet your wife picked out that tie, didn't she?"

The ice rattled in Nyman's glass. He put the glass down and said: "I don't have a wife."

The woman moved sideways again to bump her shoulder against his. "Why don't we get out of here and go someplace else?"

Nyman didn't shift his gaze from the glass. "What did you have in mind?"

"Oh, I don't know. There's lots of places to go. You're not scared of me, are you?"

He swallowed the dregs of gin. "No. I'm not scared of you."

* * *

Her name was Mara. From the Aloha Lounge they went to the MGM Grand, where the doorman of Hakkasan looked at them skeptically and said that the club was filled to capacity.

Mara, flushing under her makeup, turned to Nyman and said in a loud, artificially cheerful voice that one of the clubs across the street was more fun anyway.

It was after two o'clock when they got to the second club. This time the doorman greeted them with a smile, told them that the cover was ten dollars for women and forty dollars for men, collected the cash from Nyman, unhooked the rope that barred the entrance, and waved them inside.

The music made conversation impossible. Communicating by pantomime, Nyman led Mara up to one of the bars and ordered drinks.

She finished her drink standing at the bar, excused herself to the bathroom, and came back after several minutes with bright, glittering eyes and said that she wanted to dance.

Nyman said that he didn't dance.

"Never?" she shouted.

"Never."

"You mind if I do?"

"Not at all."

She said that she'd be back in five minutes. As she turned, the passing beam of a spotlight caught the fabric of her dress and the smooth paleness of her exposed back and neck. The bumps of her vertebrae, thrown into relief, showed the S curve of a scoliotic spine.

Nyman stood beside the bar and watched her dance—sometimes by herself, sometimes with men or women—for more than half an hour. His face as he watched was creased with the concentration of someone trying to solve a puzzle or mathematical problem.

When she left the floor and came back to him she was damp with sweat and smiling. Shouting into his ear, she said: "You're an all right guy, you know that?" and draped both arms around his neck and kissed his mouth.

* * *

They left the club at four a.m. and walked along the Strip, moving in the general direction of Nyman's motel. Once or twice they went into bars to have another drink and to continue their conversation, which consisted of comments about the people they saw on the street. Mara said that in Las Vegas there were only three classes of people and that each person belonged to only one class.

"What class do I belong to?" Nyman asked.

"Man-in-town-on-business."

"What about you?"

She patted his cheek and told him to drink up.

* * *

The sky was brightening when a taxi let them out in the parking lot of the Lady Luck Inn. Nyman, nodding to the office of the motel, asked Mara if she wanted him to book her a room.

Her playful smile went away. Standing in the blinking glow of the motel's sign, her face was muddled and confused.

"Aren't we going to your room?"

Nyman shook his head. "I don't think it would be a good idea."

"But it was your idea. A night out, then back to your room."

"That's what you really believe?"

"Of course it's what I believe." Her eyes narrowed. "What the hell's going on here, Tom?"

"That's what I've been trying to figure out."

Flinging out a thin white arm, she said: "We got a call from you. You said you saw me at Kasbah and you wanted a date. You'd be at the Aloha waiting for me."

"By 'we,'" Nyman said, "who do you mean?"

She flushed with anger. "You know what I mean, you son of a bitch."

"I'm sorry, Mara, but I never called and asked for you."

"Of course you did. When I showed up at the bar, you didn't bat an eye. You knew I was coming."

"I knew something was coming. I didn't know it would be you."

"What the hell's that supposed to mean?"

Telling her to stay where she was, he walked back along the sidewalk to the entrance of the alley that ran behind the motel. There, parked beside a dumpster, was an unmarked Ford in which two men were sitting with the windows rolled up and the air conditioner running. They were watching the back side of the motel, where the window of Nyman's bathroom stood at street-level.

He walked back to Mara and said: "There are two cops in the alley."

"What?"

It was a set-up, he explained. "Someone wanted me off their hands."

"Who the hell cares about you?"

He told her who he was and why he was in town. She dismissed the explanation with a stream of curses and said that he owed her money.

"I don't do this for free, Tom. You told us you'd pay for all night. I've seen the cash in your wallet."

"I never called you. The money I have is what I got from my client."

With an awkward thrust of her arm she hit him on the left side of his face, driving her knuckles into his eye. He took a half-step backward in surprise and put a hand over his eye.

She called him a number of names, said that he would pay her the money he owed her, said that he had wronged not only her but certain people who didn't like being wronged, and told him what he could do to himself.

When she stalked away on the sidewalk there were drunken men laughing and shouting at her from the windows of the hotel across the street.

Mara ignored them and walked off toward Flamingo Road. Nyman listened to the clicking of her heels with a face that was drawn and gray and exhausted.

Above him the sun was rising.

Chapter 22

He went into his room and turned on the light. His valise was still on the bed where he'd left it; there was no sign that any of his things had been disturbed. Going into the bathroom, he brushed his teeth and washed his face and was drying his face with a towel when someone knocked on the door and told him to open up.

He opened the door. The men from the unmarked Ford stood in the doorway. Their grim, expectant gazes went first to Nyman, then to the bed, then to the open door of the bathroom.

Nyman said: "She's not here, but you're welcome to check."

He opened the door wider. The older of the two men introduced himself as Sergeant Carrillo and showed Nyman a badge. His hair was gray and the square shape of his face was accentuated by a square gray moustache. His partner was a taller, heavier man named Parks.

Parks walked into the bathroom, pulled aside the shower curtain, came back out, and shook his head at Carrillo.

Carrillo turned to Nyman. "What happened to her?"

"She went home for the night. Or for the morning, I guess."

"You didn't want her to stay?"

"No."

"Why not?"

"Seemed like a bad idea."

Parks said: "Then why bother to hire her in the first place?"

"I didn't hire her. I met her at the Aloha Lounge and we went dancing."

Carrillo rubbed his moustache with a thick finger. "You sure about that? Because we heard you picked her up at Kasbah."

"Was it the casino manager who told you that? Emmler?"

"Just answer the question."

"No," Nyman said, "I didn't pick her up at Kasbah."

"But you were there last night?"

"Yes."

Parks said: "So you were there and she was there, but you didn't pick her up there?"

"Correct."

"Mind telling me why we should believe that?"

Nyman opened his wallet, took out the copy of his license, handed it to Carrillo, and gave him the same explanation he'd just given Mara. Carrillo wrote Nyman's license number in a small blue notepad and asked if there was anyone who could confirm his story.

"Lawrence Sutter," Nyman said. "He owns one of the agencies in town. Oasis Security."

"Larry's a friend of yours?"

"A colleague, at least. He used to work for my old boss."

"Who's your old boss?"

"Joseph Moritz."

Carrillo sat down on the edge of the bed and was silent for a time, his moustache curving in a thoughtful frown. "You're giving me your word about not picking the girl up at Kasbah?"

Nyman said that he was.

"So she thought you were just a john who'd called in for her?"

"That's what she said."

"What'd she do when she found out you weren't?"

"She said a few things."

"She threaten you?"

Nyman shrugged. "I wasn't listening very closely."

Carrillo asked him how long he was planning to stay in Vegas.

"I'm not sure. At least another night."

"Well, if you decide you want a girl, don't mess with the ones in town. Go to one of the ranches outside the city, where it's legal."

"Thanks. I'll keep that in mind."

Carrillo got up from the bed and said that he and Parks would be in touch. Nyman walked with them to the door, promised to let them know if he heard again from Mara, shut the door behind them, pulled the coverlet off the bed, lay down on the top-sheet fully clothed, and closed his eyes.

* * *

When he opened his eyes the room was filled with late-morning sunshine. He sighed, coughed, and reached to the bedside table for the pack of cigarettes. Lying on his back, he lit a cigarette and inhaled.

His eyes were gummy and rimmed in red. His thick black hair stood up from his forehead at an angle. He shut his eyes and smoked in silence for ten or twenty minutes, half-dozing. Then he coughed again, ground out the cigarette, and went into the bathroom.

He showered, shaved, put on the same clothes he'd worn the previous day, and sat down on the edge of the bed. Taking two slices of bread and an apple from the valise, he turned on the T.V. and watched the start of the Mets-Nationals game. When the food was gone he left the room.

He stopped in the motel office to fill a paper cup with coffee and tell the clerk he'd be staying another night, then got into his car and drove to Kasbah's underground parking garage.

An elevator took him from the parking levels to the casino floor. He made his way past the slot machines and gaming tables to the registration desk, where he told a smiling woman that he needed to speak to Mr. Emmler.

"I'm sorry, but he's not here this time of day. He works the swing shift."

"Do you know where I can find him?"

"Sorry. I wouldn't know."

"What about his house? Does he live here in town?"

"Can I ask why you're so interested in Mr. Emmler, sir?"

"Gratitude," Nyman said. "He sent me a gift last night and I wanted to thank him."

"Well, if you wait for the swing shift, you can thank him in person."

Yawning, he turned away from the desk and went into a café just off the gaming floor. There he bought a larger cup of coffee and sat down at a table, taking out his phone. A search for Stephen Emmlers in Las Vegas gave him the address of a house on Anaconda Road.

Fifteen minutes later he was driving along a freshly paved street in a subdivision of large, newly built homes. He left his car in the driveway of a beige stucco house and rang the doorbell.

The woman who answered was small and jittery and had a fitness tracker on her wrist. Before Nyman could speak, she said:

"Sorry. We're not buying."

"That's okay. I'm not selling."

"What do you want, then?"

"This is Stephen Emmler's house?"

Her face tensed. "My husband's sleeping. He works nights."

"So do I. If you tell him Tom Nyman's here, I think he'll want to talk to me."

"Why would he want to talk to you?"

"Because I'm the one he tried to put in jail."

She shut the door and turned the lock. The sound of heels clicking on tile came faintly through the door.

Nyman took the cigarettes from his pocket and leaned against the railing of the porch, looking out at the line of identical, xeriscaped lawns across the street.

After two or three minutes the door opened again and the woman said in a hoarse voice: "He's out back, by the pool."

The pool was a dark blue rectangle set into a quarter-acre of white gravel. Emmler sat on the edge of the shallow end with his legs in the water, wearing a t-shirt and a pair of lime-green trunks. The skin of his scalp, beneath its short blond hair, was turning red with sunburn.

Nyman walked along the edge of the pool and sat down in a lawn chair facing him. Laughter drifted over from the other side of the yard, where two small girls were playing on a jungle gym. Emmler looked down at his legs and moved them in the water, making small blue ripples.

"I haven't had a chance to check on that jackpot your friend won," he said quietly.

Nyman watched the ripples. "That's all right. I imagine you've had a busy morning."

"Pretty busy."

"What did they threaten you with? Filing a false report?"

"Carrillo and Parks, you mean?"

"Yes."

Emmler shrugged. "They didn't do much threatening. Just a lot of questioning."

"Did you give any answers?"

"Not as many as they wanted. I tried to explain that someone like me is just a middle manager. The executives tell me what they want done and I make it happen on the floor."

"Or in my motel room."

"Until a few months ago," Emmler said, "I never thought I'd have anything to do with people's motel rooms."

Nyman asked him what had changed a few months ago.

"Lots of things. Mainly it was the Swiss leaving."

"The Swiss?"

Moving his legs in the water, Emmler said: "The construction loan to build Kasbah was held by a bank in Switzerland. The original owners defaulted, so the bank stepped in to finish construction and run things until they could find a buyer for the casino. The bank is the one that hired me four years ago."

"And a few months ago they found a buyer?"

He nodded. "The new guys replaced most of the management, but they decided to keep me around. At least for now."

"Who are the new guys?"

"I doubt you've heard of them. It's a real-estate firm that mostly does new developments. Kasbah's what they call an opportunistic investment."

"Savannah Group?"

Emmler looked over in surprise. "You keep up with the industry?"

"I keep up with Savannah."

Nyman told him about Merchant South and its connection to Alana Bell's murder. When he was finished, Emmler shook his head and said:

"No—that's crazy. All Savannah cares about is the bottom line. They're not interested in killing people."

"They're interested in me, though," Nyman said. "Someone told you I might come around and ask questions about Alana Bell. Didn't they, Stephen?"

"Sorry. I don't remember."

"They told you to get me out of the way with Mara."

"Her name's not really Mara," Emmler said, "and she's been thrown out of every place on the Strip. She deserves everything she got."

"Who told you to get me out of the way?"

"Sorry. I don't remember."

"Just give me a name. Then I'll leave you alone."

"Can't help you. Sorry."

Nyman stood up from the chair. His eyes were squinting in the bright sunlight and his jaw was set hard. He opened his mouth to speak, then closed it and started to walk back to the house.

Behind him, Emmler said in a mild, conversational tone: "One thing I can tell you, though. There's a standard casino protocol for dealing with big winners."

Nyman stopped. "Yeah? What's that?"

"Well, if somebody wins big, you want to keep them in your place as long as possible, so you can win back the money they won from you."

"Makes sense."

"And the main way you keep someone in your place," Emmler said, "is by taking care of them. Spoiling them, basically."

Nyman turned around. "And who is it who does the spoiling?"

"Oh, I wouldn't know anything about that," Emmler said, glancing at his daughters, who were crouched in the shade of the jungle gym's slide. "I leave all that to the concierge."

Chapter 23

Leaving Anaconda Road, Nyman stopped at a restaurant called Peking Garden and ate a lunch of fried rice, wontons, and egg drop soup. Then he drove back to the Strip, parked for a second time in Kasbah's garage, and rode the elevator to the gaming floor.

Threading his way among crowds of gamblers, he sat down at a five-dollar blackjack table and took a stack of twenty-dollar bills from his wallet.

The dealer said: "Change on two hundred," and arranged the bills face-down on the felt. He counted out stacks of chips in white, red, and green, pushed them over to Nyman, and swept the cash into an open slot in the table.

Nyman played a single hand and lost. Standing, he tipped the dealer, gathered up his chips, and made his way into the lobby, where the desk of the concierge stood in a square of sunlight.

As Nyman walked his stride became looser and jauntier. The blank expression on his face was replaced by a genial smile and eyes that were uncharacteristically bright and self-assured. When he reached the concierge he put the stack of chips on the desk and said:

"Just the guy I wanted to see."

The trim little man behind the desk gave Nyman a polished smile. "What can I do for you, sir?"

"I have a friend in L.A.," Nyman said. "He came out here a week or two ago and won all kinds of money with you guys."

"Really, sir? That's terrific. We love it when our guests have a lucky streak."

"Yeah, well, this guy's whole life's a lucky streak. And he tells me you showed him a hell of a time after he won."

The concierge beamed. "We always try to take care of our guests."

"Well, that's what I want," Nyman said, picking up a green chip and putting it on the desk in front of the concierge. "Exactly what you gave my friend. The whole deal."

A flicker of unease went through the polished smile. "Well, that might be a little difficult, not knowing who your friend is."

Nyman described Michael Freed and Alana Bell in detail.

The concierge said: "And they were here last week?"

"Two weeks ago, actually. And thanks. I knew you'd help me out."

Nyman gave him two red chips.

The concierge looked at the chips, then at his phone, then lifted the receiver and started talking to someone in a whisper. Nyman picked up a hotel brochure and glanced through it with evident curiosity, making interested noises as he turned the pages.

The concierge hung up. "Well, sir, we might be in luck. One of my assistants is on her way down from the pool. She thinks she might've been the one who took care of your friends."

The assistant turned out to be a tall young woman in a tailored suit. Nyman spoke to her in the same self-assured way, describing Freed and Alana in the same terms. She said that she remembered both of them very well.

"His name was Michael, wasn't it?"

"Michael Freed, yes."

"I don't think I caught the lady's name. But Mr. Freed had done very well at the tables, so I asked if I could be of service."

"Poker, right?" Nyman said. "About five grand?"

"No, sir—blackjack in the high-limit room. It was twenty thousand, I think."

Nyman whistled. "Well, whatever you gave him, that's what I want. Michael said you guys know how to take care of somebody."

The woman glanced at the concierge, then back at Nyman. "Well, that's the thing. I offered Mr. Freed a suite upstairs, but he said no. All he asked for was the use of a house car and driver."

Nyman snapped his fingers. "That's right: I heard about the driver. Where can I find him?"

"Excuse me?"

"The same one Michael had. Is he around today?"

The concierge stepped between the woman and Nyman. "I'm sorry, sir, but you haven't mentioned whether you're staying with us here in the hotel."

"Haven't I?"

"No. Naturally, we like to help all of our gaming guests, but—"

Nyman stopped him with an upraised hand and said that he understood. "Can't expect you guys to keep track of the drivers. You probably get them from an outside service, anyway."

"No, we have them on staff, but my point—"

"Thanks," Nyman said, gathering up his chips. "I'll let you get back to work."

Turning, he left the lobby and crossed the gaming floor. At the cashier's window he changed his chips back into cash and said to the squat, balding cashier:

"I think I left my sunglasses in one of the house cars. They keep them parked down in the garage, I'm guessing?"

"Yes, sir. Level P5. Would you like me to call down to the attendant?"

"That's all right. I'm going down there anyway."

Nyman slipped the wallet back into his pocket and made his way to the elevator, walking normally now and without a smile.

* * *

On level P5 he found a row of identical town cars and a glassed-in office. A reedy young man sat at a table just inside the door, frowning over the pages of a book with the words *Multistate Bar Exam* on the spine.

"If you want a car," he said as Nyman came in, "you have to talk to the front desk."

Nyman said that he was looking for a driver, not a car. "Someone who drove one of your guests two weeks ago."

Looking up, the attendant asked him if he was a policeman.

"An investigator," Nyman said. "Working with the L.A. coroner's office."

"On a murder?"

"Yes."

"Really? The victim was staying here? Or the murderer was?"

"The victim was here for a while, at least. I'm trying to find out what she did while she was in town."

The attendant put the book aside. "Well, if it was two weeks ago, it was probably Arturo who drove her. He had most of the shifts."

"Know where I can find him?"

"He'll be back in twenty minutes or so, if you want to wait. He just left on an airport run."

He nodded to a molded-plastic chair. Nyman sat down and, over the next half-hour, answered his questions about the case. The attendant had just finished law school at U.N.L.V. and was trying to get a job in the district attorney's office.

"In the Criminal Division, hopefully. Prosecuting homicides. You probably see a lot of homicides, working for the coroner."

Nyman said that he was an independent investigator, not an employee of the county.

"Like for a detective agency, you mean?"

"Right."

"I heard there's not much money in that."

"You heard correctly."

Outside, tires squealed as a car pulled into an empty spot. The driver was a short, thick-bellied man with a nose that lay flat and slanting above his mouth. He came into the office and tossed his keys on the desk.

The attendant said: "This guy wants to talk to you, Artie. He's an investigator checking up on a guest."

Scribbling on a timesheet taped to the wall, Arturo looked at Nyman. "Yeah? What guest?"

Nyman showed him the photo of Michael Freed from the Pacifica website.

"Oh yeah. A few weeks ago, right? He was with the girl?"

"You remember them?"

"It wasn't the kind of night I'm going to forget."

"You mind if I ask you a few questions?"

Arturo waved a hand. "Now's no good. I'm going up to the book to watch the fight."

Nyman said he hadn't realized a fight was coming on. "Why don't you let me buy you a drink? We can talk between rounds."

"You really got the money for drinks?"

Nyman showed him the cash in his wallet.

"All right. Deal."

Chapter 24

Kasbah's sportsbook was hazy with smoke. On the T.V.s that lined the walls were horse races, baseball games, a golf tournament, and the prefight show on H.B.O. Nyman followed Arturo up to the bar.

Sliding onto a stool, Arturo said that he knew a local boxer who was fighting in the undercard. "Welterweight named Peña. Trains at the gym I used to go to when I was a kid."

"You're from Vegas?"

"Born and raised."

"Must be an interesting place to grow up."

Arturo, holding up a finger to get the bartender's attention, said to Nyman: "Real interesting, yeah, but what about those drinks you were buying?"

Nyman asked the bartender for two beers and handed over his credit card.

The T.V. was showing footage from the previous day's weigh-in. On either side of the boxers stood two women—both taller than the boxers themselves—dressed in swimsuits printed with sponsors' logos.

Watching the footage, Arturo said: "So did he kill her or what?"

"Pardon?"

"The guy I drove two weeks ago. I figure an investigator's not going to come all the way out from L.A. unless somebody got killed."

Nyman told him what had happened to Alana. Arturo listened with a blank expression that became more animated when the bartender brought over the Bud Lights. Arturo lifted his bottle to Nyman, drank, and said without emotion:

"That's too bad. I could tell there were sparks between her and the guy, though."

"Romantic sparks?"

"Plenty of those, yeah, but violence, too. When I picked them up the guy had just won twenty grand at the tables. Wanted me to take them back to the little hotel they were staying at."

"Tryst?"

He nodded. "Hands me a hundred dollars and asks if I'd mind driving them around for the night. I tell him no problem. You get a big winner in your car, you can make more in one night than you'll get the rest of the month."

"Which night was this, exactly?"

Arturo drank again and consulted his memory. "Must've been a Saturday, because I was working the same shift I worked today. Got the call from the concierge around four or four-thirty. I pick them up at the main entrance and take them to Tryst. Guy asks me if I'll wait at the hotel until they can change and get ready for dinner."

"Did they say what they were doing in Vegas?"

"Besides winning lots of money? No. Not a word. After thirty minutes or so they came back out and said they want me to drive them to the Wynn to celebrate. One of the French restaurants there."

On the T.V., the first of the undercard fights was about to start. Peña, in gold trunks, stood in his corner, his cheeks shiny with petroleum jelly.

Arturo said: "Anyway, they were inside the Wynn for an hour or two. When they got back in they smelled like champagne and the girl told me to take them someplace for another drink, so I drove them up to the Black Hat. Manager there gives me something for everybody I bring in."

"Did you hear anything they said in the car?"

"Not in the car, no. But when we got to the Black Hat I went in after them, to let my friend know I'd brought him some customers. We're standing there by the door when I hear this angry voice coming from the bar."

"Freed's?"

"The girl's. Alana, or whatever her name was. A minute or two later I hear a chair fall over and then she comes storming by me. When I get out to the parking lot she's already in the backseat, telling me to take her back to Tryst."

"What made her angry?"

Arturo shrugged. "No idea. But the guy didn't come after her. Not even out to the parking lot. The girl still had plenty of money, so I took her back to the hotel. She goes in for five minutes, comes out with a suitcase, tells me to take her to the airport."

On the T.V., the bell had rung and the two fighters were circling each other. Peña closed in, jabbed, ducked under an uppercut, and skipped away. Arturo watched with a frown of concentration, the beer forgotten in his hand.

Nyman waited for the first round to end, then said: "So you took her to the airport?"

"Hmm? Oh. Well, I took her most of the way there. Around Tropicana she leans up from the backseat and asks me if I know where Mr. Searle lives."

"Searle?"

He gestured to the walls around them. "Guy who owns this place. Well—not owns, exactly. Guy who runs the company that owns this place."

"Savannah Group?"

Arturo nodded. "The girl wanted to know if I knew where he lives. I told her I heard he has a place in Summerlin, out on Mesquite Road, but I don't know which one. She gives me more money and tells me to take her there."

With a bell the second round started and Peña's opponent moved forward, landing a two-punch combination that knocked Peña briefly off balance.

Nyman drank his beer and said after the round had ended: "So she wanted you to take her out to Searle's place?"

Arturo looked at him blankly, then nodded. "Yeah—out on Mesquite. We found it on the eleven hundred block, I think. Place so big you can't even see it from the road, because of the trees and hedges, but Searle's name is there on the gate."

"And she went in to see him?"

"Tried to, at least. She gets out and walks up to the gate, presses a little button. After a minute she gets back in and says okay, take me to the airport."

"They wouldn't let her in?"

Arturo laughed. "Why would they let her in? Some girl they'd never heard of?"

"How do you know they'd never heard of her?"

"Well, she didn't get in, did she?"

Nyman reached again for his beer. "And after that?"

"After that I took her to the airport. When we got up to the terminal she took some money from her purse and said it was the last of what she'd gotten from that son of a bitch."

"Meaning Freed?"

"Far as I could tell, yeah. She had probably a hundred there in her hand—maybe two. Said it would hardly be enough to get her back to L.A."

"So she was just going to walk in and buy a ticket?"

"That's what it sounded like. Never saw her again, at any rate."

The bell rang for a third time. Closing quickly on the other man, Peña landed a hard right hand, followed it with another, and sent the other man to the canvas.

Nyman asked the bartender for the check. By the time he finished signing the fight had ended and Arturo was laughing and clapping and signaling the bartender for another drink.

* * *

The sun was low when Nyman got out of his car at the Lady Luck. Crossing to the manager's office, he asked the clerk for directions to Mesquite Road, filled a cup with coffee, and walked back out into the heat.

Parked in one of the visitor's spots was a silver Mercedes. He walked past without looking at it and made his way to room 111, taking the keycard from his pocket.

A scrape of footsteps came from the pavement behind him. He paused with the keycard in his hand and looked over his shoulder.

The blow caught him across the bridge of the nose, turning him around and splashing coffee against the door. He steadied himself, raised an arm, and felt something clip him on the right side of the skull, above the ear.

He was unconscious by the time he hit the ground.

Chapter 25

He woke up coughing. Something warm was in his mouth and nostrils, preventing him from breathing. He spat and gasped and touched a hand to his face. The hand came away bloody.

A voice said: "Look at the mess he's making."

Nyman saw that he was lying in the backseat of a car. The leather upholstery was slippery with blood. Through the windows came the occasional flash of a passing street lamp.

He tried to sit up. In the passenger's seat someone turned around to look at him: a boy of sixteen or seventeen with a thin trickle of hair on his upper lip. In his hand was a box-end wrench as long as his forearm and flecked with blood.

The boy climbed onto his knees and wrapped his left arm around the headrest. With his other hand he lifted the wrench.

Nyman rolled into the floorboard. When the wrench touched his skull he saw a burst of light, whiter than sunlight, and then darkness.

* * *

When he woke next he was lying on hard ceramic tiles. A sound of labored breathing came from his right, interrupted now and then by the sound of licking. A blunt-faced dog was sitting beside him, licking his blood from the tiles.

Nyman put his palms on the floor and tried to raise his body. His head came up far enough to show him that he was in the entryway of a house. Behind him, locked and chained, was the front door. Straight ahead was a living room filled with the flickering light of a T.V.

Trembling, he pushed himself into a sitting position. The dog turned its head to watch him, its muzzle pink with blood. With an arm that moved as if disconnected from his body, Nyman reached up to the door and fumbled with the chain.

Instantly there were footsteps behind him, then a hand on the collar of his shirt. The hand dragged him across the tile and up to the edge of the living room, at which point a voice said:

"Not on the carpet."

The hand let go of his collar and Nyman collapsed on the tile, gasping. The boy with the trickle of moustache stood above him, looking down with blank, incurious eyes. He wore a stained t-shirt, grimy jeans, and flip flops.

"He awake?" the same voice said from the living room.

The boy nodded. "Want me to put him out again?"

"No. Get a towel and clean him up."

The boy walked out of Nyman's field of vision. After a moment there was a sound of feet on carpet, and then someone else standing above him: a man as old as Nyman or older, dressed in dark jeans and a shirt that failed to hide the rounded bulge of his stomach.

The skin of the man's face was partly covered by a dark beard; thin dark hair was combed back from a receding hairline.

"Feeling okay?" he asked with mock concern.

"Yes."

"You don't look very good."

"Thanks."

The man smiled. "Know who I am?"

"Not offhand."

"You can call me Alex. I'm Mara's friend. You remember Mara?"

"Vividly."

The boy came back with a dripping hand-towel. He tossed it on the floor and told Nyman to clean himself up.

With effort, Nyman picked up the towel and climbed to his feet. He stood swaying on the tiles and used the towel to wipe the blood from his face and head.

A long swollen ridge ran from above his left eye to the right side of his mouth. His nose and upper lip were bulbous and too painful to touch. On the right side of his skull, above the ear, was a shallow gash.

"We didn't hit you too hard, Tom. Hit somebody too hard with a wrench and you end up killing them. We don't want to kill you."

"That's considerate of you."

"All I want," the man said, "is my money back."

"I don't owe you any money."

The man smiled and beckoned for Nyman to follow. "Come on. We'll talk while we eat."

Nyman followed him through the living room and into a large, brightly lit kitchen outfitted in stainless steel and granite.

A woman stood in front of the oven, dressed in a baggy white Suns jersey that showed the curve of her spine. On the counter was an empty Stouffer's box; the room was filled with the smell of baking meatloaf.

Alex said: "Dinner ready yet?"

The woman shook her head and turned to face them. Without her makeup Mara looked worn and fragile and a decade older. On the left side of her neck were four dark bruises, one on top of the next; a fifth bruise was on the right side of her neck, where Alex had presumably put his thumb.

"The trouble with guys like you," Alex said, smiling at Nyman and picking up a glass of wine, "is that you have no class. You come in from L.A. and think you can screw any girl in town, like you're back in college. But when you ask for one of my girls, you're making a business arrangement. Right, Mara?"

Keeping her eyes lowered, she said: "Right."

"Guys like you don't have any respect, is basically what I'm saying. If you don't give Mara what she's earned, then she can't give me what I've earned. It's like going to a restaurant and not paying your bill. You're not just disrespecting the waitress, you're disrespecting the chef who made the food."

Nyman said: "I didn't ask for her, and I never slept with her."

"At this point," Alex said, "I don't care who asked for her. Maybe you called; maybe it was someone else. But you spent the evening with her. You enjoyed her company. That's a service she provided on my behalf."

Nyman asked him how much he expected to be paid.

"All I ask is two grand. And when you consider how much my girls make on a normal night, that's very generous on my part."

The oven beeped. Mara found an oven mitt in one of the drawers and used it to take a brown rectangle out of the oven and slide it onto the gas range. The bubbling surface of the meatloaf was pocked here and there by shallow pink pools of bloody water.

The boy took paper plates from the cupboard and tossed them onto the counter beside the meatloaf, which Mara was dividing into smaller rectangles.

Only now, under the bright kitchen lights, did Nyman notice the boy's sharp, angular features, the same jutting nose and hollow cheeks he'd first noticed in Mara.

"You hungry, Tom?" Alex said, nodding to the meatloaf.

"No."

"You sure? You're looking a little pale, if you want to know the truth. Maybe you should eat something."

Nyman turned away from the food, breathing through his mouth. "I'm fine."

The other three ate standing at the countertop. For several minutes there was no sound in the kitchen but the noise of chewing and swallowing and the panting of the dog, which sat expectantly at Alex's feet, its pink muzzle dripping.

Nyman asked where the bathroom was.

"End of the hall," Alex said. "But the window's not big enough to crawl through."

"I don't need the window," Nyman said, and walked unsteadily to the bathroom.

He vomited twice in the toilet, then sat for a time on the floor with his back against the wall. Reaching into his jacket, he found without surprise that his phone and the cash in his wallet had been taken.

He got to his feet, flushed the toilet, washed some of the blood from his clothes, and drank a mouthful of water from the tap. When he came back into the kitchen the meal was over.

"Better?" Alex said.

"Yes."

"Glass of wine?"

"No thanks."

The man shrugged and refilled his own glass from the bottle. "All right, Tom, this is what's going to happen. Hunter here—" he nodded to the boy "—is going to drive you to a bank, and you're going take two thousand out of your account and give it to him. After that he'll drop you wherever you want to be dropped, within reason."

"What about my phone and cash?"

"Those are ours now. Call it a service fee."

"In that case," Nyman said, "I don't see much point in giving you anything else."

"Well, that's not really up to you. Show him, Hunter."

Slowly, with a smirk of toughness that was belied by the nervousness in his eyes, the boy put a hand to the small of his back and brought out a scuffed pistol. He raised it with one arm and held it pointed at Nyman's chest, trying to keep his hand steady.

Mara glanced up from the dishes she was washing in the sink. Looking from the trembling gun in the boy's hand to the smirk on his face, she turned off the water and left the room.

Chapter 26

Ignoring the gun, Nyman said to Alex in a tone of patient explanation:

"There are two vice cops named Carrillo and Parks. They were waiting for me when I got back to my motel last night. They already know that Mara met me at the bar. They know she threatened me after I wouldn't pay her and they know she works for you."

Alex smiled with teeth stained purple by wine. "Is all that supposed to mean something?"

"It means the police are going to come straight to you if anything happens to me."

"Assuming they ever find out what happened to you, Tom. It's not hard to lose a body in the desert."

Nyman told him not to be melodramatic. "You're not stupid enough to mess with a murder charge."

"I wouldn't be so sure about that," Alex said, and turned to the boy. "Take him down there."

The boy moved forward and waved the gun to one side, directing Nyman to walk ahead of him. Nyman, exhaling, moved away from the counter and into the archway that led out of the kitchen.

They came into a carpeted hallway with bedrooms set off to either side. Inside the bedrooms were bare mattresses, tables piled with perfume bottles, suitcases, cocktail dresses strewn on the carpet, yoga mats, stuffed animals.

"How many women does he have living here?" Nyman asked.

The boy ignored him.

At the end of the hall was another bedroom. Looking into it, Nyman saw Mara sitting cross-legged on a bed, putting rouge on her cheeks. Her lips were pursed and her eyes, looking at Nyman, were blank and lifeless. Lying open beside her bare foot was a prescription bottle.

They went through another door into the garage. The silver Mercedes stood beside a pile of boxes. The boy directed Nyman into the passenger seat, then crossed to the driver's side and started the engine. He used his right hand to steer and kept the gun in his left, resting it on his thigh so that it was pointed at Nyman.

He backed the car down the driveway, swung onto the road, and drove slowly through a neighborhood that looked little different from Stephen Emmler's.

Nyman said: "Mara's your mom, isn't she?"

The boy's voice was clipped and artificially deep. "Maybe."

"What about Alex? Is he your dad?"

"No."

"You're sure?"

"I'm sure."

"That's a shame. Such a nice guy."

The boy cursed Nyman in a nervous voice and turned on the radio.

Nyman leaned back against the seat and looked out at the street. His pupils were twice their normal size and unfocused; his pale face was sweating. After a while he closed his eyes.

* * *

When he opened his eyes the car was stopped and the boy wasn't in the driver's seat. Nyman pushed open the passenger door and stepped directly into the chest of the boy, who'd come around the car.

"This way," the boy said, gesturing with the gun.

They were in the parking lot of a strip mall. The line of darkened storefronts ended at the brightly lit façade of a bank. A pair of ATMs stood beside the bank's doors. A few feet to the right the building gave way to a vacant lot of dirt and scrub-grass.

"Two thousand," the boy said, pointing to the ATMs. "Get going."

Nyman put his hands in his pockets and stayed where he was. Nausea and blood loss had taken the color from his lips and upset his balance, making him sway slightly from side to side.

"The trouble with this plan," he said, "is that ATMs only let you take out a certain amount in a day. Seven hundred, I think it is."

The boy's eyes moved uncertainly. "What do you mean?"

"I mean I can't get two thousand out of it, even if I tried. I'd have to wait another twenty-four hours, and then I'd only have fourteen hundred for you. It would be three days until I could give you the full two thousand."

The boy shook his head; the gun came up higher. "That doesn't work."

"I know it doesn't. I wish Alex would've thought of that. Maybe you should call him."

"He told me not to call him."

"Really? Why not?"

"I ..." The boy shook his head again and stepped forward; his voice was high-pitched and wild. "Just get the money."

"I'm sorry. I can't."

"Yes you can. Just get it."

"Did Alex also mention," Nyman said, "that there are cameras in the ATMs? Which means they've probably already taken a picture of you."

The boy moved back into a patch of shadow. The gun jittered in his hand.

Nyman said: "If you want to call someone, why don't you call your mom? She'd know what to do."

"Shut the hell up."

"Or we could call those vice cops," Nyman said. "If you told them what's going on, they'd help you out. Help you get away from the guy who's beating your mom."

"Stop talking about my mom."

Nyman, swaying, took the hands from his pockets and held them open. "You're a kid, Hunter. You won't be charged as an adult. You—"

The boy swung the gun at Nyman's head, hitting him hard on the chin and mouth. An eye-tooth came loose and clattered to the pavement. Nyman started to fall, caught himself, and felt something hit the base of his skull.

His next sensation was of being dragged by the collar. Vaguely he was aware of the lights of the bank and the ATMs. He tried to speak and found that his mouth was filled with blood.

Later there was a rattle of chain link. Nyman saw that he was being pulled through an open section of fencing. Under his back was gravel; in the spinning sky were stars that formed fleeting arcs of light. From somewhere nearby came the boy's grunts.

With sudden desperate energy, Nyman spun away on the gravel, tried to get to his feet, fell, and rose high enough on his knees to swing at the boy as he came near.

The punch moved through empty air. The boy had circled around behind him and was talking in a voice that sounded as if it were filtered through water.

There was a flicker of light as the gun clipped Nyman's temple; then he saw grains of dirt and gravel at close proximity. Above him a hot wind was rising, blowing sand and dirt over his body, as if to fill a grave.

In a slurred voice he repeated a single syllable—a woman's name—until he lost consciousness.

EDGE OF THE KNIFE

Chapter 27

Something dry and sinuous moved over the skin of his hand. When he opened his eyes the snake was a dark curving line disappearing into a clump of saltbush. Beyond the clump, the beam of a flashlight moved here and there in the darkness, illuminating rocks and dirt and branches of creosote.

The beam of light swept over him. He heard a sharp intake of breath, and then Mara came into view, made visible by the glow of her flashlight. She wore the same black dress she'd worn the night before; her lips were glossy and red.

"Thank god," she said.

Nyman tried to speak and failed. His mouth was tangled with strands of half-dried blood.

Mara took his arm and helped him to his feet, then led him back through the fence and into the parking lot. Parked in front of the bank was a black Nissan with a crumpled fender.

"Hunter thought he'd killed you," she said. "He's hysterical. He thought he killed you and now he thinks Alex is going to kill him."

Nyman spat blood on the pavement and said in a slurring voice: "What time's it?"

Not answering, she led him to the Nissan and helped him into the passenger seat. A beach towel had been spread across the upholstery, presumably to absorb his blood. On the dashboard was a first-aid kit.

She came around the car and sat down in the driver's seat. Her eyes were wide and bright and her hands, now that she'd gotten into the car, had started to shake. She took the first-aid kit into her lap and tried to sort through the bandages.

"I didn't know what you'd need. I told Hunter you were probably alive, but I had to check. I thought if I could get you to a hospital, or stop the bleeding myself—"

"Thanks," Nyman said, slurring. "I'll be all right."

Anger flared in her pale face. "I'm not saying I did it for you. I did it for Hunter."

"Doesn't matter," Nyman said. "What time is it?"

She put her key in the ignition; the clock read 12:03. Mara cursed and said that she'd already missed an hour of work.

"Work?"

"The Strip. Saturdays I work the casinos."

Nyman lowered the vanity mirror and looked at his face. The mass of dirt, blood, and swollen flesh was unrecognizable. He closed the mirror and slumped back.

Mara started the engine and asked him where he wanted to be dropped.

Nyman said thickly: "Summerlin."

"What?"

"Mesquite Road in Summerlin. Have to see a suspect."

She gave him a look of disbelief. "You're not in any shape to go out there."

"I'll be fine."

"You can hardly walk."

"All right," he said, reaching for the door handle. "I'll get a cab."

She locked the door with a button and started the engine. "I'm taking you back to your motel."

Nyman's head lolled to the side as she backed out of the parking spot; after a moment he leaned forward and braced himself over his knees, as if he were going to be sick. Five or ten minutes later, muttering something indistinct, he straightened up again and looked around the interior of the car as if seeing it for the first time.

Mara, watching him in her peripheral vision, said: "He's not a bad kid, you know."

"What?"

"Hunter."

"Oh."

"A bad kid wouldn't have cared if he'd killed you."

Nyman nodded and said nothing. They were approaching the Strip from the east. In the distance the sky brightened almost to daylight as they drew nearer to the lights of the casinos. Ahead on the shoulder of the road was a parked police cruiser, its siren and headlights turned off.

Mara glanced at the cruiser as they went past. "You're not going to say anything to the cops, are you?"

"Depends. Are you going to give me my money back?"

"I can't. Alex has it."

"I need it."

"Look, I'd give it to you if I could, but I can't. I don't have anything."

"How much're you going to make tonight?"

EDGE OF THE KNIFE

The flare of anger reappeared on her face. "You know I have to give that to Alex."

"You don't have to. "

"Yes I do. That's how it works. You have no idea how it works."

Nyman rested his head against the rattling window. "I told your kid the cops would help him. They'd help you too."

She laughed. "Yeah. I don't need that kind of help."

"Fine. Not the cops. A shelter or something."

"A shelter? Why don't you mind your own goddamn business? Alex loses his temper sometimes, but he's always been there for Hunter and me. He's been there a hell of a lot more than people like you."

Nyman looked for a moment as if he were going to respond, then closed his eyes. A deep flush had appeared among the bruises of his face and spread across his forehead and neck.

Looking at the road, Mara said: "You've got nothing to say to that?"

When Nyman didn't answer she turned to look at him. After that she fell silent and drove more quickly. When the car pulled up to the Lady Luck Inn Nyman's teeth were chattering and his hair was wet with feverish sweat.

Mara came around to the passenger door. Looping his arm around her shoulder, she led him to the door of his room, then bent down to get his keycard, which was partly wedged under the welcome mat.

Inside the room, she made him sit in a chair beside the door, then went into the bathroom. He leaned with his head against the wall and looked up at the ceiling, where seeping water had made yellow stains.

Mara came out of the bathroom. "Here. Take these."

She dropped Tylenol into his hand and gave him a cup of water. When he'd swallowed the pills, she used a washcloth to clean some of the dirt and blood from his face.

Then she removed the plastic sack that lined the ice bucket and went outside, leaving the door open. Nyman heard the clatter of the ice machine, then the clicking of heels as she came back along the sidewalk and into the room, the ice-filled sack in her hand.

"All right. Lay down on the bed."

"S'okay. I'll sleep here."

"Shut up and get in the bed."

Teeth chattering, he moved to the bed and lay down on the top-sheet. She went into the bathroom to get a towel, wrapped it over the ice, and put the ice in the palm of his hand.

"There. Now hold that against the swelling."

He held the ice against his mouth. "Thanks."

Acting as if she hadn't heard, she filled the cup with more water and put the cup and the Tylenol on the bedside table. Then, without a backward glance, she left the room and shut the door.

Chapter 28

He woke nine hours later. The sheets were wet with melted ice. The plastic sack was crumpled in his hand. The flush and sweat of fever were gone.

He lay unmoving on his back for half an hour, then forced himself to get out of bed and fill the bathtub with hot water. Swallowing more Tylenol, he sat in the water and smoked what was left of his cigarettes. When he came out of the bath his muscles had relaxed and he was moving almost normally.

He looked in the mirror and saw the same mass of bruised and bloodied flesh, but less swollen. In his mouth was a toothless red socket between his upper left incisors and bicuspids.

He muttered hoarsely and bent over sink, flushing blood from the socket. Then he packed the socket with toilet paper, dressed in clean clothes, used the right side of his mouth to eat his last piece of bread, and walked to the manager's office, where a woman with an expressionless face said:

"Checking out?"

Nyman leaned against the counter and took the wallet from his pocket. "Room one-eleven."

"Looks like you had a rough night."

"That would be one way to describe it."

"Vegas can be a rough town, sometimes."

"So I'm learning."

"Cash or credit?"

"Credit," he said. "All the cash is gone."

* * *

It was a thirty-minute drive to Summerlin. He stopped once to buy coffee and cigarettes, then a second time to buy a disposable black flip-phone for fifteen dollars. It was past noon when he left the Summerlin Parkway and turned onto Mesquite Road.

A dark green column of Afghan pines rose along the side of the road. Glittering in the gaps between the pines were swathes of fairways and putting greens. Rooflines came occasionally into view above the upper branches, hinting at the massive houses that lay below.

After a mile or two the road jogged to the left and narrowed, winding deeper into the villages that surrounded a network of private golf courses. The road ended in a cul-de-sac with a cluster of palms at its center and a wrought-iron gate set off at a tangent. A strip of steel on the gate's callbox was engraved with the name Searle.

Nyman pressed the callbox button and told his name to the dry, businesslike man who answered.

"Nyman with an Y? I'm sorry, sir, but I don't have you down on the visitor's list."

EDGE OF THE KNIFE

"That's because Mr. Searle didn't know I'd be visiting. Tell him I'm the investigator who's been bothering people at Kasbah."

The man said: "One moment, please."

A yellow-headed verdin sat in the branches of the acacia that rose behind the gate. It looked down at Nyman with black, inquisitive eyes and made a whistling three-note call. From somewhere nearby came the pop of a golf ball being struck.

The man came back on the line. "Mr. Searle says to pull your car around to the service entrance. He'll meet you there."

The gate divided in the center and Nyman drove forward on a path of cobblestones. The path curved among trees and shrubs, rising steadily until the ground levelled off and he saw an enormous stone house in an imitation Tuscan style. Half a dozen luxury cars were parked in the circular drive.

He followed the cobblestone path around one wing of the house and onto a wide apron of concrete. A mild-looking older man in a polo shirt and khaki pants stood waiting in the shade of a portico. He came forward with his hands in his pockets and then, stopping as Nyman climbed out of the car, said in a warm, avuncular voice:

"My goodness. What happened to your face?"

"A meeting with some friends of yours," Nyman said, and held out a hand. "Tom Nyman."

The man's handshake was dry and firm. "Howard Searle. What do you mean, friends of mine?"

"Friends of your friends at Kasbah, at least. You're the C.E.O. of Savannah Group?"

183

Searle nodded. "We've got lots of properties, though—Kasbah's just one. I don't have a hand in the day-to-day operations."

"But someone's been talking to you about me," Nyman said.

"What makes you think that?"

"The fact that you let me through the gate."

He gave a mild smile and waved a hand. "Oh, I'm not too strict about who I let through my gate. I believe in being accessible."

Nyman said he was glad to hear it. "That should make my job easier."

"And what's your job, Mr. Nyman?"

"Finding out who killed Alana Bell."

Searle looked at him with eyes that crinkled with amusement. His body was soft but not fat and his face was relatively unlined for a man in his sixties. He held himself with an air of prosperous good health.

"The name's familiar," he said. "She was a student of some kind, wasn't she?"

"A student and an activist. One who was trying to stop your Merchant South project."

"Yes, that's right. Well, I'm sorry to hear she passed away, but I can assure you that no one at Savannah Group played any part in it."

"I'm not suggesting they did," Nyman said. "But all the same I'd like to ask you some questions."

Searle glanced at the Patek Philippe on his wrist. "Actually, I have guests at the moment, so now's not the best time."

"I only need a few minutes."

"I'm sorry, but now's really not the—"

"And this way," Nyman said, "I won't have to talk to the police about the woman you sent to my motel room."

The genial smile remained in place. "There's no need to take an ugly tone. I'm happy to do whatever I can to help. Come with me."

Nyman followed him into a glassed-in solarium that ran along the backyard and gave a view of distant greens and bunkers. Interspersed among the chairs and couches were sculptures made in stainless steel.

"I'll leave you here while I have a word with my guests," Searle said, steering him to a couch. "Something to drink while you wait?"

"No thanks."

Nodding, Searle moved off toward the interior of the house and Nyman sat down. He lay back against the cushions for a minute or two, rubbing his temples and shutting his eyes against the bright desert sunshine. Then he sat forward and looked at his surroundings.

The solarium was cold despite the sunshine and immaculately clean. Through the glass, he could see two women playing a game of lawn bowling on a green that had been laid out in the yard. They held glasses of champagne and occasionally rolled a ball across the clipped grass.

Nyman watched them with narrowed eyes. The younger of the two was no more than nineteen or twenty and moved with graceful, self-conscious poise, as if aware of her own beauty. He got up and walked to the glass, shading his eyes.

A moment later, smiling, he turned away from the window and walked in the same direction Searle had gone, leaving the solarium and coming into a large vaulted gallery. Faint voices carried in from a hallway leading into the other wing of the house.

At the end of the hall Nyman went down a short flight of steps and found himself in a large room with a pair of glass doors standing open to the backyard.

Howard Searle stood beside the doors, looking at Nyman with the same amused smile. Sitting in a chair across from him, his blue eyes wide with surprise, was Ethan Kovac.

Chapter 29

The room was a study. A desk and credenza stood in one corner; a muted T.V. on the wall was tuned to C.N.B.C. Laughter came in from the backyard, where the two women had abandoned their bowling and refilled their glasses with champagne.

Nyman said to Kovac: "I recognized your wife, so I thought I'd come and see you. Sorry if I overstepped my bounds," he added to Searle.

Searle gave an indulgent shrug. "Like I said, I try to be accessible. I take it you've already met the Kovacs?"

"I have. Good to see you again, Ethan."

Kovac had recovered from his surprise and was leaning back in his chair, chewing a thumbnail. "Nice to see you too, Tom. Face got a little banged up, I see."

"A little."

Searle said: "Have a seat, Mr. Nyman. This is a working weekend for us. We're hammering out the last details on Merchant South."

Nyman sat down. Spread on a table between his own chair and Kovac's were glossy fliers and architectural plans. One of the fliers showed a rendering of the same white condo tower he'd seen sketched on the banner across from Zamora Park.

"That's the Melville," Searle said. "Eighteen stories and two-hundred-and-fifty luxury residences. We broke ground last week on the foundation."

Nyman said that he'd visited the construction site a few days ago.

"Really? You make a habit of touring construction sites?"

"I was there to look at the park across the street."

Searle laughed. "You mean Zamora? That wasn't a park; that was a public health hazard. You couldn't walk in there without stepping on a needle."

"Alana Bell thought it was worth keeping open."

Taking the thumb from his mouth, Kovac said: "She thought a lot of things, most of them pretty naïve. Once the Melville opens, you'll have people moving in who care about the neighborhood and want to improve it. Not just transients."

Nyman asked how much the apartments in the building would rent for.

"That'll depend on several different variables," Searle said, "some of which haven't been decided yet. But we expect the value of the property to increase steadily as the rest of the neighborhood gets filled in around it."

"And you have to think about what the residents will be getting for their money," Kovac said. "A pool, of course, and a spa, and a health club. In the ground-level spaces we're putting a restaurant from my company's portfolio—a Shinsen, probably—along with a private bar that'll only be open to residents."

Searle said: "That's why I wanted to work with Ethan on this. He can bring in all the brands Koda's already established, and then give us something entirely new with the hotel that'll be built alongside the Melville. It's all about facilitating a particular lifestyle—a seamless luxury experience across the development."

Nyman said it sounded very nice. "Is this the same sales-pitch you gave to Alana when you talked to her?"

Searle shook his head. "I never talked to the woman in my life."

"You're sure? She came all the way to Vegas to see you."

"Did she? When was this?"

"Two weeks ago."

Searle cocked his head, thinking. "Well, there's your answer. I was in Florida two weeks ago. We had a ribbon cutting on Key Biscayne."

"And you never invited her to Kasbah?"

"Of course not."

"What about Michael Freed?"

"Freed? The man who did the city's study?"

"He's also the man," Nyman said, "who won twenty-thousand dollars in the high-limit room of your casino. With Alana Bell at his side."

"Well, this is the first I've heard of it. Like I said, I don't keep a hand in the day-to-day operations."

Rising from his chair, Kovac took a bottle of mineral water from the refrigerator beside the credenza. Uncapping the lid, he said to Nyman:

"I've met Freed once or twice. He's what you might call a very devoted instructor of his students. Particularly the female

189

ones. If he was here in Vegas with Alana, you can be sure it was for pleasure, not for business."

"And certainly not any business with Savannah Group," Searle said. "I couldn't even tell you what the man looks like."

Nyman took the handkerchief from his pocket and blotted the blood on his lip.

"Doesn't it seem like a strange coincidence," he said to Searle, "that Freed won so much money at your casino right after analyzing one of your developments?"

"I don't see anything strange about it. We've got holdings in a dozen different states—assets of fifteen billion dollars. These little coincidences pop up all the time."

Nyman said he didn't doubt it. "But if there's nothing to hide, why won't you cooperate with my investigation?"

"Cooperate? You're here, aren't you? I've given you— what?—fifteen minutes now of my time? There are lots of people who'd like fifteen minutes of my time."

Nyman said: "Someone at your company told Stephen Emmler to get me out of the way. Emmler admitted as much to me yesterday morning."

"Ah, so you talked to Stephen. I'm afraid he's never quite jelled with our organization. He's very much a product of the old Vegas, whereas at Savannah we try to do things differently."

"You expect me to believe that Emmler acted on his own?"

"No, it's more likely there was a miscommunication somewhere down the line. Stephen can have trouble putting our directives into action."

Nyman said that the miscommunication had cost him a phone and nearly two hundred of his client's dollars.

Searle, reaching into his pocket, drew out a wallet. "If money's what you're after, you should've said so from the start. I'd be happy to make it up to your client."

"No thanks," Nyman said. "I don't want your money."

Kovac said to Searle in a tone of explanation: "Tom's adopted Alana's opinion about us. Money's the root of all evil, so anyone with money must be evil. And developers are twice as evil as anybody else."

"That's not what I think," Nyman said.

"Of course what you guys don't understand," Kovac went on, "is that every time we put up a high-density tower like the Melville, we're increasing the supply of housing, which increases the vacancy rate and drives down rent across the city. For everybody—not just our residents."

"That's fine," Nyman said. "I didn't come here to debate policy."

"No, I realize that. And you're welcome to think whatever you want about us. But sending your henchman out to harass people is going over the line."

"Henchman?"

"Well, whatever you want to call that kid. He spent the last two days making Grace's life hell, and I think that's a pretty shady thing to do."

"Grace Salas?"

Kovac nodded. "The city councilwoman. She told me you'd been out to her office to make a lot of wild accusations, and then you sent the kid to do the same thing. I really thought you were better than that, Tom."

"You think I sent someone to bother her?"

"Where else would the kid get the idea? And frankly I think you bear some responsibility for what happened to him."

Nyman shook his head. "I don't understand."

Searle said: "He's talking about the homeless kid you sent after us. Trujillo. He was killed last night in L.A."

Nyman's face, beneath the bruises, became pale and waxy. "What?"

"Stabbed to death," Kovac said. "You didn't see it in the paper? We figured that's why you came out here today."

Nyman's voice was hoarse. "Who killed him?"

"I don't think the cops have any idea. But a kid like that, harassing so many people: it was bound to happen at some point."

Nyman said: "Where were you?"

Kovac blinked. "Me?"

"Last night. When Trujillo was killed."

"You really are a suspicious bastard, aren't you, Tom?"

Nyman repeated the question.

"I was right here," Kovac said, "along with about eighty other people. Howard hosted a party for the new oncology wing at Valley Memorial."

Nyman turned to Searle. "You were here too?"

"Of course."

"What about Freed and Salas?"

Searle shrugged. "They were in L.A., I imagine. Why would I invite them out here?"

"Then you can't vouch for them?"

"No."

"And this harassment you say Trujillo was doing. It was directed only at Salas?"

Kovac said: "Mainly at her, but we got calls from him at the Rexford. I think he might've even tried to get in the door."

Searle nodded. "We had calls, too."

"Calls about what?"

"Oh, the same things you've been talking about," Searle said. "How we were somehow responsible for the Bell woman's death. How Trujillo intended to make us pay."

"I haven't said anything about making you pay."

Searle smiled. "But isn't that what this is about for you? Exacting some sort of revenge?"

"No," Nyman said, and rose to his feet. "That's not what this is about."

Telling Searle he would be in touch, he went out to his car.

Chapter 30

He stopped at a newsstand to buy a copy of the *Times*. A story in the local section said that a transient named Eric Trujillo had been found dead on San Pedro Street on Skid Row. The young man had died of apparent knife wounds; the police had made no arrests and were asking anyone with information to come forward.

He tossed the paper onto the passenger seat and drove east to the Mojave freeway.

In Barstow, he stopped for an early dinner at a roadside café and called Paul Lattimer to give him an update on the investigation. Later, reaching into his pocket to pay the bill, his fingers came across a folded cocktail napkin on which a man had written an address in Burbank.

He looked down at the address with a thoughtful frown.

* * *

Jets, their wings flashing gold and pink in the glow of sunset, circled Bob Hope Airport as Nyman walked along a sidewalk in Burbank. He climbed the steps of a stucco duplex and rang the bell of Unit B.

Through the screen door he could hear music and the tread of heavy feet. A barrel-chested man with a graying van dyke appeared behind the screen, squinting at Nyman as if trying to place him.

Nyman said: "The Green Door."

"Oh, right." The man smiled. "Tom, isn't it? You always want to hear standards."

Nyman nodded. "How's the piano-playing business?"

"Underpaid, as usual. The name's Ira, by the way. Come on in."

The duplex smelled of dogs and pot and old records. A hi-fi beside the couch was playing a record Nyman didn't recognize, seemingly for the benefit of the Chihuahua that lay beside the speakers.

Ira said: "Something to drink? There's some beer in the fridge."

"No thanks."

"Something to smoke?"

"That's all right," Nyman said, taking the cigarettes from his pocket. "I've got my own."

Ira made a permissive gesture. "The neighbors don't mind."

Nyman took a cigarette from the pack and sat on the edge of the couch, reaching down to pet the Chihuahua.

"That's Angie," Ira said, dropping into a chair. "She's survived two ex-wives and the move from New York."

"Pleased to meet you, Angie."

The dog ignored him. From the speakers, above pulsing strings and the wordless rising tones of a choir, came the insistent wail of a tenor saxophone. Ira, leaning back in the chair, rested his head against the wall and asked Nyman if he liked the music.

"This is the first I'm hearing it."

Ira smiled. "Yeah. Not exactly the kind of thing they like to hear at the Green Door."

Nyman told him not to put much stock in what people liked at the Green Door. "A person's taste deteriorates after the third martini."

"Mmm. That's the nature of the business, though. This sister-in-law of yours—the one who wants the lessons. She better know from the start that she won't get to play the stuff she loves. The jobs I get, you play to the crowd."

Nyman lit a cigarette. "I'm not sure she could make it through the lessons, to be honest with you."

"I thought you said she had talent."

"She does. Or she did. When I first met her, she was in the music program at Pacifica. I don't think she's played in years, though."

"And her sister's your wife? That's how you're related?"

For a time Nyman said nothing. Then, keeping his gaze on the smoke that rose from the cigarette, he said:

"Theresa's sister went through some bad things over the years. Mental health things, I guess you'd call them. It all came to a head last year, and Theresa took it pretty hard."

"Came to a head how?"

"The details aren't important," Nyman said, avoiding the other man's eyes. "The main thing is that Theresa's had a lot to deal with, and she hasn't dealt with it very well. She needs someone to help her get straightened out."

Ira walked to the hi-fi to turn the record over. "What's she been using?"

Nyman said that he didn't know. "Just pills, maybe. Or maybe something worse."

"Probably a lot worse," Ira said. "People tend to go as far as they can down that road. It's what you might call the occupational hazard of being a musician."

"She's a good kid, apart from all that."

"Aren't we all?"

Nyman watched the slowly turning record. "If I could do something for her, it would mean a lot to me."

"I don't doubt it, Tom. You wouldn't've come out here unless it meant something. Especially with those bruises on your face."

Nyman waved a hand. "My own occupational hazard."

"Yeah. Manny told me you were a cop or something."

"A private investigator."

"Mmm. You in the middle of a case?"

Nyman nodded. "Up to my neck. That's why I wanted to talk to you now, before I get in any deeper."

"You make it sound like life and death."

Nyman said that he had a flair for the dramatic. "But I understand if you can't help with Theresa. I know it's an odd request."

"A little odd," Ira said. "Truth is, though, this is the kind of business that chews people up. The kid needs a thick skin if she's going to make it, and even if she makes it she won't make any money."

"But you're willing to give her a chance?"

"I'm not sure I'll be much help. But you have my address. You can tell her I'm here on Sundays if she wants to talk things over. Not too early, though."

Flushing, Nyman thanked him and said: "I won't forget this."

Ira shrugged. "The least I can do for a loyal listener."

"You're playing at the Door this week?"

"Like always. Any special requests?"

"Just the usual."

Ira went into the kitchen for a can of beer. Coming back out and pulling the tab, he said:

"I've got a theory about those songs you like. Those old standards—so tightly structured. I think they appeal to people who're trying to escape from something. People who want life boiled down to three-and-a-half minutes that make sense."

Nyman exhaled a stream of smoke and said that it was an interesting theory. "I don't know if it applies in my case, though."

Ira smiled and took a drink. "Just a thought."

* * *

Darkness had fallen by the time Nyman reached downtown. Passing the towers of the Financial District, he worked his way down Broadway and Main Street and into the five square miles of Skid Row.

The warehouses and storefronts were shuttered for the night and the single-room hotels were dark. Tents and tarpaulins covered the sidewalk and spilled out into the street. The air was hot and thick and fetid.

Midway down San Pedro a spot had been cleared among the tents and cordoned off with yellow caution tape. A few stray flowers and candles lay on the concrete; a square of cardboard bore an illegible message scrawled in black marker.

Nyman found a parking space a block away and walked back to the cordoned-off area.

In the center of the street a man was pushing a shopping cart filled with clothes and trash bags. He called out to the people he passed, most of whom were hidden inside their tents. The answering voices, when they came, were punctuated by laughs and coughs and, from the next block, the sound of sirens.

A few feet from the cordoned-off area was the loading bay of a warehouse. A woman had set up camp in front of the shuttered door; sheets of plastic had been tied to the metal above her head, forming a makeshift tent that hung down around her shoulders and the box she held in her lap.

As Nyman came closer he saw that there were two blurred shapes in the box, soft and multi-colored. A passing headlight revealed two cats so young that their eyes hadn't opened.

Nyman nodded to the caution tape and asked the woman if she knew anything about the murder victim.

She seemed for a time not to realize that she was being spoken to. Then, looking up, she saw Nyman standing above her, saw the bruises and blood on his face, and shrank back among the sheets of plastic, her eyes wide with fear.

Nyman moved off down the sidewalk. Pausing in the light of a streetlamp, he took the handkerchief from his pocket and wiped the blood from his mouth.

In the street, the man had pushed his shopping cart over to the cordoned-off area and was standing beside the tape, looking down at the candles and flowers. He was in his sixties or seventies and wore a heavy corduroy jacket and pants too short to reach to his ankles.

He looked up as Nyman approached. His face, under a grizzled beard, had the expressiveness of an actor's. Nodding to the tape, he said:

"Dead and gone. And practically a boy."

"You knew him?" Nyman said.

"Not enough to know him by name, no. He didn't live down here. Died down here, though, didn't he?"

"How do you know he didn't live here?"

"Because I know, that's how. The kid got turned out."

"Turned out?"

"Of an ambulance, most likely. Some hospital in Beverly Hills or something. They don't want to take care of somebody, they bring them down here and turn them out on the pavement. Just like that."

He snapped his fingers.

"But Trujillo was murdered," Nyman said. "Surely a hospital wouldn't have brought him down here."

The changeable face became canny. "So you already know all about him. You a cop?"

"More like a friend of his. Or an acquaintance."

"A cop, in other words."

"A private investigator."

"Mmm hmm. You say murder, but I bet you never seen a murder."

"Only the aftermath."

"Well, let me tell you something about murder. When it happens, it don't happen to people. That's a lie. Murder happens on its own, like a storm or something. Kid gets caught up in the storm and can't get himself out."

Nyman asked if he knew anything about the storm that had caught Trujillo.

The man shrugged irritably and turned back to his cart. "Who knows? You think I know everything about everything? This stuff I've been telling you—you going to give me anything in return?"

"I can give you some cigarettes."

"What brand?"

Nyman told him.

The man cursed. "Guy like you, I figured you'd smoke Camels. But those'll do."

Nyman gave him what was left of the pack, keeping back a cigarette for himself.

Chapter 31

He smoked it on his walk down to Fifth and Wall, where the L.A.P.D.'s Central Community station covered the block. Aside from the desk officer, the lobby was occupied by a pair of E.M.T.s and a shirtless man who stood leaning against the wall, his twig-thin arm held in the massive hand of an E.M.T.

Nyman told the desk officer that he had information about the murder on San Pedro Street.

"What kind of information?"

"Details on the background of the victim. And on the people who might've killed him."

She gave him an appraising look. "Are these the same people who beat you up?"

"Not exactly. I think there's a connection, though."

She nodded. "Have a seat and I'll see what I can do."

Nyman sat down. Fifteen or twenty minutes later a hatchet-faced man with an ambling, bow-legged stride introduced himself as Detective Timmons and invited Nyman back to his office.

The office was a glass-walled room in which three or four desks took up most of the space. Timmons waved Nyman into a chair in front of the largest desk and sat down behind it.

Under the fluorescent lights, Nyman could see lines of weariness around the man's eyes and the tremor in his hand as he reached for his coffee.

"Don't think I've seen you before," Timmons said. "You come around here very often?"

"I came in tonight from Vegas, as a matter of fact."

"Yeah? What took you to Vegas?"

"The same people who might've killed Eric Trujillo."

Nyman handed Timmons a copy of his license and told him about his investigation.

The weary eyes watched him closely. Timmons didn't interrupt and didn't move except to take a mechanical drink of coffee. When Nyman was finished, Timmons said:

"That's quite a case."

"I know it sounds unlikely. You can verify a lot of it with the coroner's office and the Vegas P.D."

Timmons moved a hand sideways, as if brushing aside the words. "I'm not saying you dreamed it up. As far as the Bell girl goes, it sounds like there's something there. But the Trujillo thing seems a little theoretical."

"It is theoretical, at the moment. I was hoping you've found something that could make it more substantial."

The angles of Timmons' face became sharper. "Sorry, Mr. Nyman. It's an ongoing investigation."

"I'm not asking for everything. Just an idea of what you've got."

Taking a mechanical drink, Timmons said: "We've got a dead body with a hole in the chest. All that's in the papers."

"Only one hole?"

"Only one we noticed. Haven't heard from the coroner yet."

"Some people are saying Trujillo was dropped here after he'd already died. They say he wasn't a local."

"Yeah. I've heard that theory."

"You don't put any stock in it?"

Timmons made another brushing-aside motion. "Maybe; maybe not. Trujillo hadn't been around for a while, but we knew about him. He did a little small-time dealing. You get lots of big-time dealers from outside the Row who come down here to prey on the addicts. My guess is Trujillo crossed one of them and they got rid of him."

"It would be odd, though," Nyman said, "for a dealer to take an interest in city politics."

"Not if he was trying to impress a girl."

"But the girl was already dead. She'd been dead two days when Trujillo started harassing Grace Salas."

"Okay," Timmons said. "Not trying to impress her. Trying to avenge her."

"Maybe Salas didn't like being the object of his vengefulness."

"Maybe. It doesn't seem likely, if you want my opinion, but stranger things have happened. I'll make a note of it."

"Just a note?"

Timmons glanced at a clock on the wall. "I got called out of bed on this sixteen hours ago, Mr. Nyman. I'm talking to everybody who's got something to say and I'm taking notes on everything they tell me. Every tip will get followed up on, including yours."

Nyman, after a silence, said: "Thanks for your time."

"Don't mention it. I'll walk you out."

When they came back into the lobby the E.M.T.s and the shirtless man were gone. Nyman gave Timmons a business card and said:

"You don't have any evidence of a car dropping the body off, then?"

Timmons' face darkened with annoyance. "We've got lots of stories, like I said."

"Any involving a car?"

"Down here, people see cars, planes, and flying saucers."

"What about an ambulance?"

"No. There was no ambulance. The city cracked down on hospital dumping years ago."

"What about a private vehicle?"

"Ask somebody out there, and they've seen ten vehicles, all different colors, all with bodies getting rolled out of them."

"Does one color get mentioned more than the others?"

Timmons rubbed a hand over his eyes. "Red, as a matter of fact. Three different people think they saw a red sedan. They were all high at the time, of course, but they all swear about the red."

"Interesting."

"Yeah. Fascinating. Now get out of here and let me get back to work."

* * *

A quarter-moon hung low above the skyline as Nyman walked back to his car. The hot wind had died away; in its place was a thick, humid stillness. Beads of sweat stood out on his forehead as he started the car and drove south.

The lights of the Hive were still burning. The bees and butterflies on its brick walls were made garish by ground-level floodlights. Nyman went into the vestibule and rang the intercom bell.

After a pause a woman's voice said: "Sorry, we're closed for the night. We open tomorrow at seven."

Nyman told her who he was. "I came by a few days ago to ask about Eric Trujillo. I think you might've been the person I talked to."

The pause this time was so long that Nyman looked at his watch to count the seconds. When the woman responded, her voice was tight with anger.

"I've already said everything I'm going to say to you."

"Trujillo's dead."

"I'm aware of that. You really think I wouldn't be aware of that?"

"There's a good chance," Nyman said, "that the person who killed him is the same person who killed my original client. There's also a chance they're planning another murder. I'm getting close to finding them, but I won't be able to do it without your help."

He looked again at his watch. After twenty seconds the intercom buzzed and the interior door clicked open. He went through into the large, cement-floored space that served as the Hive's main room.

The T.V.s were turned off and the pool tables were deserted. A gangly teenage boy stood with a backpack on his shoulders and a laundry bag at his feet, watching as an older man talked to someone on the phone. In the air was a smell of mop-water and disinfectant.

Standing in front of Nyman, her tattooed arms crossed over her chest, was the intake counselor he'd met on his first visit. She was looking at the bruises on his face.

"Jesus. What happened to you?"

He said that it wasn't important. "I need to talk to Marissa. Trujillo's girlfriend. She told me she was staying with her aunt, but I don't know the address."

"One step at a time, Tom. Why do you want to talk to Marissa?"

Nyman told her about Alana Bell and her opposition to Merchant South. "Apparently Trujillo decided to follow in her footsteps after she was killed. I need to find out exactly what he did and who he talked to."

"And you think Marissa can tell you?"

"She's the only person I know to ask. Unless you can tell me."

The counselor shook her head. "We haven't seen Eric around here for months. And I never heard him mention Merchant South. He wasn't exactly a political kind of kid."

"That's what I thought when I met him, but now I'm not so sure. I'm hoping Marissa can give me a clearer picture."

The boy with the laundry bag and backpack was following the older man to the vestibule. The boy gave the counselor a faint, sheepish smile; she told him to sleep well and come back in the morning.

"We're getting ready for the art show, so there'll be lots of people around."

The boy murmured something noncommittal and followed the older man out into the street.

The counselor turned back to Nyman. "How are you proposing to talk to her? By phone?"

"Face to face would be preferable. And tonight, if it can be arranged."

"It's almost eleven."

"The sooner the better. If she knows anything about what Trujillo was doing, she could be in danger herself."

The counselor gave him a long, skeptical look. Taking the phone from her pocket, she told him to stay where he was and walked back to the nook that had once served as the desk of the hotel's porter. She talked to someone on the phone for four or five minutes, then came back with a look of disappointment on her face.

"Marissa's at her aunt's place in Pico Union. She says she'd be happy to talk to you."

Nyman thanked her and took out his notebook. "What's the address?"

"Don't worry about the address. I'll get my car and you can follow me down."

"Follow you?"

She gave him a grim smile. "You really think I'd let you talk to her alone?"

* * *

Marissa and her aunt lived in a large pink house on Alvarado Terrace. It had been built a century ago in the Queen Anne style; now iron bars covered the windows and the paint hung in strips from the pedimented gable. In the belvedere of the tower were two rusted satellite dishes.

The counselor led Nyman up the front steps. "One thing I want to get straight, Tom. Marissa's made a lot of progress since she first came to us, but she's still working through some stuff. I don't want you upsetting her with a lot of questions."

"If she knows Eric was killed, chances are she's already upset."

"That's my point. Someone who's already vulnerable doesn't need to get pushed over the edge."

Ahead of them, on the front porch, the door creaked open and Marissa stepped out. She'd aged visibly in the last few days. Her round girlish body was leaner; her face was patchy and red from crying.

"Come in," she said in a numbed voice. "I was just about to feed Kelsey."

Particle-board walls divided the house into separate apartments. They followed her upstairs to a door marked *3E*.

On the other side of the door Nyman found himself in a studio apartment about the size of Timmons' office, with a sink and hot-plate in one corner, a mattress and a sleeping bag on the floor, and a loveseat pressed up against the only window.

The room was filled with people. Marissa's aunt— skeletally thin, with a look of sullen anger on her face—stood leaning against the sink, holding a baby in her arms. Two older kids lay on the mattress, watching Nyman with wide, curious eyes. A middle-aged man was asleep on the loveseat.

Turning her pink, misshapen head, the baby saw Marissa and stretched out her arms, the tiny fingers wriggling.

Marissa took the baby from her aunt, sat down in a chair, and reached for a blanket. As she arranged the baby and blanket at her breast, she said to Nyman in the same numbed voice:

"It's okay, you know. I don't blame you."

"Blame me?"

"For what happened to Eric. You might've put the ideas in his head, but he's the one who did something about them."

The aunt gave a brittle laugh. "The ideas were already in his head, Marissa. He was a stupid boy and we're better off without him."

"Shut up," Marissa said calmly, not bothering to look at her. To Nyman she said: "Don't listen to her. She has no respect for the dead."

"No, I have respect for my family. And for my niece. Unlike some people."

Nyman asked Marissa which ideas she thought he'd given to Trujillo.

"Whatever it was you talked about that day under the bridge. He was like a different person after that. Obsessed, almost."

"Obsessed with what?"

"I don't know. He said he'd found out some things, but he couldn't tell me about them. He said he was the only one who could do what had to be done."

"And what had to be done?"

She brushed away a strand of hair and shrugged. "He was too excited to make any sense. He came by here yesterday morning to get some clothes and was talking so fast I couldn't keep up. Mostly about Meridian."

"Meridian?"

The aunt said: "Another fantasy. The boy lived in a fantasy world."

As if her aunt hadn't spoken, Marissa said: "He wouldn't tell me what it was, but it was all he talked about. He said Meridian was the reason Alana had been killed. I thought it was a place or something, but it doesn't seem like that from the note."

"Note?"

"Well—the message, or whatever it is. I found it with some of his stuff this morning. You want to see it?"

"Yes," Nyman said. "Very much."

Chapter 32

Marissa turned to her aunt and said something in a low voice. Her aunt, lifting her skeletal shoulders, said:

"You look for it. How do I know where you keep his garbage?"

Marissa cursed and climbed out of the chair. The blanket fell away from her shoulder; the baby sat curled in her arm, intent on her breast. Marissa moved awkwardly around the little room, searching for the note.

The counselor told her not to worry about it. "You've already gone to enough trouble as it is. Hasn't she, Tom?"

Nyman said nothing. Marissa leaned over the sleeping man on the loveseat and picked up a piece of paper that lay folded on the windowsill. With a smile she handed it to Nyman and said:

"There."

He unfolded it. Typed on the page were several questions, each of which was followed by blank lines on which someone had written answers in pencil. Under the first question— *Where were you born?*—the person had scrawled *Pacoima*.

Printed at the top of the page were the words *Life History Survey—Zamora Park Population*. Nyman glanced at the rest of the questions and answers, then turned the paper over. On the back, in ink rather than pencil, the same person had written:

Meridian:
> *1. Freed*
> *2. Salas*
> *3. City counsel...?*

He looked up at Marissa. "You're sure this is Trujillo's writing?"

"Positive."

"Why would he write it on the back of the survey?"

She shrugged. "Alana gave him lots of stuff to fill out, back when he was living in Zamora. She acted like he was her lab rat or something."

Nyman asked her if she knew when Trujillo had written the note.

"Not exactly. It's been here a while, though. He stayed here the night they closed down the park, and he brought some stuff with him. The note was probably mixed in with that."

The aunt turned her sullen gaze on Nyman. "He would stay for days and days and never do a thing to help us. No money, no food—just the fantasies in his head."

Ignoring her, Nyman took out his notebook and consulted the pages. After a time he said:

"If Trujillo wrote it when he was living in the park, then he wrote it while Alana was still alive. She was killed the day after the park was closed."

"Is that important?"

213

"It means that whatever Meridian is, he might've learned about it from her. She might've even asked him for his help."

"She wouldn't have had to ask for it. Eric would've done anything for her."

The counselor, checking the time on her phone, said that it was getting late. "I think we've done enough interrogating for one night, Tom."

Nyman ignored her and said to Marissa: "What about Grace Salas and Michael Freed? Did he ever talk about them?"

"Not that I remember."

"Or a company called Savannah Group?"

"No. I don't think so."

"You're sure?"

"Pretty sure."

The counselor put a hand on Nyman's arm. "Come on. We're leaving."

"No, wait," Marissa said. "There's something I want to talk to you about. In private."

Rising from the chair, she carried the baby to her aunt and said that she'd be back in a minute. Her aunt muttered something indistinct and took the baby from her, cradling the little body in her skeletal arms.

Marissa led Nyman and the counselor out into the hall and shut the door. She turned to Nyman and brushed the hair from her eyes. Her voice, in the narrow space of the hall, was shy and self-conscious.

"Eric didn't say anything to you, did he? That day under the bridge?"

"About what?"

Through the door, they could hear the baby start to cry.

"About me," Marissa said. "I know he probably didn't, but I just wondered. He wasn't very good about telling me how he felt."

Nyman looked from her bloodshot eyes to the eyes of the counselor, who was watching him intently.

"I don't remember the exact words," Nyman said, "but he mentioned something about how much you meant to him."

"Really?"

"Yes."

"You're not just saying that?"

Nyman said: "I could tell he cared about you very much."

Tears pooled in her eyes. Before she could ask another question, he thanked her for her help and left the house.

* * *

It was past midnight when he parked in front of the Monte Carlo Arms. Taking the valise from the trunk, he crossed the dry brown yard and climbed the steps to his apartment. Taped to the door was an index card on which a message had been written. He read the message, cursed, and unlocked the door.

Nothing had changed in the apartment. The empty packing boxes still sat on the floor, thick with dust. He dropped the valise by the door, looked again at the card, and walked outside to the apartment at the end of the landing. The flickering light of a T.V. played behind the curtained window.

The man who answered his knock was dressed in baggy shorts and an Aloha shirt. His black hair hung down to his shoulders.

Nyman said: "Sorry you had to take care of that."

215

The man shrugged. "Wasn't much to take care of. You go out of town or something?"

"To Vegas."

"Yeah? You win anything?"

"Just these bruises."

"I was wondering about that, but I didn't want to pry."

"Never get on the wrong end of a wrench. That's my advice."

"That sounds like some good advice."

Nyman waved the index card. "And thanks for talking to them for me."

The man nodded to the card. "They were a little upset you weren't here. Said they'd been by to pick up the donations twice now, but you never answer the door."

"I keep forgetting."

"That's what I figured. They said they'd come back in the morning, but that's your last chance."

"I'll get the boxes ready. Thanks."

The man grinned. "What I told them was, I can't believe he's got so many clothes to donate. Every time I see him, he's wearing the same thing."

Nyman, not returning the grin, said: "They're not my clothes. They're Claire's."

The flush of redness began at the collar of the Aloha shirt and spread to the man's face.

Keeping his eyes averted, Nyman thanked him again and turned to leave, but the man put a hand on his arm.

"Listen, Tom, I know you don't like to talk about it, but there's something I've been wanting to say about that." His face turned redder still. "I know it's none of my business, but I just hope you don't blame yourself. For what happened, I mean."

For a long time neither man spoke. Then Nyman nodded, said that unfortunately there was no one else to blame, and walked back to his apartment.

He went into the kitchen and took down a glass. Filling it with an inch of scotch, he drank it, sniffed, and poured more scotch into the glass. Then he got a box from the living room and walked to the door that had remained closed throughout the past few days.

The door opened into a master bedroom. A queen bed was covered in sheets and neatly turned down. Photos stood in frames on the dresser and side-tables; above the bed was a mirror that reflected the prints on the opposite wall and, standing in the doorway, Nyman himself.

An interior door opened into a closet filled with the clothes of a tall, slender woman. On the floor were dozens of pairs of shoes. Gold and silver boxes on a middle shelf were filled with jewelry.

Nyman raked a hand through his hair. Dropping the box on the floor, he sat down with his drink and started to pack up shoes.

He worked slowly and methodically. He arranged the shoes in neat rows in the box, handling each one with care. After twenty minutes he went into the kitchen to refill his glass.

When the shoes were packed he moved on to shirts and dresses. From the fabric came a smell of detergent and perfume and the unique bodily smell that can belong to only one person.

Another hour passed. Gradually, as he drank more scotch, his movements got clumsier and less coordinated. Tears gathered occasionally in his eyes but he didn't bother to brush them away.

An hour before dawn he went into the kitchen to pour the last of the scotch into his glass. When the bottle was empty, making a noise in his throat, he threw it against the wall beside the refrigerator.

The bottle shattered on the plaster. He took a swaying step backward, then stared drunkenly at the shards of glass that lay around him.

It was a minute or two before he noticed, reaching for his scotch, that one of the shards had sliced his left hand, leaving a thin trickle of blood.

Chapter 33

He woke to the sound of knocking. He was lying fully dressed on the couch in the living room. On the floor beside him was an empty, sticky glass.

Coughing into a fist and walking to the door, he opened it for two men who said that they'd come for the clothes. Nyman found his wallet, gave them money, and accepted a receipt. His face was a sickly gray and his left hand was streaked with blood, but he watched intently as they carried each box out the door and down to a van below.

When they were finished he thanked them in a hoarse voice and went into the bathroom, locking the door behind him.

* * *

An hour later, shaved and showered, he passed into the lobby of City Hall and took the elevator to the twenty-fourth floor. The receptionist in the office of the Ethics Commission was the same man who'd waited on him three days earlier.

"Back for more?"

"I can't help myself."

"Well, you know the routine."

Nyman sat down at the workstation. Forty-five minutes later, having copied names and figures into his notebook, he took the elevator down to the third floor. In the antechamber of Grace Salas' office he asked an efficient-looking woman if he could talk to the councilmember.

"You have an appointment?"

"No."

The efficient face became disapproving. "I'm sorry, but she's booked solid for days. This is a very busy time for her."

"Can you tell her I'm here? She might make time for me."

"I can't tell her anything at the moment. She's at an event in her district."

The woman nodded to a flyer on the desk, which advertised a tree-planting ceremony in El Sereno. According to the flyer, it had started twenty minutes ago.

Nyman copied down the address and went out to the street.

* * *

A crowd stood in front a meatpacking plant on Alhambra Avenue. Behind the plant, withered gold by drought and heat, the Monterey Hills rose above powerlines and billboards.

Freshly planted Indian laurels stood in a row along the sidewalk, surrounded by rectangles of day-old concrete. In the shade of the trees Grace Salas had brought the ceremony to a close and was talking to some local businessmen.

Nyman waited for her to finish, then asked if he could speak to her.

The smile on her face hung suspended as she squinted at Nyman, then dropped into a thin flat line. Blood rose among the folds of her neck and anger made her voice a guttural whisper.

"You. You know what I'm going to do to you? I'm going to report you to the state licensing board."

Nyman said that she could report him to anyone she liked, but in the meantime he needed to ask her some questions.

"I don't care what you need," Salas said. "And I'm not answering any questions. I've dealt with enough of your harassment as it is."

"I never sent Eric Trujillo to harass you," Nyman said.

She gave a sharp, bitter laugh. The businessmen, already moving toward their cars, glanced back in surprise.

"You could at least have the decency to admit it. A boy that age wouldn't have said those things unless someone put him up to it."

"What did he say?"

"Besides accusing me of murder?"

"He thought you killed Alana Bell?"

Salas' eyes narrowed. "You know exactly what he thought. He came by my office on Friday, hardly an hour after you'd left. He said all the same things you'd said, but in much uglier language. The two of you were obviously working together."

A familiar-looking young man—one of the aides Nyman had seen in City Hall—stepped out of the crowd and asked Salas if Nyman was causing a disturbance.

Salas gave a forced smile. "He's making a nuisance of himself, Brian, but I think that's what comes naturally to him."

"Would you like me to have him removed?"

Salas said it wouldn't be necessary and told the aide she'd see him back at the office. Taking a long look at Nyman, the aide nodded and turned away.

When he was out of earshot, Nyman said: "Trujillo wasn't working for me. I only met him once, and we didn't exactly hit it off."

Doubt or weariness softened the edge in Salas' voice. "You're lucky, then. I got to meet him twice. The second time was bright and early the next morning."

"At your office?"

"At my house. With my grandchildren sleeping inside. He banged on my door at seven o'clock, looking like he'd been up all night."

"Where'd he get your address?"

"Oh, I've never made a secret of where I live. Which was a mistake, obviously. The boy could've killed me there on the porch—and I have no doubt he wanted to. He said he was the only one who knew the truth about me."

"What kind of truth?"

She shrugged and wiped the sweat from her eyes. "He thought there was some kind of conspiracy going on and I was at the center of it. He said it was only a matter of time before the police came for me, so I might as well deal with him instead."

Nyman asked if Trujillo had mentioned any other members of the supposed conspiracy.

"God knows. The boy was talking so fast I could hardly understand him. He threw out half-a-dozen names, one right after the other."

"Names like Howard Searle?"

"Who's Howard Searle?"

"I think you know who he is," Nyman said. "According to the Ethics Commission, he's been an even bigger contributor to your campaigns than Ethan Kovac."

Salas gave another bitter laugh and started walking, as if the conversation were over, to a Prius that was parked at the curb.

"Last year," Nyman went on, walking beside her, "Searle contributed to your reelection bid at the maximum amount. His wife and his children also contributed, along with several other Savannah Group executives. All of whom are residents of Nevada."

Salas had reached the car and stood smiling beside the door. "You think people in Nevada are inherently corrupt?"

"No. But I don't see why someone in Vegas would care about who gets elected to the city council of L.A. Not unless he knew his company would be doing business here."

"Savannah Group does business all over the country."

"They also make political contributions all over the country."

"Trust me, Tom, no one wants to get money out of politics more than I do. But just because you've accepted a contribution doesn't mean you're beholden to the contributor. And even if I was beholden to Howard Searle, I would never murder someone on his behalf. The idea is crazy."

"What about Michael Freed? Would he murder on your behalf?"

"Freed? What possible incentive would he have?"

"I'm not sure. Trujillo seemed to think he was connected to you."

"That boy," Salas said, "was out of his mind. Probably on drugs. When I told the police he'd been to my house, they said he was a well-known dealer around Skid Row. That's probably what killed him—a deal gone bad."

"What about yourself? Were you anywhere near Skid Row late Saturday night?"

"I was at home with my grandchildren," Salas said. "The youngest had a fever and I was up with her half the night."

"Is there anyone who can corroborate that?"

"Besides my family? No. I'm not in the habit of manufacturing alibis. Now, if you'll excuse me, I have to get back to work."

She unlocked the door and was lowering herself into the seat when Nyman said:

"Does the word Meridian mean anything to you?"

"Not a thing, Tom."

She shut the door and started the engine. The car eased out onto Alhambra Avenue and turned west toward downtown.

It was painted a dark, metallic red.

Chapter 34

Nyman drove to his office. Apart from the mailman, no one seemed to have visited during his absence. Mail lay scattered on the floor; on the edge of the desk stood the coffee cup he'd given to Alana Bell.

He picked up the envelopes, glanced at the return addresses, tossed them into the trash can, left the cup where it was, and sat down behind the desk.

His eyes, gazing at the cup, were bright with concentration. After several minutes he took the notebook from his pocket and found the number of the coroner's office.

He asked the operator for Ruiz, got Ruiz's answering machine, and said in his message that he was calling about the Alana Bell case. "I'm wondering if you found anything in her clothes. Paint chips from the car, for instance."

He told her the number of his new phone and hung up. A shaft of sunlight came in through the window and fell across the coffee cup, showing the dark ring at the base where the paper had absorbed the liquid. He put the cup in a drawer of his desk and left the office.

* * *

The restaurant next door was mostly empty. Bottles of mescal stood on a shelf behind the bar; on the walls were faded postcards of Puerto Escondido and Monte Albán.

Nyman sat down at the bar and waited until a small gray-haired man came out of a back room. The man acknowledged Nyman with a raised eyebrow and shouted to someone in the kitchen, then picked up the phone that was ringing by the cash register.

A different, younger man came out of the kitchen and handed Nyman a plate of food. When the gray-haired man was finished with the phone, he came over to the bar and sat down on the next stool.

"All right," he said. "What is it?"

"What's what?"

"Whatever's been keeping you away. Haven't seen you around for days."

Nyman said he'd been working on a case.

"You mean a real case?" the man said. "With a client and everything?"

"You don't have to act so surprised."

"I'm not surprised. I'm happy. Maybe now you'll pay for a meal once in a while."

Nyman told him not to get his hopes up. "I already lost most of the money. A guy took it out of my wallet on Saturday night."

The man smiled and shook his head. "You sure know a lot of nice people, Tom. That's the same night the burglar tried to get in your office."

"Burglar?"

The man nodded. "Around eleven, I think it was. When we were closing up. Saw a guy trying to get in your door. Went away when he couldn't get it open."

"You're serious?"

"Don't I look like I'm serious?"

"Did you recognize him?"

"Why would I recognize him? Tall and blond—that's all I could tell. I tried to call you, but you didn't answer. I called twice."

"I had to get a new phone," Nyman said, and wrote the new number on the back of one of his cards. Handing him the card, he said: "You'll let me know if he comes back?"

A pair of customers had come in and were waiting by the cash register. The man, rising from his stool, put the card in his pocket and said he'd think about it.

Nyman ate the rest of the food, then reached for the phonebook that sat beside the mescal bottles. He found the number he wanted in the white pages and said after his call had been answered:

"Mrs. Freed? ... Tom Nyman. Sorry to bother you at home, but I wanted to catch your husband away from the office ... Ah ... Well, maybe I could stop by and ask you a few questions, then ... No, nothing too serious. I took a trip this weekend and found out some things you might find interesting ... Yes ... See you soon."

* * *

Michael and Sarah Freed lived in a low-slung bungalow in Los Feliz. Lavender and feathergrass grew along the front walk, shaded by lemon trees heavy with fruit. A boy of five or six was clinging to Sarah's leg when she opened the door; in his dark eyes and dark hair there was more of his mother than his father.

Sarah said: "You got here fast."

Nyman said that traffic hadn't been bad. "This is your son?"

"Yes. Maddox. Can you say hello, Maddox? This is Tom."

The boy said a shy hello and ran with thudding steps into the house, disappearing into another room. Sarah smiled and held out her hand.

"Nice to see you again. Come in and I'll give you something to drink."

The house had been built in a Spanish style and the Freeds had decorated accordingly. In the front room were red drapes hung on iron spears and chairs with beaded seats and straight wooden backs. Above the fireplace was a photo of the Freeds on their wedding day.

Nyman, glancing around the room, said that it was a nice house.

Sarah gave a groan of mock despair. "Oh god, don't get me started on the house. You'd think for the amount of money we pay we could get enough space, but not in L.A."

Her son came running back into the room, trailed now by an older boy and a dog. Stopping them in front of the fireplace, Sarah said to the older boy:

"What did I tell you about running with the dog?"

The boy said: "Not in the house."

"And where are you?"

"In the house."

"Can you introduce yourself to our guest?"

The boy turned to Nyman and held out a hand. "Marcus Freed."

"Tom Nyman."

"Tom's here to ask me some questions," Sarah said to her sons, "so I need you to keep the noise to a minimum. Understand?"

"Yes."

"Yes."

"Good," Sarah said, and turned back to Nyman. "Well, now we can start the interrogation."

She led him through the house and out to a patio that was partly roofed by wooden lattice-work. A grill and picnic table stood in the shade; waiting on the table were two empty glasses and a ceramic pitcher.

"The boys decided this morning they wanted to open a lemonade stand," she said. "It lasted about twenty minutes."

"No customers?"

"No work ethic. They take after me in that respect. I've also got some wine in the kitchen, if you'd prefer that."

"Lemonade is fine."

She filled the glasses, handed one to Nyman, and sat down across from him. Beyond the lattice-work, sunshine fell on the backyard, brightening the colors of the azaleas that grew along the fence. The smell of flowers and clipped grass mingled with the smell of Sarah Freed's perfume.

"Michael should be home before too long," she said. "We got back late last night and he's spent all day in the office, trying to catch up."

"Got back?"

"From Santa Barbara. We went up for the weekend together. The library at the university has a special collection he wanted to see."

"What about the boys?"

She gave a rueful smile. "We foisted them off on Marcella, like usual. We've been leaning on her a little too much lately."

Nyman asked her which collection Michael Freed had visited at the library.

"Oh, I don't know. Something about public housing or public transportation—something public. The research was really just a cover story, though. He takes me on these little trips every once in a while. It's his way of apologizing."

"Did you stay on campus?"

"No, at a boutique in town."

"Do you remember the name?"

"Does it really matter?"

"Normally it wouldn't," Nyman said, "but there's been another murder."

She sat up straighter in her chair. "One of Michael's students?"

"No. A friend of Alana's named Eric Trujillo. His body was found on Skid Row around one o'clock Sunday morning."

She exhaled with revulsion. "Do you know who did it?"

"I have a few ideas. Nothing definite."

"I thought you didn't speculate until you had evidence to speculate with."

"My standards are slipping."

She said: "Well, you can rule out Michael. He was in Santa Barbara with me the whole time."

"You went with him to the library?"

She hesitated. "Not to the library, no. I dropped him off at the campus and went to the beach. But he was only there a few hours."

"Which day was this?"

"Saturday. I dropped him off at noon and picked him up around four or five."

"So he had four or five hours to drive down to L.A. and back."

"Drive down and kill somebody? That would take some effort."

"Murder can be a pretty strong motivator."

"I'm sure it can. But if Michael murdered him during the day, he would've had to dump the body in broad daylight. And you said the body wasn't found until the middle of the night."

Nyman looked down at his glass, frowning. "He could've had someone else dispose of the body."

"That seems a little unlikely, don't you think?"

"Getting a knife in the chest is unlikely, statistically speaking."

"Well, statistically speaking, there's zero chance Michael killed that man."

"You were with him all of Saturday night?"

She nodded. "And we didn't go to bed until after midnight."

Nyman put his drink on the table and took out his notebook. "What was the name of the hotel?"

"The Surf House," she said. "On Channel Drive."

"There are employees who can vouch for your being there?"

"Of course. Lots of them. I have a brochure in the house, if you want the number."

Nyman said he would get it later. "At the moment I'm wondering if you can tell me anything about Meridian."

"As in a line of longitude?"

"As in the thing Trujillo was investigating just before he was killed. Something he thought your husband was involved in."

"Sorry. It doesn't ring a bell."

"What about Las Vegas?"

"What about it?"

"Did you know that Michael went there with Alana two weeks before she was killed?"

Abruptly the muscles of Sarah Freed's face went slack. The skin sagged, showing age-lines that normally remained hidden. She gave Nyman a bleak smile.

"Ah," she said. "So you know about that."

Chapter 35

Leaving him on the patio, she went into the house and came back out with a bottle of chardonnay and two glasses. She filled one glass with wine and offered the bottle to Nyman, saying:

"It's not very good, but it's better than lemonade."

"I'm all right, thanks."

She shrugged and sat down. "That trip you mentioned on the phone. It was to Vegas, I take it?"

"It was."

"You felt like doing some gambling?"

Nyman told her about his trip, omitting certain details.

"Personally," she said when he was finished, "I can't stand the place, but it seems to hold some kind of fascination for Michael. He goes there to blow off steam after every semester. Plays a lot of golf and blackjack."

"And takes Alana with him?"

"Not usually. He only met her last fall, when she started the program. But apparently he thought taking her to Vegas would be a nice way to relax after finishing the Merchant South analysis."

"He told you that?"

She nodded. "This weekend. That's always part of the apology. Confessing his sins."

"Did he confess anything about getting twenty thousand dollars?"

"At the casino, you mean? Just that he won it playing blackjack, and that he and Alana had a fight when he wouldn't go along with her plan."

"Plan?"

"Well, her suggestion, or whatever you want to call it. She told him he should take all the money he'd won and donate it. Give it to one of the homeless shelters downtown. She said it wasn't really his to keep, since he'd won it by dumb luck."

"And what did he say to that?"

"Something about how a man with a family at home can't afford to give away that much money, no matter how he got it."

"Surely Alana understood that."

"You'd think so, but evidently not. Michael says they'd gone to a little bar off the Strip—some place their driver recommended. When Michael said no, she got angry and stormed out."

"Does your husband know where she went after storming out?"

"Not that I know of. Do you?"

Nyman told her about Howard Searle and Savannah Group. "They're the company that's developing Merchant South. They're also the new owners of Kasbah. Where your husband won his money."

Reaching for the bottle, Sarah poured more wine into her glass. "It sounds like you're saying the money was a payoff."

"That's exactly what I'm saying."

"Is that what Alana thought?"

"Maybe. It would explain why she went to Searle's house. I was hoping your husband could tell me more about it."

From the house, a voice said: "Tell you more about what?"

Michael Freed stood in the doorway, dressed in a shirt and tie and still holding his car keys. His handsome face was gray with exhaustion.

Nyman said: "Why Alana went to see Howard Searle, and why you didn't tell me you went with her to Vegas."

Freed looked first at his wife, then at Nyman, then at the concrete floor of the patio. He said in a hollow voice:

"How long have you two been out here?"

"Not long," Sarah said. "I've been explaining to Tom that you're not a murderer, despite your best efforts to look like one."

His gaze swung upward. "I'm not trying to look like one. Why would you say that?"

"I know you're not, Michael. Relax. Sit down and have a glass of wine."

"Where are the boys?"

"Playing," she said. "They're fine."

"Marcella's car isn't in the driveway."

"I know. I sent her on vacation."

"Vacation?"

"She's been working too hard. Like you. Sit down and have some wine."

"I don't want any goddamn wine," he said with sudden anger. "And I don't want to answer any goddamn questions. You're not welcome in this house," he added to Nyman.

"Michael," he wife said sharply. "There's no reason to talk like that."

"Oh really? Do you know what this man's been doing? Filling a kid's head with so many lies that somebody murdered him this weekend."

Nyman said: "I didn't give Trujillo any ideas, professor. If anyone did, it was Alana Bell."

Freed pretended not to hear him. To his wife he said: "I forbid you to talk to him anymore. Especially in this house."

"Since when did you start forbidding me things?"

"Since now. This isn't a game, Sarah."

"I'm aware of that. That's why I'm trying to help you."

Nyman said: "Can you tell me what Meridian is, professor?"

"No, I can't. The word means nothing to me. And I'd like you out of my house."

"It would be better for you," Nyman said, "if you were more cooperative. There are three departments working on the case, and I'm sharing information with all of them."

"Three?"

"The coroner's office, the Vista Hills police, and the L.A.P.D. Last night Detective Timmons told me that Trujillo's murderer was probably driving a red sedan. What color of car do you drive, professor?"

Freed's voice was hoarse. "Black. They're both black. You can see for yourself in the garage."

His hands were clasping and unclasping in an unconscious rhythm. Rising from her chair, Sarah put her glass on the table and said to Nyman:

"We should try this again tomorrow. My husband isn't himself at the moment. He hasn't been sleeping very well."

From somewhere inside the house came the barking of a dog and peals of laughter. Nyman said he would show himself out.

"No," Sarah said. "I'll go with you."

Michael Freed ignored them and walked into the backyard, passing from shadow to harsh sunshine. He walked to the wall of azaleas and stood staring at the pink and purple flowers, his hands clenched.

Nyman followed Sarah into the kitchen, where her purse was lying on the counter. She took a brochure from one of the pockets and handed it to him.

"From the Surf House," she said. "They'll tell you he couldn't have done any of those things. And I'll make sure he gets some sleep. He'll give you a call in the morning."

"I'm not sure he'll want to."

"I don't care if he does; I'll make him. Once he's calm, you'll see that he's innocent."

"Are you sure of that, Mrs. Freed?"

"Absolutely. My husband's a very gentle man. He could never hurt anyone."

"No?"

"Never."

"What about yourself?"

She gave a startled laugh. "Christ. You mean I'm still a suspect?"

"Of course you are."

"And what's my motive?"

"Jealousy," Nyman said. "At the thought of your husband with another woman. You put up a sophisticated front, but it must've bothered you on some level."

"It did a hell of a lot more than bother me, but that doesn't mean I'd kill someone because of it. You've never been married, have you, Tom?"

"Yes, I have."

"Really? Your wife must be very loyal and devoted, then."

"My wife," Nyman said, "is dead."

Spots of color appeared on Sarah's face and neck. She opened her mouth to speak but Nyman told her not to bother. Taking the pen and notebook from his pocket, he tore out a sheet of paper and wrote down a phone number.

"My phone was stolen in Vegas," he said, "so this is the number to call if you need to reach me."

She looked at the paper, then at Nyman. "Listen, I'm sorry I—"

"Don't worry about it."

He turned and walked out of the house. Crossing the driveway to his car, he climbed in and started the engine. He reached for the rust-colored bottle in his jacket, took out a pill, put the pill in his mouth, and turned north on the first street he came to.

Chapter 36

The street took him to Griffith Park. He followed a twisting road to the top of Mount Hollywood and turned off into an empty lot beside the observatory.

He sat for a time with the engine still running and his hands still on the wheel. Then he seemed to notice the sound of the engine; he turned off the car and took out his phone and the Surf House brochure.

A jovial-sounding man answered the call. He said that he remembered the Freeds very well: an attractive couple, very polite, very good tippers. They'd stayed in Sunset Cottage and had seemed very much in love. No, they hadn't taken any trips back to L.A.: they were there for a romantic weekend.

Nyman thanked him and hung up. Getting out of the car, he walked to the wooden fence that stood at the edge of the lot.

Below him the city lay flat and glinting in the sunshine. Far to the west, the ocean was a blurred white band of air. Directly ahead were the towers of downtown; farther south, obscured by gold smog, were the neighborhoods where Alana Bell had spent her life.

He stood staring at the city as the shadows lengthened around him and the light started to change. A hawk, gliding upward on a thermal, gave a rasping cry. Nyman watched the hawk until it met the disc of the sun; then he shut his eyes and turned back to his car.

* * *

Valerie Bell's house stood on a deep, narrow lot in Carver Manor, a mile south of Watts. Elms had been planted along either side of the street and stood tall enough to throw shadows over the peaked rooflines of the houses. Nyman passed through a neatly clipped hedgerow and made his way up to the front door, which opened before he had chance to knock.

Valerie stood in the doorway. She looked calmer than she had four days ago and better rested. Examining Nyman's face, she smiled grimly.

"Looks like you're doing about as well as I am. You'd better come in."

Bookcases lined the walls of the front room. The shelves were filled with framed photos, most of which showed Alana— in church clothes, in a softball uniform, in a graduation gown— along with Valerie and a tall older man who'd presumably been Alana's father.

Valerie waved Nyman toward a sofa and sat down across from him. "Well, you said on the phone you had information for me."

"Lots of information," Nyman said.

He told her all that he'd learned. She listened calmly at first, then with a look of mounting anger as he described Alana's trip to Las Vegas with Freed.

Nyman said: "I'm sorry if this is painful. I thought you'd want to hear all of it, though."

"Of course I do. Go on."

He went on. When he was finished, she gave a curt nod, asked if he would like some coffee, and went into the kitchen. She came back a few minutes later with two mugs and a bowl of sugar. The look of anger was gone, replaced by one of resignation.

"I suppose I don't have any right to be upset," she said, handing him the coffee. "It's nothing but what I deserve."

Nyman asked her what she meant.

"Hiring a detective to go digging into my own daughter's past. It's a sort of desecration, isn't it? Desecrating the dead instead of leaving them in peace?"

He said that he supposed it was, in a way. "But there's already been a second murder. We have to do what we can to prevent a third."

"You're assuming Allie's death was murder."

"You don't think it was?"

"To tell you the truth, Mr. Nyman, I don't know what to think. All these businessmen you're talking about: why would they care enough about Allie to hurt her? She was only a girl. She wasn't a threat to anybody."

"She might've been," Nyman said, "if she had information. Do you remember her mentioning something called Meridian?"

Valerie shook her head. "She didn't do a whole lot of talking to me over the last year or so, though. A phone call once in a while, maybe, or else she'd come on Sunday for church. But her head was always up in the clouds."

"Up in the clouds about what?"

241

"Oh, just about anything. Whatever issue she'd taken up for the day. Allie always took after her father. She was always ready for a crusade."

"Her father was involved in politics?"

"Not unless you count union meetings. He worked in a factory for thirty-six years. He and I bought this house together."

"It's a nice house."

"It's small and cramped and filled with too many memories. If you know anybody who's looking, you can tell them it'll be available soon enough."

"You've decided not to stay?"

"Yes—that's exactly what I've decided. But my plans aren't any of your business. And since I'm paying for your time," she added with a trace of a smile, "I'd better not waste it. So you'd better get out there and do whatever it is you do."

Nyman said that talking to her was more helpful than anything else. "I need to know everything I can about the last few months. Anything Alana might've told you."

She shrugged. "We'd been growing apart, like I said. Or she'd started growing away from her family. I kept telling myself it was a phase."

"What do you think was causing it? Her relationship with Freed?"

"If there was a relationship, I'm the last person she would've told about it. That was the kind of thing we never talked about. Which is my fault, I know."

"Not everything can be your fault, Mrs. Bell."

"Not everything, but a lot more than you'd think. I could've kept after her. When she stopped calling, I could've gone to check on her. I could've made her come and see me. I was her mother, wasn't I?"

After a pause, Nyman said: "You don't know why she stopped calling?"

"No. I thought she was just busy with her schoolwork. Last week she finally agreed to come to lunch, and at the last minute she cancelled. Like every other time."

"Did she give a reason?"

"I don't know. Something she had to do at the clerk's office, I think."

"Clerk?"

"The city clerk. Los Angeles city clerk. She said she was down at their office and couldn't make it for lunch."

Nyman leaned forward. "Do you remember which day this was?"

She frowned. "Monday, I think it must've been. Yes, definitely Monday. She called to say she was at the clerk's office and couldn't meet me. I asked why, and she asked if I'd read the paper that day. I said no, and she started talking about something or other—some issue she was upset about. I told her we'd have to reschedule, and she said she'd call me as soon as she could. And that was the last time I ever heard her voice."

Valerie Bell's own voice, on the last word, dropped to a whisper. She closed her eyes and sat in silence, breathing unevenly.

When she opened her eyes again, Nyman asked her if she knew which issue it was that had made Alana so upset.

"No. I'm afraid I don't. I'd gotten into the habit of tuning it all out."

"There's nothing you remember? The name of the paper she'd read, for instance?"

"No. Nothing."

Her friendliness had gone away. She stared at the floor and seemed to forget about Nyman's presence. He asked another question, got no response, and said that he should probably be leaving.

"But I'd like to call you again later, if that's all right."

Glancing up, Valerie said in a distracted voice: "Fine. But not tonight."

"No. Not tonight."

Chapter 37

Leaving his car in a lot off Bradbury Square, Nyman walked between columns of cypress trees and passed under the two statues—Phosphor and Hesper in coffin-like niches—that looked down from the portico of the Central Library.

In the lobby he stopped beside a map of the collections. A circulation aide, her arms filled with books, asked him if she could help.

Nyman said he was looking for newspapers. "Local editions from last Monday."

"Of the *Times*, you mean?"

"Of anything you have."

She glanced at the clock above his head. "We close at eight, and it's already seven-thirty. You won't get much reading done."

"I'll do my best."

Shifting the books in her arms, she led him to a table and said that she'd talk to someone in Periodicals.

Nyman used the time to make a note of the things Valerie Bell had told him, starting with Alana's visit to the city clerk. A few minutes later an older man with hair tied back in a ponytail came to the table with five or six newspapers.

"This is all we've got," he said in an aggrieved tone. "They don't let us keep them around very long anymore, with everything online. People today like to have everything online."

"So I've noticed."

"If it isn't on their phones, they won't even look at it."

"It's a shame."

"I notice you're not using a phone."

"I gave mine to a man in Nevada."

"Good for you. That was smart thinking."

Nyman arranged the papers on the table.

The first was the *Times*. He turned to the local section and scanned the headlines, finding nothing of interest. He did the same with the *Daily News*, the *L.A. Weekly*, and the *Sentinel*. When he opened the *L.A. Independent* it was five minutes to eight and a voice on the loudspeaker was announcing that the library was closed.

He found what he wanted in the opinion section. At the bottom of the cheaply printed page was a column by one of the paper's reporters, Richard Voss.

> *Next time you're suffering from a bout of insomnia, try reading the minutes of the latest City Council meeting.*
>
> *In dry legalese, the minutes keep tabs on the rusty machinery of local government, documenting each creaky motion, every sputtering attempt to get the municipal wheels turning.*
>
> *For the last several years, the biggest wheel on the Council has been Grace Salas (CD-16), who's been grinding gears on behalf of the residents of District 16,*

heaping public money on the district in the form of parks and transit lines and other perks.

Now, however, Salas seems to be looking beyond CD-16's borders.

According to the minutes from last Friday's meeting, Salas filed a motion to use $230,000 from the district's Real Property Trust Fund to give financial support to more than two dozen community organizations, most of them 501(c)(3) charities.

The only trouble? Some of those charities aren't in District 16.

The Gilman Center for Women and Children, for instance, is in Leimert Park, in District 8, but Salas plans to give the center $10,000. The Robinson Repertory Theatre is in Mar Vista, but Salas thinks it deserves $5,000 of her discretionary fund money.

The same goes for Westchester Food Bank, Children United, and Meridian Resources—none of which can be found within Salas' legal domain.

Which makes you wonder why she's so eager to expand her influence. Could it have anything to do with the looming mayoral election? Could Salas be paving the way for a citywide campaign, spreading goodwill in the direction of deep-pocketed voters?

Given her handiness with the levers of local power, the smart money says yes.

Nyman looked up. The other patrons were gone; he was alone in the reading room. Copying down the address and phone number from the *Independent*'s masthead, he made his way out of the library and into the gardens.

The air was thick with the smell of cypress. Pausing on the steps, he called the *Independent*'s number. After half-a-dozen rings, a woman came on the line and said that the office was closed.

Nyman said that he was trying to reach a reporter.

"Sorry. All the reporters went home. We're closed."

"Do you know how I can reach Richard Voss at home, then? It's important."

Her tone changed. "Oh, you want Voss? He's not a reporter; he's the editor. He's always here."

She hung up.

* * *

He found the offices of the *Independent* on a street in Van Nuys, surrounded by warehouses and pot dispensaries. The door was locked and tagged with fresh graffiti. Nyman, after pressing the bell, heard the sound of footsteps inside and someone shouting indistinctly.

The man who opened the door was taller than Nyman and twice as heavy, with long brown hair brushed back from a widow's peak. His eyes were small and dark and wary. His age might've been anything between thirty and fifty.

Blocking the doorway with his body, he said: "Where's the food?"

"What?"

"You're the delivery guy?"

"No. I'm looking for Mr. Voss."

"I'm Mr. Voss."

Nyman introduced himself. "You wrote a column last week about Grace Salas. I wanted to ask you some questions about it."

The mention of his work brought a friendlier light to Voss' eyes. "You read my column?"

Before Nyman could answer, a hatchback pulled to the curb and a man got out holding a sack of styrofoam containers. Voss met him at the curb, signed a receipt, brought the sack back to the door, and motioned for Nyman to follow.

"We'll talk in my office."

His office was a room at the back of the building. A screen door let in a smell of garbage from the alley. Voss' desk was a metal rectangle pushed into one corner; the rest of the space was taken up by a T.V. and a cot piled with blankets.

Voss untied the sack and took out the food. "Ethiopian," he said. "There's a place on Victory that's pretty good. If you want the best, though, you have to go down to Fairfax."

Nyman said: "In your column, you mentioned a nonprofit called Meridian Resources."

Voss held up a hand. "Back up a little. You say you're an investigator, but I don't know what you're investigating."

Nyman told him about his case. Voss showed no surprise at the mention of murder. He gave most of his attention to the food, pausing occasionally to drink from a tall black can of Monster Energy.

"So what you're telling me," he said when Nyman was finished, "is you think Salas killed the girl and the homeless kid?"

"I think it's possible. They both visited her before their deaths. And they both seemed fixated on her involvement with Meridian."

"Sorry—I don't buy it. Salas is ambitious, but she does a lot of good work. She wouldn't kill anybody."

"You know her well?"

"Well enough. I've interviewed her plenty of times—been out to her house. She's got a big place in Glassell Park, at Verdugo and Holt."

"Have you asked her about Meridian?"

"No, but I'm planning to." Voss took a bite of *injera*. "Funny you mention Meridian, though. Out of all the charities on the list, that's the hardest to track down. Their phone's been disconnected, and the website's just a logo with some boilerplate."

"Does it give the name of the owner?"

"Not that I remember. I did some looking around online, too, and couldn't find a thing. Just a little snippet about a donation they got from Koda."

"Koda?"

Voss nodded. "It's a company that owns a bunch of nightclubs in town. Started by a guy named Ethan Kovac."

Chapter 38

Voss turned to the laptop on his desk. Between bites of *doro wot*, he found what he was looking for and tapped the screen with a greasy finger.

"Here. This is it."

Nyman leaned forward. The screen showed a page from Koda's corporate website. At the top was a photo of Ethan Kovac on a basketball court, surrounded by kids wearing t-shirts with the Koda logo.

Under the photo was a paragraph about Koda's support of local charities. At the bottom of the page, in smaller type, was a list of the organizations—including Meridian Resources—that had received donations.

"That's all I could find," Voss said. "Doesn't say when they made the donation or how much they gave. Which means there's probably no connection to Salas."

"Why not?"

"Why would there be? Lots of people give money to the same charities. It's not a crime."

"Assuming the charity's legitimate."

Voss stopped chewing. "There's reason to think it's illegitimate?"

Rather than answering, Nyman said: "This donation Salas is giving to Meridian. How much is it for?"

"You the think the amount itself makes a difference?"

"It might," Nyman said. "Particularly if it's for twenty thousand."

Voss swallowed and sat back in his chair. "How'd you know it was twenty grand?"

"Lucky guess."

"No, it wasn't a guess." He pointed a finger at Nyman's chest. "I've been straight with you, Tom. Now you need to be straight with me."

Nyman said: "According to your article, Salas filed her motion on the Friday before last. Correct?"

"Correct. July first."

"That's the same day a man named Michael Freed went to Vegas with the first murder victim. While they were there, Freed won some money at a casino on the Strip. Twenty thousand."

"Could be a coincidence."

"Could be, yes. But there was a lot of money changing hands that day. I'd lay odds that Kovac gave a similar amount to Meridian around the same time."

"You make it sound like a conspiracy."

"I'm just telling you what I've found."

"But twenty grand—that means nothing to these people. Grace Salas' office gets more than a million a year in discretionary funds. Kovac's probably worth half a billion. Twenty grand is pocket change."

Nyman got to his feet. "You have a copy of Salas' motion?"

"Somewhere around here. Why?"

"I'll make a deal with you. If you give me your copy, I promise I'll try to give you the story before any other paper can report on it. Assuming there is a story."

Voss' eyes narrowed. "You can get a copy from the city clerk. You don't need to go through me."

"The clerk's office is closed," Nyman said, "and my night isn't over."

"You really think it's too important to wait till morning?"

"I do."

Voss gave him a long, probing look. Stretching out his hand, he said: "Okay. Deal."

Nyman took the pale hand into his own. "Deal."

* * *

Moths were circling the streetlamp outside Voss' office. Nyman paused under the light to read the photocopy of the motion, which listed the charities due to receive money from Salas' discretionary fund. He found what he was looking for midway down the page:

Meridian Resources, 3203 Whitlock Terrace, Hollywood.

* * *

Crowds of sweat-soaked tourists were milling in front of Grauman's Chinese Theatre, taking pictures of the Walk of Fame. A few blocks away, Whitlock Terrace was a side-street of shops and restaurants that catered to locals. Nyman found the small, poorly lit storefront at 3203 and passed through a door painted with the words *Golden Age Collectibles*.

The only person inside was the woman behind the counter. In her late fifties, she was thick-bodied and small-featured, with reddish blonde hair, a pale face without makeup, and a faded Ramones shirt. In her hand was a teacup that smelled of bourbon.

"Montgomery Clift," she said as Nyman came up to the counter.

"Excuse me?"

"That's who you look like. Around the time of *Lonelyhearts*, when he was going downhill. I could sell you the lobby card, but you're probably not interested."

Nyman asked her what a lobby card was.

She moved her cup, indicating the interior of the store, where shelves stood in gloomy light.

"Promotional thing the studios used to put out. Like a one-sheet, kind of, but smaller. I've also got props and costumes. Are you interested in a certain kind of film?"

"I'm interested in Meridian Resources."

She frowned and took a drink. "Sorry. Never heard of it."

Nyman turned away from the counter and was silent for a time, examining the rest of the shop.

The woman said: "So what is it, anyway? Meridian?"

"I'm not sure. It's supposed to be a charity headquartered here."

"Well, we're not a charity, exactly. But you could say we're mostly non-profit."

She smiled at the joke and took another drink.

Nyman returned the smile. "How long have you been open?"

"In this space? Two or three years. We used to be down the street, but the rent's cheaper here."

"Do you remember who used to be in this space?"

"Not by name. Stores are always coming and going. It's only a matter of time before we'll be going, too."

"When you say 'we,' who do you mean?"

She pointed to the ceiling, as if to indicate someone on the second floor. "Me and my dad. He opened it in the sixties. Back then it was just a little stall by the Farmer's Market."

"Do you think he'd remember who was here before you?"

She gave him a melancholy smile. "If anyone would, he would. But I doubt you'll be able to get it out of him."

Coming out from behind the counter, she turned the lock on the front door and led him to the back of the shop, where a staircase led to an attic-like room on the second floor.

The room was taken up by a desk and more than a dozen filing cabinets. Sitting at the desk, looking at something under the lens of a jeweler's lamp, was a man in his seventies or eighties. His sparse gray hair lay in strands across the skin of his scalp; on the bridge of his nose were half-moon glasses.

"Dad," the woman said, "this guy wants to ask you a question."

The man looked at Nyman over the rims of his glasses, his eyes vague and watery. Then, with a movement of his hand, he beckoned Nyman forward.

Walking to the desk, Nyman saw that the lamp was focused on a tray lined in velvet. On top of the velvet were four or five bracelets, all painted gold and inlaid with imitation gems.

"Dad collects costume jewelry," the woman said. "Anything the studios throw out, he goes and picks up."

To her father she said in a louder voice: "Where are these pieces from, Dad?"

Holding up one of the necklaces in a trembling hand, the man gave a hoarse whispering reply that was unintelligible. Then, falling silent again, he looked at Nyman with a shy smile, as if waiting for an answer.

Nyman said: "They're very nice."

The man's smile widened and he went on whispering. He rose to his feet and beckoned Nyman over to one of the filing cabinets. He took out a succession of trinkets—fake daggers, coins, a bishop's miter—and handed them to Nyman for his inspection.

The woman, exhaling, said: "Dad, he wants to ask you about the people who had the store before us. Do you remember their name?"

The man took another velvet-lined tray from the cabinet. Lying in the center was a large silver brooch. Attached to the brooch was a ticket with the words *Metro-Goldwyn-Mayer*.

Nyman said again that it was very nice.

The man nodded and reached for another tray.

His daughter said: "The company that used to have this store, Dad. Was it something called Meridian?"

Still whispering, the man put down the tray, shuffled to a cabinet in the corner of the room, and started taking out more trinkets.

The woman turned to Nyman and shrugged. "Sorry. Once he gets started, he doesn't stop."

"I shouldn't have bothered him."

"Oh, it's not a bother. You made his day just by showing an interest."

The man shuffled back to them carrying a green file-folder. He handed it to his daughter without a word and went back to his desk.

She opened the folder and took out a bundle of envelopes. Glancing at the addresses, she gave a short, incredulous laugh.

"It's the mail we used to get when we first moved in," she said, handing the bundle to Nyman. "Stuff that came for the old occupants. I guess there are advantages to being a hoarder."

Nyman looked through the letters. Almost all were addressed to a company called Roth Printing & Design. One envelope—from the Department of Water and Power—was addressed to Meridian Resources.

Nyman said: "Mind if I open this?"

"Be my guest."

Inside was a past-due notice for electrical charges. At the top of the page, under the account number and an L.A. phone number, was the name of the account holder: Bridget Becker.

Nyman frowned and handed the bill to the woman. "That name ring a bell?"

She held it out at arm's length to read it. "Becker? No, I don't think so. Why? Do you know her?"

Nyman shook his head. "Not yet."

Chapter 39

The windows of the Palm Court were dark when Nyman parked in the alley. Walking around to the street-side entrance, he rang the bell and waited for the door to be opened by the night-nurse, who smiled when she recognized him.

"Well, it's after ten, but I guess I can make an exception."

"You spoil me."

"I have a weakness for hard-luck cases. Come on in, Tom."

Nyman followed her through the common room and down to the door with the American flag. Nyman tapped the door with a knuckle. Joseph's deep voice came through the wood:

"Yes?"

Nyman thanked the nurse and went inside. Joseph lay propped up in bed with a thick hardcover book in his hands. Nyman, turning his head to read the spine, saw that it was a biography of Lincoln.

"Light reading?"

"It was supposed to put me to sleep, but it seems to be doing the opposite. You look like hell, Tom."

"Thanks."

"It wasn't meant as a compliment."

Nyman sat down on the loveseat. "Angels win today?"

"No, as a matter of fact."

"Still think they can catch Houston?"

"Yes."

"You're an optimist."

"I can afford to be an optimist in July," Joseph said. "And I can see you're exhausted. When was the last time you slept?"

Nyman ignored the question. "In the old days you used to have a friend at Water and Power. Any chance he'd be willing to help me find someone?"

"That depends on what you're up to. This is connected to the woman's death?"

"To her murder, yes. And to a second murder that happened Saturday night."

Joseph closed the book and put it aside. "Who was the victim?"

Nyman told him about Eric Trujillo and the rest of the investigation. Joseph listened with a frown of concentration, his eyes narrow and intent. When Nyman finished, he shook his head and said:

"I never thought you'd be so reckless."

"Reckless?"

"You're lucky you didn't die out there in the desert. As soon as you got to Las Vegas, you should've asked Larry Sutter for help."

Nyman said that Sutter was the first person he'd talked to. "I had to beg him just to make a phone call for me."

"That doesn't sound like Larry."

"Times change, Joseph. People change the way they do business. Either way, I don't have time to argue."

"You're on your way somewhere else?"

Nyman said that he'd just gotten a call from Ruiz, asking him to stop by the coroner's office. "She's working late and has some new information."

"Judging by your eyes," Joseph said, "sleep would be more helpful than new information."

"You were never one to stop for sleep."

"I was a fool," Joseph said. "Everyone under the age of seventy is a fool. That's one of the things I've learned recently."

"It must be hard being around so many fools."

Joseph shrugged. "You get used to it."

Nyman, reaching into his pocket, took out the past-due notice addressed to Bridget Becker. "About that friend of yours at Water and Power."

"It's been ten years since I talked to him, Tom. He's probably retired by now. Or dead. Times change, like you say."

"It's worth a try, though. I want to know how long she was at this address and where she went afterward."

Joseph took the bill out of his hand and looked it over. "You tried the phone number?"

"Disconnected. And there's no Bridget Becker in the white pages."

"What about the I.R.S.? If Meridian's a nonprofit, you can get a copy of their 990 form."

Nyman said he was already working on it. "In the meantime, you'll check with your friend?"

Joseph made an irritated noise and slid the notice into his book. "First thing in the morning. Now get out of here and let an old man sleep. And take some food with you. You look like you've lost ten pounds since Thursday."

"I'm not hungry."

"I don't care if you're not hungry. There's some food in the cupboard. Take something with you."

Nyman took an apple and some peanuts, told Joseph to enjoy the book, and went out.

* * *

No wind rattled the leaves of the palms along Mission Road. The air was hot and still as Nyman parked in front of the coroner's office. He stayed in the car long enough to eat a handful of peanuts, then went up the concrete steps.

The guard took him down to the security floor, where Ruiz was waiting. She wore a white mask over the lower half of her face and looked at Nyman with eyes that were red and swollen. Her voice, coming through the mask, was hoarse.

"You weren't asleep when I called?"

"I gave up on sleep a while ago. And I appreciate the call."

She handed him a mask. "Truth is, it gets a little lonely around here sometimes. Remember not to touch anything."

Harsh light greeted them on the other side of the double doors. Nyman kept his gaze on the gleaming floor and avoided looking at the corpses that lay on gurneys along the sides of the hallway.

Ruiz led him into an empty autopsy suite. A plastic bag sat on a bench among the saws and forceps and dissection scissors. Inside the bag were the jeans and Pacifica shirt Alana Bell had worn during the last hours of her life; the fabric was torn and mottled with patches of dirt and crusted blood.

"We found a few paint chips," Ruiz said, carrying the bag over to the table. "Mostly in the right leg of the jeans and the bottom hem of the shirt. Consistent with angle of impact we'd already decided on."

She took the jeans from the bag and laid them on the table.

Nyman said: "Can you match it to a particular car?"

"We can narrow it down, at least. According to the initial analysis, the basecoat was a dark, high-luster red."

Nyman asked if it was the same type of paint that would've been used on a Toyota Prius.

"Possibly. Once we do the pyrolysis, we'll know more about the chemical makeup of the binders and pigment and whatnot. That should give us the make and model."

"When will you have the results?"

Ruiz rubbed a gloved finger under her eye and shrugged. "Could be days; could be weeks. We've got cases piling up right and left."

"Including the murder of Eric Trujillo?"

Frowning, she put the jeans back in the bag. "The name's familiar. When was he killed?"

"Saturday night. Or at least his body was found early Sunday morning. On Skid Row."

"Oh—that. Yeah, I was talking to O'Bannon about that. You think there's a connection to this case?"

Nyman told her about Trujillo's friendship with Alana Bell. "Some people think they saw his body get dumped out of a red sedan."

Ruiz put the bag back on the counter. "Interesting. You want to see it?"

"See what?"

"Trujillo's body."

Flushing above his mask, Nyman said that he would, if it wasn't too much trouble.

"No trouble at all."

She led him out of the suite and down to the series of small, interconnected rooms in which corpses lay stacked in plastic sheeting. One body had been set apart from the others; it lay alone on a shelf by the door, the feet dangling over the stainless-steel edge.

Stripping away the plastic, Ruiz revealed the handsome, acne-marked face Nyman had seen once before, under the 4th Street bridge. The brown eyes—flecked with gold, like his daughter's—were half-closed. On the left side of his chest was a small opening in the skin, less than an inch in length, with brown crusted blood along the edges and streaks of blood on the surrounding skin.

"Seems straightforward," Ruiz said. "The wound's clean and unabraded; judging by the width and depth, my guess would be something like a steak knife, but it's hard to know for sure. The lack of defensive wounds suggests he didn't have time to defend himself, or else wasn't aware of what was happening. Depending on the internal damage, the death could've been fairly quick."

Looking down at the gold-flecked eyes, Nyman said: "You're sure it was the knife that killed him?"

"Reasonably. Of course we'll know more after the autopsy."

"What about suspects?"

"In Trujillo's case, you mean, or Alana Bell's?"

"Either."

She shrugged. "Not my department anymore. Vista Hills P.D. are handling the Bell case, and O'Bannon's handling Trujillo. I don't think he's found anything, though."

"What about Vista Hills?"

"Same story. They brought a guy in for questioning, but I don't think it led anywhere. Some witnesses say they saw him attack Alana a few days before she was killed."

Nyman turned abruptly. "Who is he?"

"Not sure if they ever told me his name. He's some kind of nightclub bouncer or something."

"Fowler?"

Ruiz's eyes narrowed. "Could be Fowler, yeah. That sounds familiar. Is he somebody you know?"

But Nyman was already moving to the door.

Chapter 40

Customers stood in a line along Sunset Boulevard, lit by the sign that hung above the laundromat beside the Rexford. Nyman parked in a lot on Laurel and made his way past the line and down to the auto-body shop at the end of the block.

He scaled the fence that separated the shop from the street, scaled the shorter fence that led into the alley, and came eventually to the back of the Rexford, where a bouncer was standing with his hands in his pockets, keeping watch over a drunken woman in a metallic dress.

She sat slumped on a folding chair with her elbows on her knees, trying not to be sick.

Nyman told the bouncer that he needed to see Fowler. "You can tell him it's about Alana Bell."

The bouncer was a short, stocky, boyish man in his twenties. "If you want to get in, you got to go around to the front, like everybody else."

Nyman showed him the copy of his license. "Fowler's already been questioned about the murder of a woman who was seen in your club. Now a second person's dead. I don't think this is something you want to put yourself in the middle of."

The bouncer looked from the license to Nyman. "You expect me to believe that?"

"If you don't," Nyman said, "you can talk to Detective Timmons at Central Community station. He'll be interested to know you're impeding my investigation."

"Wait a second. You're serious about this?"

"Or you can talk to Ruiz at the coroner's office. She'll let you look at the two bodies your friend Fowler put in there. They're about your age."

"But Mr. Fowler's not even here," the man said, his voice breaking. "He got called out."

"Out?"

"To Mr. Kovac's house. In the Palisades. Ethan Kovac's house."

"When was this?"

"Just now. Thirty, forty minutes ago. I was in his office when he got the call."

"You realize the trouble you'll be in if I find out you're lying?"

"I'm not lying. Ask anybody."

Nyman, making a show of being reluctantly convinced, took a card from his wallet. "If he comes back tonight, you'll let me know at this number?"

"Of course. Absolutely."

Beside them, the woman shook her head and said thickly: "Goddamn men."

* * *

He was walking back to his car when his phone rang. The number on the screen belonged to the restaurant next door to his office. A man's voice, rising above the clatter of dishes, came over the line before he could say hello.

"Tom? You there?"

"This is Tom, yes. Is this Martín?"

"He's back."

"What?"

"Your burglar friend. Hanging around your door."

"Who is he?"

"You think I'm going out there to ask him? I'm washing up and going home."

"You can't see his face?"

"I'm not getting close enough to see anybody's face, Tom. You want me to call the cops for you, I will, but I'm going home."

"No, don't call the cops," Nyman said. "I'm on my way."

* * *

Twenty minutes later he turned off the freeway and followed Sepulveda to his office. The parking lot was empty and the restaurant next door was deserted and dark. A faint light could be seen through the glass of his office door.

Parking at the end of the lot, beyond the light of the street lamps, he opened the trunk of his car, took out a long-handled flashlight, checked the bulb, and walked through the shadows to the door.

It opened to his touch. Stepping noiselessly into the entryway, he stood for a moment in semi-darkness, the flashlight raised but unlit. A sound of metal scraping metal came from the space behind his desk, where someone was kneeling on the floor, bent over the box in which he kept his petty cash.

The light of the desk lamp showed the curving back and short blonde hair of a young woman. In her hand was the carpenter's hammer she was using to pry open the box.

Nyman let out the breath he'd been holding and lowered the flashlight. Not bothering to turn on the overhead light, he sat down in one of the chairs and said:

"There's no money in it, Theresa."

She jerked away from the box and stepped back, putting a hand on the wall. Her eyes, caught in the light of the lamp, were wide and yellow and frightened. Sweat covered her face and neck; the hammer quavered in her hand.

Nyman said: "Try the second drawer on the right. There should be an envelope taped to the underside. I keep a hundred there for emergencies."

Her mouth opened and closed. It opened again and she said: "I can pay you back. Next week, I can pay you back."

"We both know you're not going to pay me back."

"I will, though. I promise."

"How'd you get the door open, anyway?"

She wore the same shirt he'd seen her in before. On the left sleeve, below the elbow, was a brown dot of dried blood.

"A friend of mine showed me," she said.

"Showed you what?"

"How to pick a lock."

"Nice friends you have these days."

She tried to smile. "They don't make friends like they used to, Tom."

"If you'd asked me," Nyman said, "I would've let you in myself."

"That's what I tried to do. I kept coming by, but you were never here. I went by the apartment, too."

As she talked, without shifting her gaze from Nyman, she opened the middle drawer and ran her hand along the underside.

"Find it?" he asked.

She nodded. Pulling the envelope free of the tape, she opened the flap and counted the bills inside. The fear had gone out of her face; now her eyes were heavy-lidded and sluggish.

"I was thinking the other day about the first recital I saw you give," Nyman said. "You remember that? Claire kept telling me how talented her little sister was and how I had to come and hear her play. I remember sitting there in the audience, thinking how alike the two of you were. Claire was so nervous and proud."

Theresa put the envelope in her pocket. "Sorry, Tom. I don't remember that."

"No?"

"No. Sorry."

"What about the first time she hurt herself, and you came with me to the hospital to see her? The nurse took us back to her bed, and you held onto my arm."

"I don't remember that either."

"Yes you do, Theresa."

"Look, I'm sorry, but I have to go. I'm not feeling well."

Nyman said: "I talked to the guy I was telling you about. The one who plays at the Green Door. He says he'll help you get some work lined up."

Pale with nausea, she shook her head and moved unsteadily to the door. "I can't do that stuff anymore, Tom. I haven't played in years."

Reaching for his wallet, Nyman took out the napkin with the Burbank address. "His name's Ira. He's a good guy."

She said with sudden anger: "Why the hell does it matter to you? If I'm not interested, I'm not interested."

"Maybe if you got interested again, you'd start feeling better."

"You have no idea how I feel."

"I'm not saying I do. But I want you to be happy."

She rolled her eyes. "Find someone else to worry about, Tom. I'm not Claire, and I don't need you."

"You need my money, though?"

Her mouth opened in surprise and her hand went to her pocket, as if she'd already forgotten about the money. Lowering her gaze, she said she would pay him back.

"Pay me back by going to see Ira."

"No, I mean with money. Next week I'll have some and I'll pay you then."

"I don't want money." He rose from the chair and held out the napkin. "Just take it. As a favor to me."

"I'm not going to see him."

"Just take it and think about it. For me."

Cursing, she snatched it from his hand and went out the door, turning toward the street and not looking back.

Nyman stood in the doorway and watched her go. When she was out of sight, he picked up the petty-cash box and put it back in his desk. Then he turned off the lamp, muttered something to the empty room, and went out to his car.

* * *

He left the coast highway at Channel Road and wound his way up into the Palisades, passing neighborhoods of deep leafy lawns and massive houses. Turning onto Kovac's street, he doused the lights of his car and took his foot off the gas, letting it ease to a stop.

A black Mercedes was parked beside the ivy-covered wall that separated the house from the street. A little farther on, parked in the opposite direction, was a silver Nissan. Both were unoccupied.

Leaving his car behind the Nissan, he walked to the door that stood in the center of the wall and tried the handle. It didn't turn. Glancing over his shoulder, he got a grip on the vines of the ivy, put his foot on the handle, hoisted himself to the top of the wall, and dropped down on the other side, crouching in the grass.

Moonlight shone on the glass-and-steel house. No lights were on inside and there was no sign of Kovac or his staff. A faint breeze brought the smell of seawater up from the beach below.

Moving silently, Nyman made his way around the house to the backyard, where the olive trees were dark shapes among the beds of sage and mallow. Beyond them, the guest house was filled with light.

271

He kneeled in the shadow of the trees. Through the glass walls, he could see the furniture in the front room and the strip of corkboard pinned with blueprints and architectural plans.

Kovac, his face flushed and distorted, stood in the center of the room, arguing with a man whose back was turned. When the man moved, Nyman recognized the bland face of the security director, Fowler. Dressed in a gray suit, he sat down on the couch and faced Kovac, smiling coldly as he listened.

A few feet from the couch, perched on the edge of a chair and taking no part in their argument, was Michael Freed.

Their voices didn't carry through the glass. The only sounds were the hissing of the waves and the occasional hum of a passing car.

The argument seemed to be coming to an end. Fowler's cold smile had given way to a look of contempt. He listened to the rest of what Kovac had to say, nodded, said something in reply, and walked to the door. Slamming it behind him, he crossed the backyard with angry strides and disappeared around the edge of the main house.

Nyman hesitated. In the guest house, Freed had moved closer to Kovac and the two men were talking calmly, unbothered by the other man's exit.

Nyman watched them for another half-minute, then jogged after Fowler. He reached the front yard as the door was swinging shut in the wall.

Crossing the yard, he went through the door and out into the darkened street.

Fowler was waiting in the shadows.

Chapter 41

The first punch caught Nyman in the stomach, knocking the air from his lungs; the second struck his temple, putting him on his knees in the gravel. Fowler took a pistol from his jacket and pressed it against the back of Nyman's head.

Nyman's breath came in ragged gasps. Fowler adjusted his grip on the gun and stepped back, keeping the gun steady. He edged toward the road until he had a view of Nyman's face. Then he let the gun swing down to his side and said:

"Jesus Christ. What the hell are you doing here?"

Nyman sat down on the gravel. His eyes were pink and watering. When he'd caught his breath, he said in a hoarse voice:

"Kovac fire you?"

Fowler put away the gun and told Nyman to go to hell. "I've done enough talking for one night."

He turned and walked to the Nissan.

Nyman forced himself to his feet and hobbled after him. He got to the car as Fowler was opening the driver's door.

"He fired you, didn't he?" Nyman said.

Fowler stopped with his hand on the door. "What makes you think it's any of your business?"

Nyman said that it wasn't. "But it makes sense that Kovac would do it. You got questioned by the cops. If he fires you, he shifts the blame. Makes you look like the guilty one."

Fowler looked hard at Nyman, then at the part of Kovac's house that was visible from the road.

"I've been with Koda six years," he said. "One big family— that's what he said we were."

"Sounds like the family's breaking up."

"Yeah. Sounds like it."

Nyman nodded in the direction of the canyon. "There's a bar on Channel Road. Let me buy you a drink."

"I don't need your sympathy."

"It's not sympathy. It's an exchange. I buy you a drink; you tell me what you did to Alana Bell."

Slamming the door, Fowler came back around the car and pointed a finger at Nyman's face. "I didn't do a goddamn thing to her. She's the one who attacked me."

"Alana? When?"

"The night she came to the Rexford. She talked to Kovac for a few minutes, then stormed out when he said he wouldn't abandon the project. He told me to go after her. Told me to try and talk some sense into her."

"And knock her around if she wouldn't cooperate?"

"Don't be ridiculous. When I caught up to her she was on Laurel, walking over to her car. I said her name; she ignored me. I tapped her on the shoulder; she turned around and attacked me, fists and everything. I pushed her away and told her she was crazy. That was the end of it."

"And the bruise on her cheek?"

Hesitating, Fowler said: "That might've been from me pushing her. She hit the ground pretty hard."

"And later? When you killed her?"

"For Christ's sake, you think I'm that stupid? Why would I kill her? She was nothing to me. Kovac wanted her to stop fighting the new development—fine. That's his problem. It had nothing to do with me."

"Unless Kovac ordered you to kill her."

Fowler laughed and turned away. "If that's what you think, you don't know anything about anything. Kovac wouldn't kill anybody."

"Who would, then?"

Fowler started to lower himself into the car, then stopped. Looking at Nyman, he nodded to Kovac's house. "If I were you, I'd take a closer look at your friend Freed."

He shut the door and started the engine.

* * *

Nyman went back to his car and sat behind the wheel. He took the peanuts from the glovebox and ate them mechanically, watching Kovac's house. When the peanuts were gone he smoked cigarettes. An hour and a half later, Freed came out and climbed into the black Mercedes.

Nyman waited for the Mercedes to get midway down the road, then put his car in gear.

* * *

EDGE OF THE KNIFE

It was ten minutes to three when Freed pulled into the driveway of his house in Los Feliz. Nyman, following a block behind, continued to the end of the cul-de-sac and parked along the curb.

Freed got out of the Mercedes and mounted the steps of the porch. A light came on in the front room as he took the keys from his pocket; the door opened and Sarah stood framed in the doorway, dressed in the same clothes Nyman had seen her in earlier. Freed pushed by her without speaking and shut the door.

Nyman left his car and knocked on the door. Sarah, opening it, looked at him in surprise and said:

"It's a little late, don't you think?"

Her husband was standing beside the fireplace. Above him, on the mantle, his younger self smiled down from the black-and-white wedding photo. Freed grabbed an iron poker from a stand beside the fireplace and took a step toward Nyman, his voice low and guttural.

"Get out of my house."

Nyman put his hands in his pockets and nodded to the poker. "You don't think a knife would be more appropriate?"

"What the hell is that supposed to mean?"

"Eric Trujillo was murdered with something like a steak knife. The kid you were so eager to put suspicion on when I first talked to you."

"That has nothing to do with me."

"Then you won't mind letting me have a look at your knives?"

Sarah moved between the two men and held out her hands. "It's too late for this. What we all need is some sleep."

Freed threw the poker against the fireplace and moved off into the hallway, walking with long, lunging strides. His wife picked up the poker and put it back on its hook.

Nyman said: "I need to talk to him, Mrs. Freed."

"So you keep telling me."

"He went to Ethan Kovac's house tonight. In the Palisades. Did he tell you he was going there?"

Before she could answer, Freed came back into the room holding a glass and a fifth of Jack Daniels. Without looking at Nyman or his wife, he stalked into the hallway; after a moment came the sound of a door closing and a lock being turned.

Sarah looked helplessly at Nyman, then followed her husband. When she was gone, Nyman went into the kitchen.

Beside the sink, slotted into a block of wood, was a set of kitchen knives. Taking a handkerchief from his pocket, he brought the knives out one by one and examined the blades. There was nothing on them—no blood or scuffs or damage—to suggest that any had been recently used.

"You're certainly persistent, aren't you?"

Nyman slid the last knife back into its slot and turned to look at Sarah, who'd come in from the front room. She went to the refrigerator, took out the bottle of wine she'd drunk from earlier, poured two glasses, and handed one to Nyman.

"He locked himself in the study," she said, leaning against the counter and taking a drink. "Our entire marriage, he's never locked me out before. I've never seen him like this."

"Will he talk to me?"

"He says if you go near him, he'll kill you. I think a part of him even thinks he'd do it."

"Why'd he go to Kovac's tonight?"

"I have no idea. I didn't know he was friends with Kovac."

"What about a woman named Bridget Becker?"

"Becker?" Sarah shook her head. "Never heard of her."

Nyman took a drink and put the glass aside. "Your husband's acting like a guilty man, Mrs. Freed."

"Trust me, I'm aware of that. But he couldn't have killed those people. He was in Boston on Wednesday and in Santa Barbara with me on Saturday. It's impossible."

"He could've hired someone to do the killings for him."

She gave a little shiver of revulsion. "You think of the worst scenarios."

"It's part of the job."

"What about trusting your instincts? Isn't that part of the job? Don't your instincts tell you Michael's innocent?"

"I don't put much stock in instincts."

"No, I'm not surprised. You're very clinical, aren't you?"

Nyman didn't answer. Beside him the ticking of the wall-clock seemed to echo in the quiet house. Sarah looked down at her glass and shook her head.

"I wish I could give you my instincts. Being married to someone for so long, you find out who they are, the good parts and the bad. I know every side of Michael, and none of them could commit a crime like that."

Nyman told her she was lucky. "In my experience, there's always a part of another person that stays hidden."

"If they want it to stay hidden, then yes. But Michael's never been like that."

"You're lucky."

After a pause, she said tentatively: "Your wife. She kept things from you?"

"No, that's not what I meant."

Nyman took the cigarettes from his pocket, started to take one out, then stopped. With a restless movement he put the pack in his pocket and reached for his wine.

"Have you ever noticed," he said, "that when you first wake up in the morning, there's always a moment when you can't remember who you are? It only lasts for a second. Then you think about your job, or something you did the night before, and that brings it back. The memories."

Sarah's eyes narrowed in confusion. "I hadn't noticed, no. Does it matter?"

"That's what I meant about the hidden part. There's an emptiness at the center of a person, I think. All your thoughts and feelings come out of it, but you only get a glimpse of it occasionally and indirectly. Out of the corner of your eye, so to speak."

"I don't think I follow you, Tom."

"My wife," he said, "had certain problems, and for a long time I thought I could save her. I thought there was some kind of core inside her, and if I could heal the core, she'd be the person she was supposed to be."

Sarah waited for him to go on.

"I don't know if your husband's guilty or not, Mrs. Freed, but don't waste time thinking you can save him. There's no core you can get to, in him or in anyone else."

She said that her husband wasn't in need of saving. "And I don't agree with anything you just said. You might've been through something bad with your wife, but that doesn't mean it's true of everybody."

"It doesn't matter much either way, in the end."

"I think it does," Sarah said. "And I'm sorry about what happened to her, whatever it was."

It seemed for a time that Nyman wasn't going to respond. Then, with a grim smile, he said:

"There are jugular veins on either side of the neck. If you cut one of them"—he took a knife from the block of wood and gestured with it, moving it above the skin of his neck—"if you cut one of them deep enough, even if you miss the artery, death from hemorrhagic shock will come within a few hours."

She looked at him and said nothing.

Looking down at the blade, Nyman said: "Of course she was very considerate. There's a place down by the marina—a jetty that goes out into the water. On one side is a little sliver of beach where nobody ever goes. She did it down there, where I wouldn't be the one to find her."

"I'm sorry, Tom."

"It took three days," Nyman said, "for someone on the jetty to notice. The coroner's office called me and I went down to identify her."

Nyman put the knife back in its slot.

In the darkness beyond the kitchen, there was a sound of soft footsteps. The Freeds' younger son came in from the hallway, holding a stuffed dog.

The boy looked warily at Nyman, then walked stiff-legged to his mother, saying that he'd had a bad dream. She kneeled down and spoke him to him in a quiet voice, putting an arm around his shoulder.

Nyman left the house and went out into the night.

Chapter 42

It was almost five when he parked in his usual spot on Via Marina. Sailboats bobbed at their berths across the channel. Farther away, among the houses in the Del Rey hills, lights winked on here and there as the earliest risers left their beds.

He followed the grass along Channel Walk until he came to the concrete path of the jetty. The brackish smell of seawater was mixed with the smell of tackle and live bait.

At the end of the jetty, sitting on overturned buckets, fishermen were preparing their lines with mackerel and anchovy. To Nyman's left, lapping with small waves, was the sliver of beach no one ever visited.

He sat down on his usual bench and looked back at the land. The lights of Venice ran away to the north, merging with those of Santa Monica and the Palisades and then, as the land jutted west, bleeding into the glow of Malibu.

He sat for half an hour with his arms crossed and his face creased in thought. More than once he opened his notebook to make a note in the margins or draw a question mark next to a note he'd made earlier.

Sometime before six he closed his eyes. When he opened them again the sun was above the mountains and the L.A. basin was filled with light.

He got up from the bench and paused for a moment to look down at the sliver of beach. The tide was rising and waves were moving closer to the wall of the jetty, washing away the tracks of birds and leaving clean white sand behind.

He walked back to his car.

* * *

In Glassell Park, at the corner of Verdugo and Holt, he found the house Voss had told him about: an old Craftsman painted a dusty green, its eaves inlaid with stained-glass windows. Parked in the driveway was Grace Salas' red Prius. Walking around the car, Nyman found no major dents or scratches.

Laughter came through the front door as he rang the bell. The door was opened by a smiling young woman who looked at him expectantly, her eyebrows raised.

Nyman said that he needed to speak to the councilmember. "My name's Tom Nyman."

"Mom's in the kitchen with the kids. You're one of the new aides?"

"I'm a private investigator."

Her eyebrows dropped and her smile went away. Without a word, she turned and led him down a hallway that opened into a kitchen. Grace Salas, in the same black suit he'd first seen her in, was cooking pancakes. Three young kids were waiting at the table.

"You have a visitor, Mom," the woman said.

Salas glanced over her shoulder, recognized Nyman, and looked away again, busying herself with the pancakes. By the time she brought the food over to the table her features were composed.

"Let me see your hands," she said to the kids.

Two of the kids held out their hands; the third ran to the sink. Salas put down the plates and said to Nyman:

"You can wait in the office down the hall. I'll be with you in a second."

Nyman followed the hallway to a cluttered room lined with bookshelves. An orange-and-white cat, thin with age, lay stretched in the patch of sunshine that fell across the rug. Nyman was reading the spines of the books on the shelves when Salas came in.

"Well, now you've tracked me down at home, just like your friend. I hope you're not planning to be as rude as he was."

Nyman said that he wasn't planning anything. "I just want to know why you decided to give twenty thousand dollars to Meridian Resources."

Salas walked to a chair and made a show of clearing away the papers that were piled on the cushion. With her face averted, she said:

"You're referring to the council motion?"

"Yes."

She put the papers on a shelf. "That's just part of the job. Making sure local organizations get support."

"Even if the organization isn't in your district?"

She smiled. "You read Voss' column."

"I did."

"That's Richard for you: always looking for a controversy. The fact is, in a place like L.A., councilmembers have to look beyond their own little neighborhoods. The city's too interconnected."

"But why Meridian?"

"Why not? They do good work."

"What kind of work?"

"Environmental advocacy, for the most part. I believe their main focus is alternative energy."

"You believe?"

"That's what I've been told, yes."

"By who?"

Her gaze went to a clock on the wall. "By Michael Freed, as a matter of fact. Meridian's director is a former student of his."

"Bridget Becker?"

"That's right."

"So Freed asked you for twenty thousand dollars for his former student?"

"Of course not. You make it sound like a payment. He told me that Meridian was a deserving organization."

"And what's his relationship with Becker?"

"Well, he was her professor. I assume he's kind of a mentor."

"Where female students are concerned, he has a reputation of being more than a mentor."

Salas laughed. "Trust me, Tom, I'm not interested in academic gossip. All I know is that Freed assured me Meridian was worthy of our support."

"Have you ever dropped by Meridian's offices, councilmember?"

"Not personally."

"Have you tried calling them?"

"Not that I remember."

"Would you be surprised to hear that their phone's been disconnected and that their office has been leased to someone else?"

Nothing surprised her anymore, she said. "And it's not my job to keep tabs on every charity in the city."

"But it's your job to give Michael Freed twenty thousand dollars when he asks for it?"

"He didn't ask for it. I've already told you that. There's no need to badger me with the same questions."

Nyman said: "You've heard these questions before, haven't you? First from Alana, and then from Eric Trujillo."

"No."

"Did they threaten to expose you?"

Looking again at the clock, she said she was late for a meeting at City Hall. "You'll have to find another time to harass me."

"How can I get in touch with Bridget Becker?"

"I don't have the slightest idea. I've never met the woman."

"What about Ethan Kovac? Did you know he also donated to Meridian?"

"No, I didn't, and it means nothing to me. Now if you don't leave, I'm going to call the police."

Nyman said he would show himself out. When he reached the driveway Salas' daughter was loading the kids into the Prius. She pretended not to see him and Nyman went by without speaking to her, making his way back to his car.

He was lowering himself into the driver's seat when his phone rang. Recognizing Joseph's number, he opened the phone and said:

"I hope you have good news for me."

"A little good and a little bad," Joseph said. "The good news is, I found our friend at Water and Power, and he's not dead."

"That is good. What's the bad news?"

"He can't tell us much about Bridget Becker, aside from the fact that Meridian leased the shop in Hollywood for a brief time three years ago."

"And then disappeared?"

"More or less. She left a forwarding address, but the bills they sent there never got paid."

"What's at the forwarding address? Another store?"

It was an apartment, Joseph said, on Gossett Drive in Beverly Hills.

Nyman took down the number, thanked him for his help, and drove west in the thickening morning traffic.

Chapter 43

Gossett Drive was a palm-lined street of closely set houses and apartment complexes. The address Joseph had given him belonged to a cream-and-beige, two-story complex with an open courtyard at the center. A stepladder was leaning over the bottlebrush hedge at the front of the building; in the grass was a toolbox and a new mesh window-screen still in its cardboard frame.

The security door stood open, held in place by a rubber wedge. Nyman passed through the door and came into the central courtyard, where the sun shone down on a murky swimming pool.

Apartments were ranged around the courtyard, each with its own stoop and letterbox. Crossing to number six, he pressed the button beside the door.

A bell chimed in the front room, but there was no answering sound of footsteps. Moving to one of the windows, he was looking through the glass when a voice said behind him:

"Don't bother. They moved out three weeks ago."

Nyman turned. A man in slippers and a robe stood beside the pool, holding a coffee mug. He was in his late thirties or early forties; his eyes were dark and sleepy and bored.

"Saw you from my kitchen," he said, nodding to another apartment. "You see everything in this building. I'm Chris, by the way. The manager."

"Tom Nyman."

The man nodded but didn't come any closer. Running his gaze over Nyman, he seemed to come to a conclusion.

"You're a cop."

"Close," Nyman said. "A private investigator."

"And you're looking for the Egans?"

"Who are the Egans?"

"The people who lived in number six. Nice couple. Moved out at the end of June."

Nyman said: "I'm looking for Bridget Becker."

Some of the boredom went out of the man's eyes. "In that case, you're a little late. She hasn't lived here for two or three years."

"Do you know where I can find her?"

Yawning, Chris turned toward his apartment and gestured for Nyman to follow. "Come in and sit down," he said, "and we'll talk about it."

His apartment was crowded with furniture, all of it heavy and ornate. Cheap oil paintings in gilt frames hung on the walls, interspersed with playbills and cast photos from theater productions. Nyman recognized Chris in a few of the photos, younger and thinner.

He waved Nyman into a wingback chair and sat down in a matching chair across from him, so close that their knees were almost touching. Reaching into the drawer of a side table, he took out a plastic bag filled with loosely rolled joints.

"Smoke?" he said.

"No thanks."

"Mind if I do?"

"Go ahead."

He lit a joint and sat back in the chair. The robe hung loose at the sides of his body, exposing patches of hairy skin.

Exhaling smoke, he said: "She left him, didn't she?"

"Pardon?"

"Bridget. She had a fiancé when she lived here. I always figured she'd leave him after a few years."

"Why?"

"He didn't really seem like the type of guy who could hold onto her. Not for very long, at least."

"What kind of guy was he?"

"Oh, he was all right. Kind of a young-executive type. Not real interesting to talk to."

"Do you know where they are now?"

Chris gestured in a vague direction. "Whatever town he was from—I can't remember the name. He came from a lot of money, which of course is why she married him."

"She told you that?"

"She didn't need to tell me. A woman who looked like her—she wouldn't be with a guy like that unless he had money."

"Maybe they were in love."

Chris smiled. "You don't strike me as the naïve type."

"I cultivate a little naivety. For my health."

"Is it working?"

"Not at the moment. What about the fiancé? Do you remember his name?"

Drawing on the joint, he held the smoke for a moment, then let it escape through his nostrils. "Tyler, I think it was."

"That was his first name or his last name?"

"His first. I don't remember the last. I don't know if he ever told me the last. It was an unusual arrangement, their living here."

"How so?"

It had been a sublet, Chris said. "The guy who had the lease was a student at Pacifica. He left to do a semester abroad and Bridget came in to use it while he was gone, which was only a few months. After a while the fiancé starting living with her."

"Bridget was a student too?"

"She said she had some kind of business, but I never saw her do much work. Mostly she sat out by the pool. Used to wear a little green-and-white bikini that drove the guys nuts."

"She was attractive?"

He nodded. "A real California type. Blonde and curvy. Tall. I figured she was an actress, but she claimed she was a social worker or something."

"Claimed?"

"Well, someone tells you something, you never know how much to believe. You say you're not a cop, but you ask questions like one. You're sure you don't want to smoke?"

"I'm sure."

"What about a drink? I can fix you something."

"No thanks."

Chris smiled, but there was no happiness in it. "All business?"

"Today at least."

"It's all right. Thing is, when I took this job, I never figured how lonely it would be, just staying home all day. When you go to an office, you at least get to talk to people."

"Unless it's a one-person office."

"Is that what you have? Just yourself?"

"Just myself."

"So you know what it's like to be lonely."

Nyman asked him for the third time if he knew where Bridget had gone after she'd moved out.

He let more smoke dribble from his nostrils. "Somewhere with her fiancé, like I said. I think maybe they bought a house. He was from a town up north."

"In L.A.?"

"No, farther than that. Up toward Ventura."

"Vista Hills, maybe?"

"Could've been. Who knows?"

"And you can't remember his last name?"

"No." And then, as a thought occurred to him, he said: "But Victor might. The handyman. He's been here as long as I have."

He pushed himself out of the chair and moved toward the door. Nyman followed him back across the courtyard and out to the front of the building, where a pot-bellied man was removing the cardboard frame from the window-screen.

Chris pointed a thumb at Nyman. "This guy's looking for Bridget Becker. You remember her?"

Victor nodded. "Blonde, right?"

"She used to sit by the pool," Chris said, brushing ash from his shirt. "Remember?"

"I remember."

"In a green-and-white bathing suit."

"I don't remember the bathing suit."

"What about her fiancé's last name? This guy's trying to find them both."

"Collins," Victor said, tossing the frame aside and climbing the first two steps of the ladder. "Last name was Collins. He used to give me a few bucks for taking care their plants."

Chris looked at Nyman with a smile. "There you go. Tyler Collins."

Nyman took out his notebook and turned rapidly to the page on which he'd made his first note of the case. He looked up at Victor and said:

"Was the last name Collins, or Collinson?"

Victor paused in his climb; he tipped his head to one side and frowned. "Could've been Collinson, I guess. Sounds right."

Nyman put away the notebook and took the keys from his pocket.

Chris watched him. In full sunshine, the branching veins along his cheekbones stood out beneath the pallor of his skin.

"Got what you wanted?"

"Yes. Thanks for your help."

"Sure you don't want to stay for that drink?"

"I don't really have the time."

Chris looked up at the man on the ladder. "What about you, Vic? You want to have a drink with me?"

"Sorry, man. Too much work to do."

Still smiling, Chris nodded. "Oh well. Maybe next time."

He walked back into the building alone.

Chapter 44

Nyman drove back into Vista Hills the same way he'd driven into it five days earlier, passing shopping malls and office parks. The roses had been torn up and replanted in the median where Alana's body had been found. Apart from the fresh earth beneath them, there was no sign of what had happened.

He parked beside the Spanish Colonial house. Walking to the gate and pressing the intercom button, he saw that the flowers of the jacaranda had started to fall from the limbs, melting into a dark ooze on the concrete.

After a burst of static, a woman's voice said: "Yes?"

Nyman told her his name and occupation. "I came here a few days ago to ask you about Alana Bell. You told me you didn't know her."

The static crackled in the quiet air. Finally the woman said: "Sorry—I don't know what you're talking about."

"I think you do, Bridget. It's time you and I had a talk."

The static crackled on, then stopped. Nyman was reaching again for the button when a motor whirred and the gate rolled aside.

He walked up the driveway to a colonnaded porch on which a blonde woman in her thirties was waiting. She wore white shorts and a baggy t-shirt streaked with fresh paint. Without offering Nyman her hand, she asked him how he'd known that she was Bridget Collinson.

"I didn't know. Mostly it was a guess."

"You're a good guesser."

"It's an advantage in my line of work."

"You're really a detective?"

He showed her the copy of his license. Reading it, her tanned face became paler. "Well, I guess you'd better come in."

They walked together into the entry hall. The woman's feet, in leather espadrilles, slapped on terra cotta tiles as she led him to a room that had been made to serve as a painter's studio. In front of the window stood a canvas and easel and brushes.

She'd been painting a view of the foothills. The layers of brown and gold paint were thick and impressionistic; a sliver of robin's-egg sky stretched across the top of the canvas. Nyman said that he liked her work.

She shrugged. "On the good days it's not too bad, I guess."

"Today is a good day?"

"It was until you came."

Nyman nodded. "I tend to have that effect."

She stood for a moment in front of the painting, looking at it with eyes narrowed in self-criticism. Then, shaking her head and turning away, she said:

"So you're here about the dead woman."

"And the dead man."

"Man?"

"There've been two murders," Nyman said. "Both involving a red sedan. Can I ask the color of the cars you and your husband drive, Mrs. Collinson?"

One was black and one was white, Bridget said, "and they're both mine, not my husband's. He moved out a few months ago."

"I'm sorry to hear that."

"You shouldn't be. He made it very clear that it was better for both of us, in the long run. But you didn't come here to talk about that."

"No, I didn't," Nyman said. "I'm more interested in Meridian Resources. Are you still the director?"

She picked up a brush and ran her fingers through the bristles. "That was never a very accurate job title," she said. "The only employee I ever had was myself, and I wasn't what you'd call diligent."

"Your former landlord says you spent most of your time by the pool."

She looked up in surprise. "You mean the place on Gossett? I guess I probably did spend a lot of time at the pool. It's amazing how you forget things."

Nyman said that he'd also visited her old shop on Whitlock Terrace. "No one remembered you there."

"No, they wouldn't have. I was a kid in those days. I didn't know what the hell I was doing."

"You'd been a student at Pacifica?"

She nodded. "A master's student. Studying with Michael Freed, as I'm sure you know."

"Was Meridian his idea?"

"Michael's? Oh no. It wasn't even an idea, really: just a way to spend some money my parents had given me. I had a lot of big plans, but I didn't know what I was doing. I printed up some letterhead and came up with a website and that was about it. When Tyler came along I gave it up and assumed my natural role."

"Which is what?"

She gestured to the walls of the house. "Showpiece wife. Pretty and vacuous. Unfortunately I screwed that up too."

"You don't seem vacuous to me."

"There are different kinds of vacuity. In any case, Meridian was a total failure."

"Grace Salas," Nyman said, "seems to think it was worth a twenty-thousand-dollar donation."

From somewhere nearby came the sounds of conversation and the whirring of a kitchen appliance. Bridget walked to the window and looked out at the dry gold hills.

"You know about everything, then."

"Not everything," Nyman said. "Ethan Kovac gave you money, too, but I don't know how much. I'm assuming it was also twenty thousand."

"Does it really matter?"

"I'm just trying to get it all straight. The scam itself seems simple enough, but the details are complicated."

"And what's the scam, as you see it?

A quid pro quo, Nyman said. "Grace Salas convinced the city council to give a favorable development deal to Koda and Savannah Group, both of which had contributed heavily to her campaign. When people started to object, she and the developers went to Freed to help them hide the fact that it was a bad deal for the taxpayers."

"You make it sound so sordid."

"Wasn't it?"

She turned to face him. "You'll be going to the police with all this?"

"I've already gone to them with some of it. I'll take the rest to them when I have it."

"And what will you tell them about me?"

"Everything I know," Nyman said. "So you might as well start with the truth."

She nodded and leaned back against the windowsill. Calmly, she said: "The development would've gone ahead either way, no matter what Michael did. Even if his report had said it was a terrible deal, Salas would've gotten someone else to say it was wonderful. It would've been a minor bump in the road."

"Then why the donations to Meridian?"

She shrugged. "Because of Alana Bell, basically. She'd gotten into Michael's head. Convinced him that the homeless people in the Merchant District were some kind of moral crusade. She got him to write a scathing analysis, which he turned around and submitted to Salas."

Nyman said that Salas couldn't have liked that.

"That's putting it mildly. She told him that any deal this big was going to involve some back-scratching, and there was no reason to make the perfect the enemy of the good. She said he owed it to the city to rewrite the report."

"Which he did."

"Yes. He turned in the second version just before he left for Vegas."

"Where he knew Savannah Group owned the Kasbah casino."

"Maybe—I don't know the details. All I know is he went to Vegas, won some money, and told Alana he'd turned in a revised report. Which is when she went through the roof. She thought the money he'd won in the casino was a bribe, and she said she was going to expose him."

"Was it a bribe?"

"Honestly, I don't think even Michael knew what it was. Salas had told him that Savannah and Koda would be grateful for the revised report, but I don't think she promised him anything explicit. Michael would've refused an outright bribe."

"And the donations to your company?"

She lifted her paint-stained hands. "Same thing. Michael told Salas that one of his students had a charity worth supporting, but I don't think he ever asked for money directly. When I got the check from Koda, I didn't know what the hell it was. I'd never even heard of Koda. And pretty soon there was another check from C.D. 16."

"What'd you do with the money?"

After a pause, Bridget said: "I don't see any reason why I should answer that."

"Obviously you gave the money to Freed."

"Why obviously?"

He repeated her gesture to the walls of the house. "Forty thousand dollars wouldn't mean much to someone like you, Mrs. Collinson. To someone like Freed, it would make a difference."

"You really think I'd be that generous?"

"Yes. Particularly if you were in love with him."

"With Michael? That's absurd. He's a married man."

"With a history of seducing his students."

"I'm not going to dignify that with a response. He's been a mentor to me and a friend. That's all."

"When was the last time you saw him?"

She flushed. "It's been months."

"Then how do you know so much about his business?"

"We talk on the phone. Like all friends do."

"Soon," Nyman said, "there are going to be cops here asking you these same questions. You're going to have to find a better way to answer them."

The flush extended to her hairline. "Infidelity isn't a crime, you know. I don't have to answer questions about my friendship with Michael. To you or anyone else."

"Murder is a crime, Mrs. Collinson."

"Thank you—I'm aware of that. And I'm not a murderer."

"What about Freed?"

"Michael could never do something like that. Never. Neither of us had anything to do with that girl's death."

"No?"

"No."

"Then why," Nyman said, "did she come all the way up here to die?"

Chapter 45

Her reply was cut short by a knock at the door. Leaning into the room, a man in khaki work clothes said that lunch was almost ready. "They're setting it up for you in the conservatory."

Bridget nodded. "Thanks. I'll be there in a second."

The man stepped out of the room and shut the door.

Turning to Nyman, she said: "I don't suppose you'd let me answer your questions another time?"

"It's your choice. But it would be easier to get it over with."

Her gaze went to the clock on the wall. "Are you hungry?"

"Not really."

"Neither am I, but it'll hurt their feelings if I don't come."

"Is it a special occasion?"

"If you can believe it," she said, walking to a chair in the corner of the room, "today's my birthday."

Draped over the back of the chair was a change of clothes. Laying them across her arm, she said that he was welcome to join her for lunch. "But I need to change first."

He waited for her in the hall. She came out a few minutes later dressed in dark jeans and a trimly cut blazer. Her face was still without makeup and her hands, long-fingered and as large as Nyman's, were still flecked with paint. On the third finger of her left hand was a diamond wedding ring.

He followed her through the house to a glass-walled conservatory filled with tropical flowers. She led him in among the flowers and over to a table where the man in khaki was waiting beside two women who were, judging by their clothes, a cook and a maid.

On the table were several covered dishes and a cupcake with a candle in it. The man, seeing Nyman, slipped behind a wall of ferns and came back carrying a second chair.

Bridget said: "You shouldn't have done all this. It's so beautiful."

She blew out the candle, opened the card they'd given her, opened the gift, and gave each of them a hug. When they were gone, she let out her breath in a long exhalation and sat down at the table, motioning for Nyman to do the same.

"I'm sorry you had to see that," she said. "You probably think I'm ridiculous."

"It's all right. I have to do the same thing with my servants."

She took the candle out of the cupcake. "For the record, I never wanted servants in the first place. Tyler's the one who hired them."

"They seem fond of you."

"They do, don't they? I'm not sure why. I'm grateful to have them, though. They're almost the only friends I have left."

"What happened to your other friends?"

"You don't really care, do you?"

"I'm curious."

She cut the cupcake in half with her knife. "Well, Tyler grew up in Vista Hills, so after we got married, I sort of moved into his social set. My old friends drifted away and his friends became my friends."

"And now you're separated."

"Right. Which leaves me having birthdays with the hired help and the guy who wants to put me in jail."

Nyman said that the only person he wanted to put in jail was the person who'd killed Alana Bell and Eric Trujillo.

"Which you think is me."

"Not necessarily. But I think there are things you haven't told me. Such as why Alana came all the way up here to see you."

Putting half the cupcake on a plate, she pushed it over to Nyman. "I know you won't believe this, but I never actually saw her in person. Here or anywhere else."

"You talked to her, though?"

"I heard from her, but I never responded. She sent an email to my old Meridian account, saying she knew I was one of Michael's students and I was mixed up in Merchant South."

Nyman took the notebook from his pocket. "When was this?"

"That she sent the email? It would've been Monday or Tuesday, I think. Of last week."

"So two or three days before she was murdered."

"Yes. I think that's right."

"What else did she say?"

Bridget made a sweeping movement with one hand. "All sorts of things. She said she knew about the Vegas money and Salas' donation to Meridian, which she'd read about in the paper. She said Michael had betrayed her and now I was complicit in the scam, but if I helped her make it all public I could redeem myself and my reputation. Then she gave me her phone number and asked for a time to meet."

"And what did you do?"

"I called Michael. He told me about the trip to Vegas and their blow-up at the bar."

"Did he tell you to talk to her?"

"Just the opposite. He said he'd handle it himself. He said he'd made a terrible mistake with the rewritten report and now the only way to correct it was by admitting everything and returning the money. He was even going to send a letter to the *Times*, explaining what he'd done."

"That would've been quite a gesture."

"That's the way he is, though. Deep down he's a very honest and caring man."

"But not caring enough to actually follow through on his gesture."

"Well, that's because he didn't have a chance to follow through. I talked to him on Tuesday afternoon; that night he flew to Boston for a conference. And he was still in Boston—or on the plane coming back—when Alana got hit by the car."

"Right outside your front gate."

She leaned forward eagerly. "But don't you see? That's what proves it was an accident. She sent me the email, and I never responded. She'd already been up to Salas' office to harass her about the donation, so it makes sense she'd come up here to harass me, too."

Nyman said: "You think she drove up here to harass you, and just happened to get hit by a car as she was crossing the street?"

"I know it doesn't fit whatever explanation you've come up with, but it seems logical to me. There are hit-and-runs around here all the time."

"And what about Eric Trujillo?"

The eagerness went out of her face. "He's the other victim?"

"That we know of so far. He was stabbed to death Saturday night and dumped on Skid Row an hour or two after midnight."

She shook her head. "I don't know anything about that. Michael told me there'd been another killing, but he didn't say who it was."

"So you've talked to Freed since Saturday?"

Alarm widened her eyes. "Well—yes. We talk sometimes on the phone, like I said."

"Did he tell you who killed Trujillo?"

"Of course not. He doesn't know anything about it."

"What about you, Mrs. Collinson? Where were you on Saturday night?"

Nodding to the door her servants had passed through, she said: "I was here with them. We had dinner and I drank too much wine and made them listen to all my problems, like usual."

"And they'll confirm that?"

"If you want to humiliate me even more, yes. You can do it now, if you want to. I'll call them in and we'll establish that I'm a flake and a bad wife but at least I'm not a murderer."

"You're laying it on a little thick, aren't you?"

"That's the only way I know how to lay it on. Do you want me to call them in or not?"

Nyman rose from his chair and said that it wouldn't be necessary. "But I meant what I said about the police coming by. You need to think carefully about how you're going to answer them."

"Because I'm guilty?"

"No," Nyman said, turning toward the door, "because you're protecting someone who doesn't deserve it."

Chapter 46

He drove south to Pacifica.

The campus was mostly deserted. The only people in sight as he crossed the quad were three or four students lying on the grass in front of the library, books piled beside them. No one joined him in the elevator as he rode up to the School of Public Policy.

The same bearded secretary was at the front desk. Nodding as he walked by, Nyman made his way down the hall to Freed's office, where he opened the door without knocking and went in.

Freed looked as if he hadn't slept. His face, no longer gray, was an angry red. The smell of Jack Daniels filled the room and was mixed with a smell of sweat. Half-rising out of his chair, he looked at Nyman with jaundiced eyes.

"Get out."

Nyman ignored him and sat down. In Freed's hands was a photo of himself and his wife and children. They were standing on a beach with the water behind them; Freed's arms were wrapped possessively around the shoulders of his sons.

Nyman said: "I called your house, but no one answered."

"If you don't get out of here, I'll call the campus police."

"That's fine with me, professor. They can make sure you behave yourself."

Freed put the photo aside and laid his hands flat on the desk, as if trying to steady himself. Rather than a jacket and tie, he wore a polo shirt with two red spots on the collar.

"Cut yourself shaving?" Nyman said.

"What?"

"Your collar. There's blood on it."

Freed blinked. "Yes, I know. I had a nosebleed."

"Last night?"

"This morning. When I woke up."

"Why'd you go to Ethan Kovac's house last night, professor?"

Freed shook his head. "I've never been to Kovac's house."

"I saw you there," Nyman said, "along with Kovac's director of security. He told me you were acting like a guilty man."

Freed's hands, still flat on the desk, were trembling. "Is there anything you won't stoop to, Nyman?"

"I take it that you and Kovac needed to get your stories straight about the murders?"

Freed said half-heartedly: "It was a fundraising visit. Kovac offered to give money to the university, and I went to see him about it."

"At two o'clock in the morning?"

"We stayed up late, talking."

Nyman reached for his notebook. "I think I've got the timeline figured out, but maybe you can fill in some gaps. Sometime during the week of June 27th, you submitted an analysis of the Merchant South development to the city council.

This was your original report—the scathing one you'd written with Alana Bell."

Freed said: "I don't know what you're talking about."

"Later that week," Nyman went on, "Grace Salas asked you to write a more favorable version. She promised you—either explicitly or implicitly—some sort of financial reward for your trouble."

Freed said nothing.

"That Friday," Nyman said, "Salas donated twenty-thousand dollars from her discretionary fund to Meridian Resources, which was founded by your friend, Bridget Collinson. The same day, you left for Vegas, where you got another twenty-thousand in the high-limit room at Kasbah casino, which is owned by Savannah Group. Around the same time, you got the final installment of the bribe from Kovac's company—also in the form of a donation to Meridian."

Nyman looked up from the notebook. "Is all this correct?"

Again Freed said nothing.

"Now what I don't understand," Nyman said, "is why you took Alana with you to Vegas. You had to know she'd be angry when she found out about the revised report. And it wouldn't have been hard for her to connect the blackjack money to Savannah."

Freed gave the approximation of a smile. "You think you know her that well?"

"Based on what other people have told me, yes."

"You don't know anything about her. She was far more complex than anyone gave her credit for—especially her family. She wasn't immune to money or the things it can buy."

"You thought you could bribe her?"

"Absolutely not. I thought I could convince her to relax. Make her see that it's all right to indulge yourself once in a while. She was a brilliant woman, but too rigid—emotionally and intellectually."

"So she got angry with you."

"Yes. Very."

"And when she got back to L.A.," Nyman said, "she read Richard Voss's column in Monday's issue of the *Independent*, which mentioned Salas' donation to Meridian."

For the first time, Freed showed a hint of interest. "Is that how she found out?"

"At least in part."

"I wondered about that."

"And that was about the time Kovac sent his director of security to harass her when she wouldn't cooperate. Eric Trujillo noticed the bruise on her face the next day, and at some point she told him about your connection to Meridian and Salas."

"Trujillo," Freed said, "was not just an innocent kid. He was obsessed with her."

Nyman shrugged. "Maybe he was. Either way, he knew who to blame when she got killed. He went to Salas' home and office; he made calls to Koda and Savannah Group. And I'm guessing he came to you too, professor. Was it here in this office?"

Freed got up and walked to the window. With his back turned, he looked less impressive than he had five days earlier. The broad shoulders had started to slump forward in the manner of an old man's.

After a time he said: "I killed them both."

Nyman's face showed no change of expression. "Is that right?"

"Yes."

"How'd you do it?"

Freed didn't turn around, but his head twitched to one side. "What do you mean?"

"Well, you were in Boston when Alana was killed, and in Santa Barbara when Trujillo's body was dumped. I've already talked to people who saw you in both places."

Freed sat down again behind his desk. He looked squarely at Nyman, his gaze calm and level. "I paid to have it done."

"Both times?"

"Yes."

"Who'd you pay?"

"I don't know his name. It was a man I'd met at the park. He was homeless and desperate. He said he'd do it for money."

"How much?"

Freed swallowed. "Two thousand dollars."

"In cash?"

"Yes."

Nyman picked up his pen. "Describe him."

Freed gave a vague description of a man in his thirties, tall, dark-haired, dark-eyed.

Nyman said: "Where'd he kill Trujillo?"

"What do you mean, where?"

"When he stabbed him, where were they? Here in your office?"

"Of course not. It was downtown. On Skid Row."

"The man didn't dump the body there later? Out of a red sedan?"

Freed swallowed again and shook his head. "No. It all happened on the street."

"Have you told your wife about your murders, professor?"

"God no. I could never do that to her."

"Why not?"

"What do you mean, why not? You've met her. She could never understand why I'd do something like that."

"She's too innocent?"

"Yes. Exactly. I know you judge me for the way I've treated her, and you're right. I've been terrible to her. At some point you see yourself for who are, Nyman, and I've seen myself. I'm a weak man, and I've thrown away a perfectly good marriage."

"With your affairs, you mean, or the murders?"

"The affairs. What else?"

His voice, no longer lifeless, quavered with self-pity.

Nyman looked at him with narrow eyes, then looked at the watch on his wrist. Climbing to his feet, he said in a brisk, businesslike voice:

"There's a detective at Central Community station. His name's Timmons. I suggest you go down there, professor, and tell him everything you just told me."

"What? Now?"

"As soon as possible. And you should take a lawyer with you. Do you have a lawyer?"

Freed stared at him in bewilderment. "No. I mean, I've used firms in the past, but never for anything like this."

"Well, it's your decision. Good luck."

Nyman opened the door, started to go out, then paused. "One other thing. The nanny who watches your sons. Is she still on vacation?"

"Marcella? Yes, I think so. Why?"

"Just curious."

Chapter 47

As the carillon rang the four o'clock hour, Nyman stopped under the shade of a palm to dial Marcella's number. Getting no answer, he went into the student union, bought a coffee at one of the cafés, came back out into the sunshine, and tried the number again.

This time a woman's voice, low and guarded, said hello. He told her who he was and asked if they could meet. She said that she was on vacation and too busy for a meeting.

"Where are you?" Nyman said.

"Long Beach."

"I can come to Long Beach. What's the address?"

"No, I'm sorry, it's not possible."

"Are you frightened of something, Marcella?"

"I'm not frightened."

"Then there's no reason not to meet me, is there?"

For a time he heard nothing but her breathing and snatches of what sounded like the mournful tones of a church organ. Then she said that she wasn't in Long Beach.

"Where are you?"

"At La Concepción," she said, and gave him the address.

It was a church in East L.A. Nyman made the drive in half an hour and left his car on Cesar Chavez Avenue, beside a *tortilleria* fragrant with the smell of cooking masa.

Palms outstretched, a statue of the Virgin stood above the doors of the church, framed by a stained-glass oculus. Shafts of colored sunlight followed Nyman across the lobby and into the nave, where the pews stood in semi-darkness.

Marcella was in a middle pew: a small woman with a stack of sheet music on her lap. Thick black hair fell to her shoulders, accentuating the narrowness of her face. Aside from the skeletal, gold-painted Christ above the altar, they were alone.

Sitting down beside her, Nyman thanked her for meeting with him. "You're here for the service tonight?"

She shook her head. "Choir practice. But it doesn't start for a few minutes."

"I'll try to make this quick, then. Have the Freeds told you anything about my investigation?"

They'd told her bits and pieces, she said. "But none of it's true, you know."

"None of what's true?"

"The things you're thinking about Mr. and Mrs. Freed. No one in that house could hurt anyone."

"Why not?"

"Because they're good people. You know how they dote on those boys? If every parent was like that, this would be a better world—I can tell you that."

Nyman said: "I called you once before to ask about last Wednesday. The night Alana Bell was killed."

She nodded. "I told you the truth then and I'm telling you the truth now."

"I don't doubt it, but I need to ask one more thing. Did you drive to the Freeds' that night?"

The question seemed to take her by surprise. "I always drive."

"And you parked in the driveway? Not the garage?"

"Of course. It's only a two-car garage."

"And last Saturday night, when Eric Trujillo's body got dumped on Skid Row: you were at the house then, too?"

She consulted her memory. "The day I watched the boys, you mean? Yes, I was there."

"Alone?"

"No, the boys were with me the whole time."

"Apart from the boys, I mean. Did you see the Freeds?"

Footsteps came from the lobby behind them. Other members of the choir were making their way into the nave, carrying hymnals and sheet music.

Marcella gestured for Nyman to get up. "We'll talk outside."

He followed her back through the lobby and down the front steps. Across the street, a line of customers angled out the door of the *tortilleria* and ran halfway down the block.

"Last Saturday," Nyman said. "Did you see the Freeds that day?"

Nodding, Marcella said that she'd gone to the house in the morning, like usual. "Mr. Freed was packing for Santa Barbara, to go and see the library. I played with the boys in the yard for an hour or two and then Mrs. Freed came out and asked me if I could stay the night."

"Did she seem upset?"

"Not at all. A little shaky, maybe. I thought maybe she was getting sick. But she said they needed to get away for the weekend and I'd be doing them a big favor."

"Did you leave the house at any point after that?"

"That day? No, I don't think so. I have my own little room at the house—clothes and everything. We stayed out in the yard for the rest of the morning, and then I made them lunch. In the afternoon I think I watched T.V. Then in the evenings we always have the same routine. The boys like to play video games."

"And you parked in the driveway?"

Irritation showed in her narrow face. "I already told you that."

Nyman asked if her car was somewhere nearby.

"How else would I get here?" She nodded to a red Ford parked along the street. Despite the dents and scrapes on the bumpers, the exterior was immaculately clean.

"Did you wash it recently?"

Marcella, flushing, looked over his shoulder at the pitted concrete face of the Virgin. "It's not important, is it?"

"It might be very important, depending on your answer."

"I don't know why I have to give you an answer. I don't know why you're so suspicious of Mr. and Mrs. Freed. They never did anything to you."

"Did you wash the car, Marcella?"

She lowered her eyes and said in a reluctant voice: "Mr. Freed felt so bad about the Santa Barbara trip, he paid for me yesterday to get it cleaned. At a place in Boyle Heights."

"Inside and out?"

"Yes. But it doesn't mean anything."

"Thanks for your help, Marcella."

"Do you hear what I'm saying? It doesn't mean anything."

Nyman turned and walked back to his car. Behind him, echoing inside the church, the choir was singing a hymn he didn't recognize.

* * *

He drove to Skid Row. On San Pedro Street, at the spot where Eric Trujillo's body had been found, the flowers and candles were gone but the cardboard sign was in the same place, its message still illegible.

He parked in front of Central Community station, took the phone from his pocket, and made two calls.

The first was to Valerie Bell. He told her where he'd been and where he was going next, and warned her that the police and the press would be contacting her soon, possibly that night.

The second call was to the Surf House in Santa Barbara. The phone was answered by the same man he'd spoken to a day earlier.

"The married couple I asked you about," Nyman said. "Mr. and Mrs. Freed. You're sure neither of them left the hotel that evening?"

The man was sure. "I saw them having dinner in the restaurant, and one of our waiters took some champagne to their room afterward. It must've been close to midnight."

"And they weren't acting strangely?"

"Not at all. They seemed very much in love. It's nice to see a married couple still so affectionate."

"And Mrs. Freed," Nyman said. "How would you describe her?"

"Physically, you mean? A very attractive woman. Tall and blonde—a good deal younger than Mr. Freed. A real California type, if you know what I mean."

Nyman thanked him and hung up.

In the lobby of the station he stood for ten minutes in a line of people waiting to talk to the desk officer. Late in the day, the room was hot with streaming sunshine and sour with the smell of bodies. The officer beckoned him forward and looked at him expectantly.

Nyman said that he needed to talk to Detective Timmons.

"Sorry, but Timmons isn't here. Is that all you wanted?"

"Do you know when he'll be back?"

"No, sir, and I have no way of getting in touch with him. Now can I do anything else for you?"

"I have information about one of his cases. I think he'd be interested to hear it."

"If you have a tip, sir, you can call our tip line. The number's there on the wall."

"There's no way I can speak to him directly?"

The desk officer said: "If it's really this important, you can use the paper there to leave him a message."

Nyman moved off to the end of the counter and scribbled out a brief note that ended with the Freeds' address in Los Feliz. The desk officer, after she'd read it, looked at him more closely.

"You're sure he'll know what this is about?"

"Yes," Nyman said. "And if he comes, tell him to come armed."

Chapter 48

It was after seven when he got to the bungalow in Los Feliz. The tufts of feather grass moved lazily in the front yard, stirred by the breeze. Climbing the steps of the front porch, Nyman went to the door and found streaks of fresh blood on the knob.

He stood for a moment without moving, then looked back at the street. Aside from his own car, there were no cars in the street and no one on the sidewalks. Several houses away, a girl was playing basketball in a driveway. There was no sound apart from the bouncing of the ball.

He cupped his hands and looked through the front window, but the view was blocked by curtains. Taking the handkerchief from his pocket, he gripped the doorknob and tried without success to turn it.

Still with the handkerchief on his hand, he pressed the doorbell and listened to its dull ring. He looked at his watch, waited until a minute had passed, then left the porch and crossed to the driveway.

On the concrete in front of the lowered garage door were two more drops of blood. He went past the driveway to the side of the house.

A window stood midway along the wall. Stretching up on his toes, he looked through the glass and saw only a section of blank wall and ceiling. He stayed for half a minute beside the window, listening, and then moved on toward the backyard.

It was enclosed by a pine fence. Putting his hands on the top edge, he scrambled awkwardly against the wood until he was perched on top of the fence and looking down at the azaleas that grew on the other side. Beyond the flowers was a short stretch of grass that ended at the patio, where a sliding glass door showed no sign of movement within.

He dropped down and jogged to the patio. The door opened to his touch; he slipped into the house and left the door open behind him.

He was standing in the kitchen. On the wall was a thick smear of blood, still so fresh that he could smell it.

The bottle of Jack Daniels, with only a ring of whiskey at the bottom, stood on the table. On the counter was more blood, some of it mixed with water from the tap. In the sink, in a puddle of bloody water, was one of the knives from the block of wood. The blade caught the light of the bulb above the sink and glittered.

He went from the kitchen to the living room. The drapes hung on their iron spears; the chairs stood just as they had on his last visit. Lined up beside the front door were two pairs of boys' shoes.

He went into the hallway. The first door opened into an empty, bloodless bathroom. The second door was closed. Using the handkerchief, he turned the knob, stepped through, and found himself in the boys' bedroom.

The boys were lying side by side on the floor. Piled around them were pillows and sheets from the beds, both of which had been stripped down to the mattresses.

The older boy raised his head and looked at Nyman with frightened eyes. He held a book open in his hands; on the page was a drawing of a knight on a horse.

"He was scared," the boy said, nodding to his brother, "so I was reading to him."

The younger boy's eyes were wide and red from crying.

Nyman cleared his throat and said: "That was a good idea. What book did you pick?"

The older boy showed him the cover.

"That looks like a good one," Nyman said.

"It's all right."

"Are your parents around? I can't seem to find them."

"Mom had to go out," the older boy said. "She told us to stay here and not answer the door."

The younger boy said: "We made a fort, but the dog knocked it down."

He pointed to the corner of the room, where the dog lay with its head between its paws, looking at Nyman sleepily.

"Did your mom say where she was going?"

The older boy shook his head. "Dad called a couple hours ago, and after that she had an accident, I think."

"With a knife?"

"I think so. She wouldn't let us come out of the room."

"What about your dad?"

"He's still at work, I think."

Nyman nodded. "Well, I'm sure they'll be back soon. You mind if I go out in the hall and make a phone call? I'll be back in a second."

The boys said they didn't mind.

He stepped out of the room, shut the door, and went quickly down the hallway, pausing to look into other rooms as he passed. The first was the study in which Michael Freed had locked himself the previous night. The second was the master bedroom: tidy and unmarked by blood.

Taking the phone from his pocket, he called Marcella and asked her to come to the house. "The boys are here alone and I can't find their parents."

"What?"

He repeated what he'd said and told her to come as quickly as she could. "There's blood all over the house."

"Blood?"

"I need someone to look after the kids."

"Okay. Hold on. I'm leaving now."

Nyman hung up. He went back to the study and stood in the doorway, looking at the desk, the bookshelves, the framed diplomas on the wall. Going to the desk, he searched the drawers until he found a box of Michael Freed's business cards.

He called the number on the card. After five or six rings he heard the recorded message of the Department of Public Policy. He cursed and hung up. On the desk was the glass Freed had carried in the night before, still sticky with Jack Daniels.

As he stood staring at the glass there was a rumbling noise at the front of the house.

He left the study and went to the front room. Beyond the fireplace was a door leading into the garage. He stood beside the door, listening, and then opened it when he heard a car pulling in.

A black B.M.W. stood in the nearer of the two spaces. Sarah Freed was visible through the windshield, her face partly obscured by her hair. Moving stiffly, she got out of the car and shut the door. Clasped in one hand was a paper sack with the logo of a pharmacy. Her eyes, when they came up to look at Nyman, were bloodshot and unfocused.

"Oh," she said. "Hi, Tom. Michael said you'd probably be here."

Nyman said: "I was worried about you."

"Really? About me?"

"Yes."

"There's no reason to worry. Everything's fine."

"You left the boys here alone."

"Did I? Yeah, I guess I did. Well, I'm back now."

"Where'd you go?"

"Oh, that's not important," she said, and waved her left hand.

Wrapped around the wrist was a bandage of bloody gauze.

Chapter 49

He offered to carry the paper sack for her, but she held it close to her chest and shook her head.

"No thanks. It's just something I picked up."

"Is your wrist all right?"

"My wrist?"

"There's a bandage on it," Nyman said. "And blood in the house. Your son said you had an accident."

"Yes," she said, leading him inside, "it was an accident. It was very silly, actually. You made it sound so simple."

"Made what sound so simple?"

She went ahead of him into the kitchen and didn't seem to hear the question. Dropping the sack on the counter, she picked up the bottle of Jack Daniels and looked at the bourbon at the bottom, her mouth turned downward in distaste.

"I've never liked whiskey. Such a man's drink. What do you think about some vodka?"

Nyman said he wasn't in the mood for a drink.

"No?" She looked at the clock on the wall. "It's after five. You can have a drink if it's after five."

She took a tumbler down from the cabinet and found a bottle of Stolichnaya in the cupboard. Unscrewing the cap, she filled the tumbler half-full and took a drink, wincing at it.

"Christ, that's harsh."

Nyman said: "How did the accident happen?"

"What?"

"Your wrist. How'd you cut it?"

"Oh, that." She looked down at her arm and took another drink. "That's what I was saying—you made it sound so easy. It's not easy at all."

"What's not easy?"

"Well, your wife, I mean," Sarah said. "Slitting her throat like that. You made it sound simple, but it would've taken a lot of nerve. It took me hours to make the first tiny cut."

Nyman, pale and sweating, said: "You must've been pretty upset."

She made another dismissive gesture. "Please don't waste any pity on me, Tom. I don't deserve it."

"I think you do."

"That's a nice thing to say, but you're wrong. You can't deserve anything until you've done something to deserve it. I've done nothing."

"Did you kill Alana Bell, Mrs. Freed?"

She gave him a pained smile. "Of course I did. That's why you're here, isn't it?"

"What about Eric Trujillo?"

"I killed him," she said, "almost exactly where you're standing. The poor kid."

She lurched forward against the counter, her face crumpling as if she were going to cry; but no tears came.

Instead she steadied herself on the countertop with an elbow and brought the drink to her mouth. She drank, winced, put the glass down, and nodded to the block of wood that held the knives.

"That's a new set. The old set's in the trash somewhere. I don't remember where."

"Trujillo came here to confront you?"

"Me? Of course not me. He wanted Michael."

"But Michael wasn't here?"

"No, he'd already left for Santa Barbara." She swung her glass toward the backyard. "Marcella was out there with the boys, and Michael had left for his supposed research trip. Of course I knew what it was all about."

"A weekend with Bridget Collinson?"

"What else?" She grinned and drank. "Someone to comfort him in his grief. That's always been Bridget's role. The shoulder to cry on whenever he comes knocking."

"So your husband went to Santa Barbara with her," Nyman said, "and you got left here."

"As usual. And that poor kid Trujillo. If he'd just gone away, like I told him to, he'd still be alive. But he wouldn't listen. He'd been up all night, and he'd already been out to see Grace Salas. He was completely unreasonable."

"So you killed him."

"Well, I didn't have much choice. He knew about the money and where it came from. He said he was going to make it all public, for Alana's sake."

"The money, then, is all that mattered to you?"

Ignoring the question, she pointed to the sack from the pharmacy. "Can you hand me that, Tom? It's my medicine."

Nyman took an orange bottle out of the sack and looked at the label. "What kind of medicine?"

"Nothing. Just something I needed to get filled."

"Tell me more about Trujillo."

"Give me the pills," Sarah said, "and I'll tell you whatever you want."

"He was a strong kid. Surely he would've tried to defend himself."

Exhaling, she said in a weary voice: "He never had a chance to defend himself. We were in the living room, arguing, and I said we should have a drink and talk things over like adults. I came into the kitchen, got the knife, and asked him to come in and help me with the glasses. Then I waited for him to come around the corner."

"And that was it?"

"More or less. I thought there'd be a struggle, but all I remember is the blade going into the skin—like into a piece of fruit. I put it there," she said, pointing to a spot on Nyman's chest, "and the next thing I knew he was on the floor, looking up at me. It was probably ten minutes before I realized he was dead."

Nyman asked her why she'd waited until midnight to dump the body.

"Did I wait that long?"

"According to the witnesses on Skid Row."

"I don't remember any of it very well, to be honest. I remember putting some sheets in Marcella's car and dragging him out there. I had to be quiet, because she was still in the backyard with the boys. I asked her if she could stay the night, and then I drove around for a while, trying to think of where to put him. It was a lot harder than the first one."

"Alana, you mean?"

She nodded. "Can I have the pills now, Tom?"

"According to Bridget Collinson," Nyman said, "your husband had decided to make a full confession to the *Times*. It would've meant the end of his career."

"And the end of sixty thousand dollars," she said. "Do you know what that would buy? Marcus is starting fifth-grade at Saint Anselm's. That's two full years of tuition."

"It was about the money, then."

"It was about the money," Sarah said, "and the fact that she could sit there and talk about compassion and justice and meanwhile have sex with the father of my children. Does that strike you as particularly noble, Tom? Does that sound like the kind of person we should be venerating like some kind of saint?"

"I don't think she was a saint."

"No? What do you think she was?"

"An ordinary person with ordinary problems."

Sarah squinted at him for a moment, then smiled and shrugged and made an expansive gesture with her glass. "You're probably right. That's probably exactly what she was."

Nyman, putting the pills back in the paper sack, asked her how she'd done it.

"With the car, you mean?"

"Yes."

"Well, that wasn't very hard. Bridget called down here as soon as she got the email, asking Michael what to do. He was all over the place—packing for the Boston trip and giving her his spiel about admitting everything to the newspaper. All I had to do was get Alana's number from his phone before he left for the airport."

"And you called her?"

"Yes, the next day. Bright and early."

"Did you tell her who you were?"

"Of course not. I said I was Bridget Collinson and I wanted to talk to her at my house as soon as possible. She said she couldn't get there till that night, because she was going to see a private investigator. I said the later the better. Marcella fell asleep around ten o'clock, after the boys went to bed, so I took her car and went up early and waited by Bridget's house."

"It sounds very simple."

"It was simple. That's what no one tells you: that there's no great moment of panic. You do what you need to do and it's over before it starts."

"Like suicide," Nyman said.

"Yes. Precisely. Will you give me my medicine, Tom?"

"No."

The look of pleading went out of her face. "It's my choice. You of all people should understand that."

"I don't understand much about what you've done."

"Oh, don't deceive yourself. You made it very clear. There's no secret part of us waiting to be saved. If you couldn't save your wife, how could you save me?"

Nyman said: "There are still your sons. I know you care about them."

She shook her head vigorously—too vigorously—from side to side. "For Christ's sake, don't talk about them. They wouldn't want to grow up in a world with me still in it."

Nyman was opening his mouth to reply when a squeal of tires and the sound of car engines came in from the driveway. He put down the paper sack and started to walk to the front door; behind him there was a rustle of movement.

He turned in time to see Sarah take a knife from the block of wood and run to the back of the house.

He ran after her. She was through the door and into the yard when he came onto the patio. She ran to the back fence, stopped, and turned to face him.

Raising the knife in her right hand, she slashed it against her left forearm, then against the soft skin of her neck.

The blade made clean, shallow cuts. Nyman crossed the yard in a dozen strides and caught her in both arms, knocking her to the ground and pulling the knife by its blade from her hand. Beneath them the grass was still wet from the evening watering.

Sometime later there were footsteps and voices. Timmons, hatchet-faced, came forward and kneeled beside Sarah Freed, telling Nyman to move away.

Staggering to his feet, Nyman walked sideways until he found his path blocked by the fence. At his feet, rising out of black earth, were pink and purple flowers. He stared at the azaleas as if he didn't recognize them, then turned to look at Timmons.

The detective was putting handcuffs on the wrists of Sarah Freed, who lay writhing in the grass, her voice a shrill animal scream. Nyman shivered and sagged back against the fence. He said a woman's name—a single syllable—and looked down at his hands.

They were red with blood.

Chapter 50

A cool September wind rattled the windows of a building on Culver Boulevard. Inside, on a red-leather banquette, a man and a woman sat leaning over their drinks, whispering to each other and giggling. Nyman, on a stool at the end of the bar, finished what was left in his glass and signaled the bartender for another round.

The bartender walked over with a careful smile. He dabbed with his towel at a wet spot on the bar and said:

"What about a cup of coffee instead, Tom? I just started brewing some."

"No thanks."

"You sure? Or maybe just a glass of water?"

"Another Gibson, Manny. I've got the money for it."

The bartender hesitated, then nodded and reached for the bottle of gin. Nyman, leaning on his elbows, looked across the bar to the man who was playing "Skylark" on a keyboard. In the fishbowl beside him were a handful of dollars and some coins.

Nyman's eyes were narrowed in concentration. His face, always lean, now showed dark hollows in the cheeks and blue sockets around the eyes. On the palm of his left hand was a crosshatching of pink scars.

"Been meaning to ask you something, Tom," the bartender said, setting the fresh drink on the bar.

Without shifting his gaze, Nyman picked up the drink. "What's that?"

"Friend of mine's been having some trouble lately. Trouble with the police, I guess you'd call it. I told him I knew an investigator who might be able to help."

Nyman went on watching the piano player and said nothing.

"Is it all right if I send him by your office, Tom?"

Taking a drink, Nyman said: "I'm not spending much time at the office these days."

"No?"

"No."

"He could give you a call, then, if that would be easier."

"I'm sorry, Manny. I can't help you. Or your friend."

Reddening, the bartender nodded and turned away. At the keyboard, Ira had finished the song and was rearranging his sheet music. On the bar beside Nyman's glass, neatly folded, was a copy of the *L.A. Independent*.

Nyman opened the paper to an interior page and found, under a caricature of Grace Salas, the latest column by Richard Voss.

Hard evidence seems to be in short supply these days. Take the announcement made last week by the Los Angeles City Ethics Commission, which has been investigating the questionable campaign donations received by Grace Salas (CD-16) in the last City Council election.

The Commission's verdict? "Despite irregularities in the councilmember's fundraising reports, there is insufficient evidence to justify a fine for misconduct."

Never mind that those questionable donations came from employees of the same two development companies. Never mind that both companies were later chosen by Salas and her colleagues to build Merchant South, a massive real-estate project with links to a pair of grisly murders.

And never mind that the murderer's husband, Prof. Michael Freed, who recently resigned his post at Pacifica University, is the same economist Salas hand-picked to write a glowing review of the project.

According to the City Council, all this fails to provide sufficient evidence of guilt. In an August meeting, the Council declined to censor Salas for her role in the boondoggle.

"Although Ms. Salas did not follow proper procedure in the allocation of her district's discretionary funds," the Council wrote, "we have found nothing to indicate that she was aware of the criminal behavior of other parties."

Those "other parties" might include Savannah Group, the lead developer of Merchant South and the owner of the Kasbah casino in Las Vegas. After allegations surfaced that Savannah had used its blackjack tables as a one-stop A.T.M. for Freed, the Nevada Gaming Control Board launched an investigation.

The result? "There is no conclusive evidence of gaming irregularities at Kasbah Casino and Resort."

In fact, the only person who seems swayed by the evidence is the murderer herself, Sarah Freed, who earlier this month admitted her guilt as part of a plea deal with prosecutors. According to her statement, the murders were crimes of jealous passion, not part of a broader conspiracy.

It's possible she's telling the truth about that. The evidence, however, suggests otherwise.

Nyman tossed the paper onto the bar and reached for his drink. Across the room, the woman on the red-leather banquette was resting her chin on an upraised fist and snoring softly. She wore a sleeveless dress that exposed her arms, the skin of which was just starting to be discolored by liver spots. The young man beside her, shaking her by the knee, told her it was time to leave.

They rose together and made their way unsteadily to the green-lighted door. For a moment, as the door opened, there was a sound of traffic and distant voices, then silence as the door swung shut again.

Ira had left the keyboard and stood now beside Nyman at the bar, waiting for a cup of coffee.

"That slow enough for you, Tom?" he said.

Nyman looked up. "Hmm?"

"'Skylark.' I know you like a slow tempo."

"Oh. Sure. It was perfect."

Ira's eyes narrowed. "You doing all right?"

"Just fine."

"If this is fine, I'd hate to see what not-fine looks like."

"It looks about the same," Nyman said, "just with more gin."

Ira smiled. "That sister-in-law of yours came to see me, by the way. Theresa, or whatever her name is. Yesterday afternoon."

Nyman paused with his hand halfway to his glass. "She did?"

"Talented girl. Rusty, obviously, but she was better than I thought she'd be."

Still with his hand in the air, Nyman asked if she'd agreed to come back for more lessons.

"If she can stay clean, she'll probably be the one giving me lessons. I told her I knew some people she could audition for. She said she'd think about it."

The bartender came forward with the coffee and Ira busied himself with cream and sugar.

Nyman, frowning, drank the last of his Gibson. He looked up at the clock on the wall, then down at the scars on his palm, some of which still showed the redness of fresh blood beneath the skin.

Draping the wet towel on his shoulder, the bartender came out from behind the bar and sat down on the stool beside Nyman's. Together they watched as Ira went back to the keyboard and started to play another song, a quiet melody in a minor key. The last of the other customers had gone away and the three men were alone in the dim little room.

"All right," Nyman said, turning to the bartender. "Tell me about your friend."

Printed in Poland
by Amazon Fulfillment
Poland Sp. z o.o., Wrocław

54661400R00197